PSYCHOLOGY AND OTHER STORIES

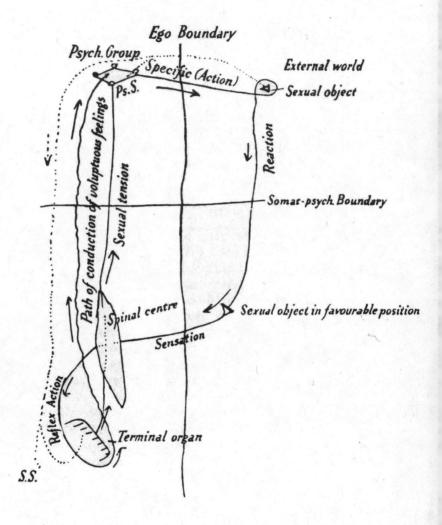

C.P. Boyko

Psychology and Other Stories

BIBLIOASIS

FIRST EDITION

Library and Archives Canada Cataloguing in Publication

Boyko, C.P.
        Psychology and other stories / C.P. Boyko

Short Stories.
ISBN 978-1-926845-50-0

        I. Title.

PS8603.O9962P79 2012   C813'.6   C2012-901701-9

 Canada Council   Conseil des Arts   ONTARIO ARTS COUNCIL
for the Arts   du Canada   CONSEIL DES ARTS DE L'ONTARIO

 Canadian   Patrimoine
Heritage   canadien

Biblioasis acknowledges the ongoing financial support of the Government of Canada through the Canada Council for the Arts, Canadian Heritage, the Canada Book Fund; and the Government of Ontario through the Ontario Arts Council.

The author would like to thank the Canada Council for the Arts, which provided financial assistance during the writing of this book.

PRINTED AND BOUND IN CANADA

What we can call by no better name but accident or idiosyncrasy certainly plays a great part in all our neural and mental processes, especially the higher ones. We can never seek amongst these processes for results which shall be invariable. Exceptions remain to every empirical law of our mental life, and can only be treated as so many individual aberrations.

William James

Contents

for Richard Linklater
for Robin, Glen, and Hank, three friends I made in the psychology department
and for Hubert T. Ross, my therapist

PART I

REACTION-FORMATION

At first this struck me as ridiculous. But nevertheless, like all the rest, it had to be carefully analyzed. When I came to look at it more closely it seemed to have some sort of meaning after all.

Freud

"*I* HAD A DREAM LAST NIGHT," said the doctor at last, then lapsed again into pointed silence.

Archie shifted uneasily on the couch. "Oh?"

"Yes. I dreamt that I had to go somewhere, somewhere far away from where I felt safe and comfortable and appreciated, and after a long and arduous journey I arrived at the designated place *only to discover* that the person I was supposed to be meeting ... was there waiting for me. It was very gratifying, and I did not feel at all foolish or maltreated."

"I'm sorry I was late," said Archie for the second time.

"No," corrected Dr. Pringle. "You're not. If you were sorry to be late you would not *be* late."

"I guess that's true." He had hoped the session would not go this way. "I guess I must be resisting something?"

This mollified Pringle, to Archie's relief. His question could just as easily have prompted another of the doctor's transparent wish-fulfillment dreams: one in which, for example, he, the doctor, was skillfully digging a hole or erecting a wall or something *without* any clumsy oaf coming along to take the shovel or the trowel out of his hands.

"I don't have to tell you that you're only harming yourself," said Pringle. "You need all the time I can give you. You know that I see most of my patients *three* times a week. And they haven't half the complexes you have."

"What about the Gerbil Man?," Archie asked, using Dr. Pringle's code name for his prize patient—a fellow psychoanalyst who believed that invisible rodents were nibbling on him at the most inopportune times.

"As a matter of fact," said the doctor with strained modesty, "I've made rather something of a breakthrough with him."

Archie let the doctor talk; he had no choice. Most days he was quite content to have Pringle go on about his other patients: it took some of the heat of scrutiny off himself, and occasionally some of what the doctor said was actually interesting. Today, however, Archie felt strangely anxious to speak. He was, he realized, happy.

Archie extended his legs, careful not to appear restless. He was, for once, thankful for the more traditional arrangement of the furniture in this office, which Pringle borrowed from a local colleague for this one hour each week. In Pringle's own office upstate, the couch faced his desk and consequently one had to take care to look interested or attentive when he talked about his colleagues or his other patients. The doctor did not return this courtesy when Archie talked about his own life, preferring to stare out the window or make notes or mutter to himself. Once, waving Archie on, he had even taken a phone call. Apparently, Dr. Pringle did not think that it was important that he see his client, but that his client see him. "It aids the transference," he had once said. So, to compensate for the unfavorable position of his colleague's couch, instead of simply turning it around, Pringle brought with him a framed photograph of himself, which he hung on the wall opposite Archie at the start of every session and removed at the end. In the picture the doctor looked startled, as if the photographer had snapped it without first explaining to him what photography was.

"And this," Pringle was saying, "is exactly what one would expect to find in a subject with such a perfect manifestation of castration anxiety produced by an affection-withholding mother and an emotionally absent father."

As something seemed to be expected of him, Archie said, with as much thoughtfulness as he could cram into two syllables, "I ... *see*."

"I fully expect to be able to write the case up now in another six months or so."

"That's ... smashing."

"But enough about him," said Pringle with sudden violence. "Why are you resisting treatment?"

Archie supposed he did arrive late rather often. Most of the time this was just good sense: the doctor himself was almost never punctual. But perhaps this was, after all, only an excuse. There always remained the remote possibility that, like today, the doctor would be on time; and if he, Archie, nevertheless insisted on coming late, thereby risking Pringle's bitter inquest into his deeper motives, he really must be resisting some facet of what Pringle called the treatment.

He said honestly, "I don't know."

Dr. Pringle barked with laughter. "Of course you don't. That's what I'm here for. Well," he sighed. "Tell me about your week." A glottal film of detachment entered the doctor's voice.

Archie took a quavering breath and said, "Well, you know, it's silly but I think I've finally ..." Not wanting to say something as puerile as "made a friend," he finished: "finally met someone." But this, he realized with embarrassment, made it sound like he'd met a girl, a potential lover.

"Ah ah ah," said the doctor. "Dreams first."

Archie hated Parcliffe at first. Everything was different here.

At Templeton the boarders had outnumbered the day boys by three to one; here, because the nearby town was so much larger, the ratio was inverted, and consequently it was the boarders, not the day boys, who were the second-class citizens. At Templeton, poverty had been disgraceful; here at Parcliffe, for some reason, it was *chic*. Even the masters dressed shabbily and let their hair grow long, like refugees or filthy beatniks. Here at Parcliffe there were no tennis courts, no swimming pools, and no one played chess. At Parcliffe, instead of a semiprivate room, tenth formers were stuck in dorms; so, instead of the one roommate that his age and status should have entitled him to, Archie had three. And all three were asinine simpletons.

In fact, as Archie told his mother on the phone one week, all the boys at Parcliffe were either stupid or stuck-up. He tried to say this in the same lightly bitchy tone that she and her friends used when complaining about their exes, their analysts, or the filthy beatniks that had moved in next door. But he must have done it wrong.

"Darling, is it really so horrible as all that? Have I done perfectly the wrong thing?"

This should have been his cue to say something stoical, but her sympathy unmanned him. He held his eyes open, so the tears would evaporate.

Parcliffe Academy had been modeled on the English public school, but without any slavish adherence to verisimilitude. Little was known about Henry Parcliff, its founder. There was the rumor that, prior to the more lucrative inception of academies, he had made his living dowsing for water, coal, and gold with a forked stick. Aside from this, one fact could be inferred about Parcliff: he had never been within miles of an English public school. The school that took his name had probably been fashioned from what he remembered of a few English memoirs or Bildungsromans read in his youth. His intent, no doubt, had been to suggest the chilly, aristocratic (and expensive) atmosphere of those schools, but with as few strokes (and at as little cost) as possible. He must have found that the easiest way to do this was to give things impressively English-sounding names. Thus, Parcliff's school was christened Parcliffe Academy; its teachers were called Masters; its dormitory residences were called Houses; teacher's pets were called Prefects; grades were called forms; final exams were called A-levels; French was called Latin; and baseball was called cricket.

This scheme allowed the boys' parents to say to their friends things like, "My Arthur has just scored a beta-alpha on his Tenth-Form A-levels," which sounded more lovely to their ears than its American translation ("My boy just passed grade ten with a B average"). They could also say that their boys "up at" Parcliffe were on the rowing team and in the First Eleven at cricket. This, indeed, was a privilege bestowed upon every parent—included, as it were, in the price of tuition—because participation in both these impressively English-sounding sports was mandatory; and, by the same sort of linguistic legerdemain that made every hall monitor a house prefect, every cricket team was called a First Eleven.

Cricket, indeed, was a perfect example on a small scale of the school's philosophy of style over substance, or nomenclature over reality. The cricket played at Parcliffe (unbeknownst to any of the boys who played it there) bore only the most superficial resemblance to the bona fide article. It was nearer to baseball than perhaps any other sport, but it was not very much like baseball. The returning boys knew the rules, or claimed to (though it soon became clear that there was as much scope here for interpretation as in biblical exegesis); the new boys were put in the harmless outfield positions and assured that they would "pick it up."

Archie, who at Templeton had been excused from all team sports as a conscientious objector to their symbolic bellicosity, watched the game closely at first—demonstrating his active interest in the proceedings by hunkering down into a limber half-crouch; occasionally slapping his hands together with rugged alacrity, like a lumberjack preparing to climb a tree; calling out scrupulously generic encouragement to his teammates; and expressing his chagrin, when the opposing First Eleven stole a wicket or scored a base, in the catchphrase then popular at Parcliffe: "Suck my *cock*," or simply, "*My cock*." Like a scientist working in the best Baconian tradition, he began by merely collecting data, without presumption; but soon this approach yielded, under a prolonged barrage of bewilderment, to wild conjecture. Desperately he tried to impose upon the scene of intermittent bedlam before him some underlying logic or rationale, some hypothesis that could guide his behavior or at least streamline his options should the ball come near enough to him and to no other player that he was forced to interact with it. But when this did not happen and continued to not happen, he found himself unequal to the effort of sustained attention. His mind began to wander.

Freykynd the Elvin Warrior, who wielded his dagger like a sword, observed from a safe remove the goblins performing their strange and barbarous rituals ...

At Templeton in the dorm they had played a sort of game after lights out. Perhaps, he thought, it originated in a reflexive flouting of authority: to go to sleep when they were *told to* would be to surrender a portion of their priceless autonomy. So, instead of sleeping, they talked. It didn't matter what one said, as long as one made one's voice, the voice of revolt, heard. (On second thought, perhaps the game had even deeper roots in a simple fear of the dark?)

As the game and the night progressed, the boys' eloquence waned, and words deteriorated into mere noise—grunts, animal calls, belches. The goal, at least as Archie saw it, was to be one of the last to make a sound—but not *the* last, because if no one replied you never knew whether your witticism (or sound effect) had been deemed unworthy of reply or whether you were the only one still awake. The best outcome, the clearest victory, was to say something, ideally after several minutes of silence, and be greeted with a chorus of groans, laughs, or weary and defeated *shut UP already*s. Then at last you could sleep, secure in the salience of your individuality.

They did not know this game at Parcliffe. One night, five minutes after lights out, Archie moistened his lips, raised his hands to his face, and blew a great sloppy mouth-fart into his palms. He held his breath, trembling with mirth, in the absolute silence that followed. When the silence continued, the twitching worm of suppressed hilarity in his guts became a twitching worm of apprehension. Why was no one saying anything? They couldn't be asleep, surely, not all of them, not already! The only explanation was that they did not think it was funny. Well, it wasn't meant to be brilliant—only an opening move, something to get the game started, like pawn to king four.

He pretended to be asleep, praying that no one had traced the sound to its origin. He lay there on his bunk, stiff with shame and loathing, for an hour before the dense, rotating knot of his thoughts finally began to break up and fly apart. He was given a moment's respite in which he was almost no one and nowhere; then his eyelids became transparent and the nightmares began.

He sat in the crowded dining hall, eyes on his book, and listened disdainfully, despite himself, to the stupid boys around him telling jokes.

"What's the difference between Master Perkins and a rock?"

"I'll buy."

"Perkins smells like shit."

"How can you tell Fatty Roberts from a bouquet of roses?"

"How."

"Fatty Roberts sucks your cock."

"Oh, hey, um, hello?"

Archie looked up. He recognized the boys who stood over him as Ambrose Tench and somebody Greaves from the Ninth Form—a year below him. (Tench, with his slouching posture and close-set eyes, Archie had already transported into the Kingdom of Yllisee as a minor character, Harpnox the Man-Bear, a dim-witted shopkeeper whose every line of dialogue was "snuffled.") Like everyone else at Pervcliffe, these two did not, apparently, know his name. He felt a pang of refreshingly pure hatred.

"Yes?"

"You *are* a catamite, aren't you?"

Though he did not recognize the word—that was the point—he did recognize the game. He and Lyle had played it at Templeton. The idea was to find some scurrilous word in the dictionary, then try to get other boys to admit that they were, for instance, steatopygous coprophiliacs or anencephalic monorchids or whatever it might be. The trick was to pose the question casually, as if only seeking confirmation of some humdrum, well-known fact.

"Oh, you know, I *used* to be," he said, "but then your bloody union fees just got out of hand."

The boys stared at him, faces slack as masks. "Yes, well, uh, all right …" They giggled uncertainly and moved off in search of their next victim.

"Clever clever," said a voice Archie recognized.

He was brought out of his reverie by some commotion. Instantly he was overwhelmed by the dread, so familiar to him from his nightmares, that some specific but mysterious action was required of him, and that if he flubbed it he would be exposed before everyone as the fraudulent and altogether inadequate specimen that he was.

He looked up; there was the ball; he ran to meet it.

It seemed he would never reach it. His legs were heavy and unco-operative, as if he were running through some invisible fluid—

As he climbed to his feet, dazed and ashamed, the ball landed, with a prim *pat-pat*, on the turf a few feet away. It had not, after all, been his moment. He had run clear across the field and collided with Mawthorn who, with his eyes on the ball that was rightfully his, had not seen Archie coming.

He began to help the other boy up, but dropped him like a leper when his teammates' screams revealed to him that the ball was still in play! He lunged at it with simian abandon, snatched it up with both hands, drew back his arm and ... Where? Where to throw it? The boys were all shouting at him but he was far beyond the reach of human language.

He hesitated for only a moment. His arm knew what to do, if he did not. He fired the ball, as hard as he could, at the bobbing, unhelmeted head of the running batsman.

He had time to admire his throw—its speed, its precision, the geometrical perfection of its arc, like the illustration in a physics text-book—before a twinge of disquiet tugged at his guts.

Luckily, his arm had not taken into account the fact that its target was moving. The ball missed the oblivious batsman's head by several inches, but came close enough that the infielder who had been run-ning to catch it felt obliged to shout at the batsman to duck. The ball swooped to earth and rolled gracefully out of bounds. The opposing First Eleven had time to capture four more bases and break seven more wickets before it was retrieved.

Archie trudged back to his corner of the field, muttering and kicking at the turf as he went. This display of remorse did not express his disappointment, but concealed it: he was playing the part of the passionately engaged and ordinarily competent athlete cursing himself, unfairly, for the sort of mistake that anyone might make.

But this pantomime could no more evoke the true depth and complexity of his anguish than a tin whistle could perform a symphony of Rubbra's. To truly give vent to his feelings, he would have had, at the very least, to die.

No one chided him; no one even tried to cheer him. It was as if he did not exist.

He hated Parcliffe at first. Then he met Clayton Fishpool.

Fishpool was, in Archie's scheme of classification, perhaps the most stuck-up boy at the school. He wore an ascot and socks with sandals—either of which in isolation would have qualified him as the most eccentric character Archie had ever laid eyes on. He was idiotically handsome, with just the kind of soft lank hair that Archie believed, on his own head, would have made him look rakish, carefree, and sensitive, yet with a capacity for beautiful cruelty—but which, on Clayton Fishpool, only looked foppish. Aside from his physical appearance, Fishpool had about him an aura of self-sufficiency and complacent grandeur. He was sixteen, and he carried himself as though he had arrived at this sublimely remote age through his own foresight and diligence. For *The Lyre*, the school's snobbish literary newspaper, he wrote poems and editorials which he signed "C.S. Fishpool."

(He was known, in the gold and green groves of Yllisee, as Dartagnan the Disreputable, Dartagnan the Demi-Mage.)

"What's that you're reading?"

Archie held the book at arm's length and eyed it indifferently.

Fishpool emitted a high-pitched squeak. "Oh, *Strachey's* all right, but if you go in for that whole Bloomsbury thing you should really read Firbank."

Archie told his face to take on the expression of a man who had long ago resolved to look into Firbank and was now grateful for this reminder. In fact, he was appalled: He had chosen this book, as he chose all his books for public consumption, for its obscurity. He would not read "classics": to do so was, first, to admit unfamiliarity with them, and, second, to reveal a prosaic and unoriginal soul. In the dining hall he therefore read *Two Noble Kinsmen* instead of *Hamlet*, *The Holy Sinner* instead of *The Magic Mountain*, *The Eternal Moment* instead of *Howards End*, George Meredith instead of George Eliot, Edward FitzGerald instead of F. Scott Fitzgerald, William James instead of Henry James, and someone like Lytton Strachey instead of someone whose work he actually enjoyed, like John Buchan or Aldous Huxley. He believed, or anyway sometimes imagined himself saying he believed, that the duty of the serious student of literature was not to tread the same old well-worn paths, but to blaze new trails, to seek out the unknown and unsung masterpieces. (Or was he simply afraid to read any book that someone might know better than he did?) He had thought Strachey safe; but now here was C.S. Fishpool, not only wearily familiar with Strachey, but able to name an even more obscure author whom Archie should have been reading instead.

"Well yes, Strachey's *all right* all right," Archie began his prepared statement with heavy if undirected irony, "though I do find at times that his prose can be a bit what you might call flowery in spots." (Twelve hours later, lying in bed and replaying this conversation in his head, he was wracked by remorse that he had not said "florid.")

Clayton Fishpool pushed his chair back and narrowed his eyes at Archie. "You say that like it's a bad thing, Archer old cock."

"Well, I suppose," Archie drawled, becoming defensively more languorous the more fretful he felt, "it's just that I feel sometimes that he's a bit, well, pleonastic." He fairly vibrated with tension as he waited for this bomb to drop; he had never said or heard the word spoken aloud and had no idea if he was pronouncing it correctly.

Fishpool threw back his shoulders. Archie would soon come to recognize this gesture as characteristic: it always preceded a diatribe. As Fishpool spoke, his shoulders would slowly roll forward again; periodically he would throw them back again, as if winding a clock.

Archie listened to him talk, his attention cutting in and out at random, as if by some mysterious physiological process. On a conscious level, he found Fishpool's apparently impromptu speech on the role of language in literature clever and thought-provoking. But on an unconscious level? Perhaps he was only flattered to have someone talking to him at all—and someone who knew his name, no less.

A week later, Fishpool found Archie in the dining hall dutifully reading *Valmouth* (and holding it up rather conspicuously, for by this time he had also read, but without being discovered doing so, two other Firbanks—working his way chronologically backwards on the assumption that, like wine, writers improved with age).

"Tell me what you think," said Fishpool expansively, as if Archie's opinion of the book were only one of many things he wished to know.

"I find it to be," he said, taking care to make this sound not like a criticism but a dispassionate appraisal, "a bit, shall we say, thin on the ground insofar as plot is concerned."

"That is of course the *point*, cock. What makes Firbank so brilliant is that he has tossed out plot, story, action, chronological progression—all that dreadful muck. Plot is dead—and Firbank, before even the Moderns, helped kill it." Fishpool threw back his shoulders. "Literature," he said, "is not about *story* but about character—and by character one means the intricate machinations of the individual psychology. Say what you will about the sins and excesses of Joyce"—and here he paused gallantly, as if to allow Archie to say what he would about the sins and excesses of Joyce—"he did at least do one important thing for literature: he moved the stage into the mind where it belongs; he brought *thought* into his characters' heads ..."

Several minutes later, Archie's face felt like it had cramped permanently into an expression of engaged receptivity, like that of a wise judge listening with a painstaking suppression of bias to a sympathetic witness.

Fishpool was saying, "Firbank of course works the same ground but from the opposite direction. His characters, or quote characters unquote, are all surface, all gorgeous glittering sound and light— 'The play of shine and shade on the trees as the supple boughs wag.' We enter not at all into their thoughts. That is the clue, of course, the key: they are but the thoughts, the psyche incarnate, of Firbank himself. You see, Archer, you have to read Firbank's *characters* as an expression of *Firbank's* character. And that is just what literature must aim to be, if it is to be literature at all: an expression of, a monument to, its creator's individuality. Or don't you agree?"

Archie, furrowing his brow and jutting out his jaw, said: "Well, *yes*, but ..."

A black panic seized him by the throat. He had no idea what he was going to say next.

That evening, Archie had the room to himself; Rodney, Hollingsward, and Caulkins were out on some mission to waylay a group of Downsfield girls who were rumored to be making a foray into town. Archie went to his bedside locker and removed the latest five or six hundred pages of the manuscript of *The Adventures of Freykynd The Elvin Warrior* from its hiding place beneath his retired tennis shoes. His gaze hovered above the page for a moment, circling vulture-like, before swooping down to tear apart that which something else had already killed.

"Elf!" cried Snodlock thickly in his gruff troll's voice. "I must have parley with you!"

Freykynd looked over his shoulder, slowed, and finally stopped. Still he held aloft Cawlwyn his dagger, which he wielded with two hands like a sword. "You will have parley from that remove, troll!" snarled Freykynd softly.

Snodlock halted suddenly and began nervously to wipe his fat hirsute troll's hands on his filthy apothecary's apron.

"Speak, troll!" snapped Freykynd impatiently. "Speak! I am in haste to Lawdimor, where the elder demi-mages convene this midnight!"

"It is precisely that," gasped Snodlock resolutely, "I mean to speak of."

"Well?" shouted Freykynd.

"Dartagnan the demi-mage," hissed the troll malevolently. "He is not what he has seemed heretofore."

Freykynd tightened his grip on Cawlwyn.

Archie, in desperation, picked up his pen, changed the final period to a comma, and added: *thinking that ...*

But he did not know what Freykynd was thinking.

He did not tell Dr. Pringle about his nightmares.

Nor did he think of them as nightmares. Nothing really nightmarish ever happened in them. He dreamt that he was called on in class and didn't know the answer. He dreamt that he was writing an A-levels but had forgotten to study. He dreamt that he was rowing but his paddle would not pierce the water. He dreamt that someone was watching him. He dreamt that something important was happening but he could not open his eyes. He dreamt that he was searching for a book that he could not find. He dreamt that he was late. He dreamt that he was lost in a dark forest. He dreamt that he was being followed.

It was not the content of the dreams that made them terrible, but the feelings that accompanied them. He felt hunted; he felt that time was running out; he felt that he was making an irrevocable mistake; he felt that all his sins were about to be made public—that he would be exposed to all the ridicule and contempt that in his weakness and ineptitude he deserved.

Archie did not tell Pringle about his dreams because it was the doctor's opinion that dreams were only clumsily disguised sexual fantasies. The (always disguised) object of Archie's sexual desire was usually, according to Pringle, Archie's mother. When Archie dared to deny an Oedipal fixation, the doctor only added homosexual longings (also disguised) to his diagnosis. So, instead of arguing, Archie took preemptive measures, concocting false dreams to bring to the sessions: drab, sterile dreams that could not possibly betray the slightest whiff of submerged longings or unconscious urges, or indeed the existence of longings or an unconscious at all.

This week, however, his hands full with Firbank and a self-guided crash course in Latin, he had forgotten to prepare a dream. He had no choice but to improvise.

He felt frozen and aphasic; he felt as if he had never in all his life dreamed and would not know a dream were he in one; so he began by saying how incredibly vivid his dream had been, how forcefully it had impressed itself on him, how really just amazingly *dreamlike* it had been. He paused dramatically, as if mustering the strength to spill his fertile secret. What did people dream about? What did *normal* people dream about?

He closed his eyes and saw himself (or someone) ... standing. Around him was ... nothing.

"I am in a large room," he said recklessly. "A very large room ..."

The doctor, behind him, was silent.

"Or perhaps it's outdoors. I don't see walls or a ceiling ..."

The doctor, behind him, grunted.

"Yes, it's outdoors. There is someone there with me ..."

Two or three minutes later, when the doctor's grunts had become almost continuous, Archie drew to a close: "That's all I remember."

"Very revealing," Pringle said. "Yes, very revealing indeed. To begin with the room, which is at the same time not a room but the as you put it 'outdoors,' by which can only be meant the world, the universe, all of existence. A room is an enclosure, but what kind of enclosure is it that you cannot see the walls of? An enclosure, of course, that you *do not know* is an enclosure. A fish, it is said, does not see the water in which it swims. Likewise, the *unborn child* does not see the walls of the womb *as* walls. It does not know its little room *is* a little room, but takes it for the world."

Dr. Pringle, having crested this first foothill of interpretation, paused for a moment before continuing in a lower, steadier tone, like one conserving oxygen for the peak.

"That explains the appearance of the 'woman,' as you called her, who is at once your mother and not your mother. Her identity is indistinct and spectral because in this place she is both present and not present; that is, she is omnipresent—she is all around you. She is, like the walls and the ceiling of your womb-room, everywhere and nowhere ..."

Half an hour later, the doctor began summing up his findings in the ringing tone of a mountaineer driving home his flag: "And the significance of the breadbox—which we have seen to be an instrument of concealment, a symbol of shame—outside the expected or prescribed setting of a kitchen or pantry—which I need hardly tell you is richly associated in your unconscious mind with the mother-figure, the wife, the housewife, the *feminine*, the *female*—but instead displaced to a highly irregular context, that of the lawn—which you will recall we identified without trouble as a symbol of growth, of fecundity, of fertility, that is to say, of *procreation* or, quite simply, heterosexual intercourse—the significance of this displacement is that it reveals a deep-seated anxiety about being discovered in the classically feminine domain, that is, in the sexually passive role of the woman; and the shifting of the urge for concealment onto the lawn is obviously a feeble attempt to convince yourself of your own masculinity, your own virility, your own heterosexuality. But the breadbox, alas, is empty."

Archie had seized on a breadbox as the dullest, most common-place object he could think of. He did not know why he had placed it on a lawn (he should have known better), except that a breadbox in a kitchen had not seemed sufficiently dreamlike. Now he objected: "But I didn't say it was empty."

"Exactly as one would expect. Any *empty* breadbox would have been too revealing, too disturbing. Even through the dream-veils of condensation, displacement, and distortion, the realization of your homosexuality would have been too distressing to face. We have discussed the function of the reaction-formation before. When you want something that you are at the same time ashamed to want, you push it out of your mind. Though there *is* no 'out of your mind'—there is only the unconscious, which receives and stores everything, like a landfill. Out of sight, perhaps, but *never* out of mind—there, in a rather clever inversion of the famous proverb, is perhaps the most succinct expression of Freud's theoretical framework. Out of sight, but never out of mind. Yes. 'Inversion,' incidentally, is another word, which Freud and Havelock Ellis among others used, for homosexuality. This *is* to the point, for homosexuality is a kind of inverting, a turning upside-down—a reaction-formation, to use the technical term. I know you have no aversion to technical terms." The doctor grunted several times, like a hunter practicing a birdcall. "When you push something, some disgusting desire, out of your mind, you are left with a puzzling absence to explain. 'Why is it I do not care for such-and-such?' The most effective explanation, the one that will provide the greatest defense against a rebirth of the desire, is that you *hate* such-and-such. Take for example the anal retentive person who, frozen at the anal stage of psychosexual development, does not forthrightly display his enthusiasm for, as Freud puts it, 'what is unclean and disturbing and should not be part of the body,' but rather pushes these things away and becomes fixated, through the mechanism of the reaction-formation, on cleanliness, orderliness, and trustworthiness. By the same token, one of the surest indicators that someone has homosexual inclinations is the fact that he finds persons of the same sex—and, *a fortiori*, acts of homosexual intercourse—disgusting and repulsive. The clearest proof that the breadbox is empty—that your heterosexual libido is absent—is the fact that, in the dream, it is not. And now I'm afraid we've gone past time."

The problem with this explanation, thought Archie on the cab ride to the bus that would take him back to school, was that he did not find men, or other boys, especially repulsive. Did he? Well, *some* he did (he thought of Master Perkins's big greasy head, or the prefect Jelroy's cleft palate, or Fatty Roberts's fat)—but that didn't prove anything, since he also found many girls and women repulsive (the Matron came to mind). It was true that he wasn't especially *attracted* to men or boys—but wasn't that also true, by definition, of any heterosexual male?

He realized that, to refute the doctor's theory, he would have to prove that the idea of homosexuality and homosexuals did *not* especially bother him. If he was disgusted by the sight of, say, even two men kissing, then perhaps the doctor was right—perhaps he was resisting something.

"Here all right, sir?"

They had arrived at the bus stop. Archie, embarrassed by his thoughts, overtipped the cabbie and climbed out.

Having established the necessity of the thought experiment, and realizing that further delay would only be incriminating, he quickly, but nonchalantly, closed his eyes and pictured two men kissing.

He didn't like it.

Oh God—then it was true.

But hold on. He'd made the men especially manly: stout and muscular and hairy—he could almost hear their day-old stubble rasping like sandpaper when they touched …

So he made them younger. (This was, he assured himself, fair play: he was not especially attracted to older women either—or, without begging the question, *no one* was especially attracted to a much older person.)

This was, at first, an improvement. Yes, he could almost believe that he felt nothing, not the slightest twinge of any sexiness or (what would have been even more damning) any disgust. He was just a heterosexual watching two homosexuals express their affection; what of it? He felt no more nor less than he would have felt at the zoo watching a couple of birds feed each other or a couple of monkeys groom each other.

But his relief was short-lived. Try as he might, he could not prevent the kissers from assuming identities. His slim, blond, featureless statuary kept slipping into sudden focus, becoming one person after another like the amorphous characters in a dream; and despite himself—yes, *despite himself!*—he saw Rodney kissing Hollingsward, then Hollingsward kissing the Man-Bear, then Jelroy kissing Caulkins, then McMichaels kissing Fatty Roberts, Fatty Roberts kissing Lyle, Lyle kissing the Headmaster, the Headmaster kissing Master Perkins (oh Jesus wept!), Perkins kissing Clayton Fishpool …

He clamped his eyes shut as if they were sponges that could be wrung out, then opened them wide and drank in great draughts of clean, sterilizing sunlight.

This was stupid. Dr. Pringle didn't know what he was talking about. He was always going on about homosexuality; it was his *idée fixe*. Archie was taking the man too seriously. All his mother's friends mocked their analysts. Archie, who had first been sent to Dr. Pringle when he was ten, understood that these sessions were in some way necessary and bettering, like piano lessons, chicken pox, or a visit to the dentist, and that their necessity and benefit were in some way inseparable from their unpleasantness. But if your dentist told you that your oral hygiene was deplorable, you did not take it to heart; after all, that was what he *had* to say. If Dr. Pringle hadn't decided that all Archie's problems stemmed from repressed homosexuality, he would have had to come up with some other reason for them.

"You idiot," he muttered. A fat woman waiting at the corner for her signal scowled at him; blushing, he threw himself into the perpendicular crosswalk just as the light turned yellow.

It wasn't fair: even a fat, ugly woman could make him feel stupid and inferior. That was the difference between boys and girls: only intelligent, handsome boys made him feel uneasy, while all girls, even stupid ones, even ugly ones, filled him with panic.

He crossed the street briskly, but refused to break into an undignified run. He was acutely aware, as always, of the waiting drivers' eyes on him. Like an actor getting into character, he tried to see himself as he would have liked them to see him: rangy, insouciant, wise. When he reached the opposite sidewalk he slowed his pace to show them, by contrast, just how quickly he had been moving to get out of their way.

Still blushing, his mind lashed out again at the fat woman across the street. How could anyone let herself get so fat? Then his disgust gave way to a flare-up of vicious lust: How he'd like to fuck her, the fat pig. That would teach her to scowl at him. That would teach them all.

There were not many places one could go to be alone at Parcliffe. There was the corner of the library, behind the expired periodicals, where he worked on *Freykynd*. There was the derelict lavatory in the basement of the Masters' House. (He knew it was derelict, unvisited even by Sawchins the custodian, because he had discovered in one of the toilets, lying lengthwise like a wedding band in a jewelry box, a massive crap whose progenitor had evidently been too proud (or perhaps too traumatized) to flush; and it was still there a week later, a little furry around the edges but instantly recognizable.) And then there was the Wood.

Generations of boys had trampled the bush into a vast, alluring warren of criss-crossing paths and passageways, crawl spaces and trenches and grottoes. But, down by the muddy creek, there was a grassy clearing which, because it gave no cover, because it left nothing to the imagination, was ignored by the younger boys who came here to play war. At one end of this clearing there was a little depression, bound on one side by the creek, on the other by the trunk of a tree, and concealed from view by the tall stalks of grass that tasted like licorice when chewed. It was here that Archie came to masturbate, or, sometimes, to think.

Somehow, the open air always felt cooler and fresher on his cock than on any other part of his body. Was this just an illusion of contrast, produced by the fact that this part of his body was so seldom exposed, and therefore felt nakeder when it was? Or was the skin of this organ more sensitive than the skin elsewhere? As he pondered the matter, the wrinkled little fleshy stub came to life, increasing in size by an implausible factor till it had reached a regal stature—standing there, indeed, proud and quivering with purpose, just like a queen.

He closed his eyes and mentally perused his cousin Patricia's letters, lingering over the most-nearly-pornographic phrases: "I want to lick you up," "We will touch each other all over," "My hot lips yearn and ache," "I want you to crush your sweetness into me." As usual, he eked out these maddeningly vague words with phrases committed to memory from the scientific article on "intercourse" that Lyle had ripped out of the Encyclopedia last year: "Respiration becomes shallow and rapid ... heartbeats are stronger and quicker ... tendency to trembling, constriction of the throat, sneezing, emission of internal gas, are due to diffusion of the motor disturbance ... dilation of the pupils, the expansion of the nostrils, the tendency to salivation and to movements of the tongue ... movements of the tongue ... erectile tissue charged with blood ... perceptible to touch in an increased degree of spongy and elastic tension ... face becomes red, and exactly the same phenomenon takes place in the genital organs ... the erection of the male organ which fits it to enter the female parts ... fluid which copiously bathes all parts of the vulva ... onset of muscular action, which is largely involuntary ... muscular action ... under the influence of the stimulation furnished by the contact and friction of the vagina ... involuntary rhythmic contractions ..."

But soon even the biological facts were swamped by a surge of emotion, and his cousin's individual features were washed away in a tide of abstraction: instead of one girl, he thought of girls in general; instead of one body, bodies in general; instead of one love, *love*. In a vision that seemed less like a dream for the future than some memory of former happiness, he saw himself on a dark desert highway, being embraced from behind by his soulmate, the beautiful genius who forgave him completely. He turned and crushed her in his arms, tore off her clothes with his teeth, carried her away, laid her down and lay down on top of her, and *had* her, *took* her, *possessed* her …

And yet it all remained dim and vague: she was resplendently nude but he could not quite see what she looked like; he himself was still clothed, or only half present, or half himself; and though she was soft and yielding she remained somehow pristine and inviolate, even in her subjugation.

As he made his way back through the Wood he was suddenly reminded of a similar spot he had once discovered on the edge of town outside Templeton. It too had been cross-hatched with pathways that twisted and curved out of sight in just the right way, revealing nothing of their direction or destination, enticing one irresistibly with the thrill of discovery. He prowled around in that wood like a wolf, like a panther, like the last man alive on the planet, surviving by his wits and strength alone. Then he encountered the other.

Well hiya.

Hi.

Hail fellow nature-lover well met and all that jazz I'm sure.

There was something furtive and smug about the man, as if he had expected to find someone like Archie in a place like this.

I was taking a shortcut, Archie explained. The words caught in his throat and betrayed a sudden, inexplicable guilt.

The man was blocking the path, and made no move to step aside. *In a hurry?* he asked, his voice rich with amusement and knowingness.

Bloody right, said Archie, and turned and fled.

At the time, his guilt and shame, so seemingly groundless, had bewildered and angered him. But now, at last, he understood their origin.

That wood had been on the same end of town as the public toilets.

Homosexual men often made dates with one another in public toilets (indeed, while standing at the urinals, if some of the books he'd read could be believed).

The man in the wood had been a homosexual. A homosexual had made a pass at him.

Surely, of all people on the planet, it was homosexuals who were most attuned to the telltale signs of homosexuality in others.

Did the man know something that Archie did not?

"Come in, come in, whoever you are," sang a voice distinctly not Fishpool's. Archie looked again at the number on the door, then pushed it manfully open, an explanation ready on his lips: *Sorry, old cock, I thought these were C. S. Fishpool's rooms …*

But the words died before they were born. At the sight of the naked boy on the bed, apparently trying to twist himself into a pretzel, Archie fell speechless.

"Come on you bastard, close the door will you?"

Though run together, the two parts of this sentence were uttered in such radically different tones—the first part growled, the second part tinkled—that they seemed to come from different personalities altogether. Archie shut the door.

The "bastard," as a compulsive second glance revealed, was the boy's leg: he was trying to get a look at the bottom of his foot. The second glance also revealed that the boy was not in fact fully naked, but wore a white towel around his waist which nevertheless, in his present posture, completely failed to conceal any part of his anatomy whatsoever.

"I *think* I've got another *bas*tard of a *wart*," said the boy, jumping from one end of his register to the other and back in the space of "bastard" alone. "Can *you* see the cunt?"

With simulated naturalness Archie kept his gaze averted, looking with roving absorption at every object and furnishing in the room. "I wouldn't know what one looks like," he said regretfully, so that the boy would not think that his wartlessness was for him a source of pride or superiority.

"Like a little prick of an asshole of a wart right on the bastard bottom of your asshole *foot*."

Archie, like an amnesiac clutching at some inconsequential but precious memory, shouted, "I think I've probably got the wrong room."

"Fishie's in the bog; he'll be out. I can *feel* him, the cunt. Just look. Here. *Please*."

Archie turned his head far enough to see that the boy had fallen back on his elbows and extended his long pink leg, with all its toes wriggling, in Archie's direction.

"It could very well be a wart."

"No, but come on. It's not contagious to *look* at. It won't hurt you to *look*, will it?"

He thought of his session with Dr. Pringle. He looked at the boy's foot.

It was easy, after all, not to stare down the leg at the exposed groin; he'd had plenty of practice in the locker room. Encouraged, he even grabbed the boy's ankle to steady it. But the pink skin, which he'd expected to be warm and clammy, was as cool and dry as a corpse. He dropped it at the sound of Fishpool's voice.

"Is Deivers going on about his ineffable bloody warts again?"

Archie felt a sinking panic, as if he had been dropped into a foreign city, as if this moment did not connect to any other moment of his life.

"It does look like a wart," he said. "But one never knows."

"I'll cut it off," wailed Deivers, rolling back and forth on the bed. "I'll cut the whole damn cunt of a foot right *off*."

"Oh *poo*," said Fishpool. To Archie he said, "Let's away."

"Are we ... Is he not ..."

"No. Deivers isn't literary."

"The distinction between form and content," one boy in an ascot was saying to another boy in socks and sandals, "is an insidious one. You cannot say *what* a poem says without saying it *the way* the poem says it."

"In other words," said another boy wearily, "*form has content*. No argument here. But can the inverse be said? Does *content* have *form*?"

"Ah—*pétition principe*. You are still treating them as distinct entities. Content *cannot* be extracted; meaning *cannot* be abstracted. A paraphrase is not the same as a poem. A synopsis is a lie."

Archie nodded and grumbled his agreement. It was the only response he'd managed to muster since their arrival.

"But then," someone else was saying, "as Lucretius so aptly put it, you will not feel death because you will not be. By the same token, you will not feel fame either."

"Lucretius is overrated as a philosopher—underrated as a poet."

"Ah!—but it is the desire of posthumous fame that inspires one to create great works of art in the here and now."

"The here and now is overrated. No one lives there anymore."

"Ah!—but!—the esteem of future generations, as Seneca so felicitously phrased it, is no more valuable than that of the present one!"

"Give it to us in Latin, Bowling."

"One little known fact about Seneca is that he often spoke a lot of balls."

"Often speaking a lot of balls is underrated."

Archie laughed with the others, but this only made him feel more excluded, like a ghost excluded from the gaiety of those he haunts, which he can never hope to contribute to.

He saw now that Fishpool was speaking: "... On the other hand, you can't rule it out entirely."

Archie felt harpooned with awe and envy. To be the sort of person who always knew what to say, and at just the right moment! When he looked at Fishpool as an example of what he himself was not, Archie almost hated him.

"I need solitude for my writing," someone was saying. "As Kafka said, not 'like a hermit,' but like a dead man."

"Firbank was a hermit, wasn't he?"

"That's *one* word for what he was, yes."

Archie glanced at Fishpool, but he seemed not to have heard. But a minute later he stood, and the other members of the Club fell silent.

It was time for the story.

"One summer, when I was thirteen, my parents got into their heads the notion that I was in need of a tutor. Nor was this notion completely unfounded, I must confess. I was not exactly, at that time, setting the world afire. The fact was that my interests had begun to migrate outside the academic realm. I was thirteen. Perhaps you know what I mean.

"Money, as always among the Fishpools, was scarce. My parents could not afford a 'proper' tutor, but had to cast their flimsy net among the teaching trainees at the local college. I gathered that only one candidate had, for the rate they could offer, presented herself to their scrutiny. I overheard my parents discussing this candidate's qualifications one night. Wasn't she too young? my mother worried. My father agreed, but the advanced state of my nescience left them no choice; in spite of their reservations, the girl was hired.

"As if deliberately to combat my parents' fears, 'Eileen,' as I will call her, acted not like the seventeen-year-old girl that she was but a sexagenarian schoolmarm. She dressed like a matron and ruled like a martinet. Not a day went by without her finding some excuse to slap my hand with her ruler. The most common indictment was inattention. If the object of my alleged inattention was my schoolwork, I plead guilty; but emphatically not guilty, if the object was my tutor. Despite her formidable demeanor, there was no question but that she was the most exquisitely lovely creature I had ever laid eyes on. It was the most delicious torture to sit beside her day after day, pretending to grapple with algebraic functions or dangling participles while in fact grappling with the overwhelming urge to take into my arms and grapple with Eileen.

"Nor was she blind to my misery—I made sure of that. I called her cruel, vicious, uncaring, cold; she feigned to believe that I referred only to her pedagogy. I asked if she treated all men this way; she slapped my hands for my impertinence. I began to find these slaps strangely pleasurable. It was as if the ruler were an extension of her flesh. I became more impertinent, inciting her to more frequent thrashings, and trembled in anticipation when she reached for the instrument; at night in bed I caressed the smarting welts that blossomed on the backs of my hands. She understood what I was up to, but saw no way to relent without acknowledging the passion that underlay my impudence. She was committed to her course of action, as I was to mine. More than once I provoked her to the brink of tears. I was shameless; I was in love.

"Then my parents went away on holiday. My scholastic performance had not improved; as punishment, they left me at home, alone with my tutor, to study.

"By the second day we were both utterly frazzled. I refused even to pretend to work, and she, for her part, abandoned all attempt to control me. Even the ruler disappeared. Instead of liberating me, this rather intimidated me. Had I gone too far? I teased her; she made no reply. I jabbed my pencil at my books; she took no notice. We sat in agonized silence, heads hanging, frozen with fear—each frightened of what the other would do.

"When, after an eternity, I looked up, I perceived that she had been weeping. Quite thoughtlessly, I put my hand on hers. A spasm, as of malaria, shook her thin frame, and tears began to roll down her cheeks. She looked at me then, and I saw that her eyes, though moist, were not sad.

"'Oh Clayton,' she said, 'we mustn't ...'"

Archie, who had been listening raptly, captivated as much by Fishpool's eloquence and self-possession as by the tale itself, noticed that some of the boys in the circle were fidgeting. Now one of them stood and, moving with exaggerated delicacy, like an usher in an opera house, went to the door and locked it. Another withdrew something from beneath his chair.

Archie felt a stirring of panic: something was about to happen, and he wouldn't know what to do.

"I told her that it was not wrong, that nothing that two people both wanted so badly could be wrong. She smiled at me then—and it was as though she had doffed all her schoolmarm's sternness. She shook her head as if shaking off a dream. She had regained possession of herself, but no longer had to smother anything, or lock anything of herself away. She grasped my hand firmly and led me to the bed, saying, 'But you must not forget that in this, as in all things, I remain your *tutor.*'"

Another boy withdrew something from under his chair, and another. Archie saw that they were readying their towels. He felt a flood of relief that spilled over into gratitude; though Fishpool had not told him what the towel was for, he *had* told him to bring one. Archie rummaged in his book bag for his.

"I applied myself to her instructions with a fervor that I had never shown in scholastic pursuits. And, as our passions mounted and intermingled like the smoke of two cigarettes climbing towards the ceiling, a strange inversion occurred. I, for one ineffable moment, became the tutor, and she the pupil. I taught her the calculus of pleasure, showed her how to bridge the split infinitive of joy. I clutched her like a pencil, spun her like a protractor, measured her every dimension with my ruler—repeatedly, patiently, pedagogically. She gasped; she understood; she saw the light.

"Like the Jabberwock," Fishpool concluded, "she burbled as she came."

There was no applause, no plaudits, not even any smiles. It was as if they had all been waiting impatiently for him to finish. Fishpool left the pages of his address on the podium and returned to his seat without a word. Without a word, the towels were unfurled and laid on the floor at the center of the circle, like the long petals of a flower. Then, without a word, the boys of the Literary Club unbuttoned their trousers.

Archie followed suit. He draped his pants over the back of his chair; he sat on the edge of his towel, facing the others; he spread his legs and grabbed his cock—which he was alarmed, then relieved, to find fully erect.

Afterwards, the boys put on their pants, rolled up their towels, and proceeded to mingle and chat as if nothing extraordinary had occurred. "I thought C.S.'s story this week rather good, didn't you?" "Have you read the new Isherwood?" "When's the bloody *Lyre* deadline anyway?"

He was reminded of parties of his mother's, when someone had puked in a vase, or broken the punch bowl, or begun weeping in the bathroom, or pawed at the wrong person, and so had to be politely shown the door. This fall into disgrace always marked the climax of the party, but the guests lingered awhile through the dénouement, chatting extra loudly, grinning extra brightly, mixing their drinks extra strong, as if to deny that anything disgraceful had happened at all.

Archie, who wished for nothing more than to disappear, found himself consistently not alone. A steady file of boys came round to introduce themselves, shake his hand, welcome him to the Club. They asked him questions: "What's your stance on rhyme, Archer?" "Archer, how do you feel about this Beat thing?" "Have you read the new Isherwood?" Gone now was the frosty atmosphere of the symposium; but, friendly as they were, he could not clear from his mind the image of what they had all just done.

"Say, Archer, what's your favorite poem? I know, I know—but if you *had* to pick one."

He struggled to think of the title, or indeed existence, of a single poem. He remembered *Don Juan*, but wasn't sure that something so lengthy qualified as a poem. Could he get away with something like Shakespeare's Sonnet 163?

"Well, if I had to pick *one*, I guess it would have to be 'The Windhover,'" he said, recalling the quantity of praise that Master Royd had heaped on a poem by that name in Advanced English last year.

"Manley Hopkins, eh?" The boy lifted his brows, as if impressed by Archie's audacity. "How about that. Old manly Manley Hopkins."

Ms. Hastings looked up from her knitting and smiled warmly. As one of the few women on staff at Parcliffe, and the only one under forty, it was perhaps strange that the librarian had so utterly failed to inflame the ardor of the student body. Though amicable and by no means deformed, she was nevertheless not only thoroughly unsexy but downright unsexual. It was simply not conceivable that she could be the owner of organs of procreation. (Though Archie had to admit that he could not muster much faith in the existence of, for instance, his cousin Patricia's vagina, either.)

Today, he keenly resented Ms. Hastings's sexlessness. It seemed an ambiguity expressly designed to confuse and dismay him, like a bit of doggerel introduced into an otherwise intelligible play.

"Title, author, or subject?"

He was prepared for this. "Subject, please. I'm looking for information—whatever I can find—I don't know if you'll have anything—on *honorary degrees*."

But she was unwilling to deviate from the script: "Under what letter, please?"

"H, please."

"H what?"

"What?"

"H what? H-A, H-E, H-O, what?"

"Oh. H-O, please."

"H-O what?"

"H-O, um, well, N, I guess. H-O-N."

"In that case our choices are two. We've got Homo to Hone or Hone to Hot."

His heart sank. His eyeballs started to tremble.

"What are we looking for again?"

"Honorary degrees." His mouth was too fast for his brain.

"That's easy, then. We'll be wanting Hone to Hot."

"Well yes and hominids too, if possible. It's a sort of anthropological angle that I'm taking to ... honorary degrees."

"Then we'll be wanting Hoc to Homo. 'Hominid' is with an I, isn't it?"

"Well, yes. However," he went on, his speech slowing to a panic-stricken crawl, "it just occurred to me that it's not *hominids* it's likely to be under but, come to think of it, more likely, ah, homonyms."

Ms. Hastings put her hands on where her hips would be if she'd had hips. "With an O?"

"With an O, yes."

"H-O-M-O, *homo*. As in *homo*-nyms."

"Yes."

"Then it's not Hoc to Homo that you're wanting at all, but Homo to Hone."

"I guess you're right."

After an epic search in which something more esoteric than mere alphabetization must have been involved, she lugged the two drawers over to the counter and dumped them with a grunt. Then she waited.

He attacked Hone to Hot first. There was nothing for "honorary degrees." The nearest heading was "honorary titles," but that said "See: Titles of honor and nobility"—and he was not about to ask to see the Tit to Todg (or whatever) drawer. Instead he turned to "honorifics" and jotted down call numbers with one of the stubby, never-to-be-sharpened pencils provided. He lingered a little longer, riffling forward and backward through the cards with a scholar's conscientiousness, so that Ms. Hastings's effort might not seem so inordinate. He gave her a quick smile, like a man who takes such easy-going pleasure in his innocent task that he positively welcomes observers; then he turned to Homo to Hone.

He pulled forward half the cards and found himself staring at "homosexuality—mythology." Panicking, he jumped to the back of the drawer and loitered for a while amid "Honduras" and "Hondschoote, Battle of, 1793." Making a thoughtful face, as of a yokel contemplating a manual transmission, he pushed back all but one inch of the cards and was rewarded with "homo erectus." He felt himself blushing, and flipped quickly forward through "homo-cysteine—pathophysiology," "homogenization (differential equations)," "homografts (moral and ethical aspects)," and "homologous organs (see also Anatomy, comparative)," before pausing, without quite remembering why, at "homonyms." Had Ms. Hastings gone back to her knitting? He didn't dare look up. He pretended to write down a call number, then realized that it would be just as easy to copy out a real one. This done, he leapt forward, landing on "homosexuality and literature—France—20th century." Time was slipping away. He flipped madly through "homosexuality, female (see also Lesbians)," "homosexuality, female—fiction (see also Lesbians—fiction)," "homosexuality—folklore," "homosexuality—in animals," and "homosexuality—religious aspects" before it occurred to him that he was moving further away from the generic category. What must Ms. Hastings be thinking? He could imagine the censorious scowl coming over her normally affable features, the look of disgust as she began to wonder what malicious, plagiaristic, or pornographic use he was putting her poor card catalogue to. He jumped back—too far: "homophile movement," "homophobia—history," "homoptera," "homoscedacity." She must know, from his place in the drawer, what he was up to. He jumped forward—too far: "homosexuality—law and legislation," "homosexuality—miscellanea," "homosexuality—mythology." Back where he started! Enough!

"All done?" she asked dazedly, as if she had just been wakened from a lovely dream.

One evening on his way back to his House from the Wood, he saw someone coming towards him across the quad.

It was Clayton Fishpool. He did not want to talk to Clayton Fishpool.

So he changed his direction, but subtly: he did not want to be seen, but he did not want to be seen wanting not to be seen, either.

Had Fishpool spotted him? It was dusk; perhaps he had not. But he was getting closer. And each of Archie's own steps only brought him nearer. He did not dare swerve off to one side or (what he most wanted to do) turn and go back the way he had come. He had to content himself with slight, imperceptible deflections. Gradually he veered away from the encounter.

But still Fishpool came his way! He had altered his course to compensate for Archie's drift. Or had he? Maybe Fishpool had been walking in this direction all along, and it was Archie who had inadvertently put himself in his path. Or maybe he *had* changed his course, but for some other, innocent reason; maybe he'd remembered someplace else he was supposed to be.

No, it was impossible! Even as Archie turned more and more sharply, till he must have looked like a tilting drunkard, Fishpool continued to stroll directly toward him. Archie walked a little faster. If Fishpool saw him speed up, then all pretences would have to be dropped—the chase would be on. Fishpool was not fooled. Fishpool was keeping pace. Worse than that, he was gaining. Archie could *feel* him getting closer, though he dared not turn his head. He could feel the boy's proximity, like the heat from a fire, on the side of his face and the back of his neck. And the heat was increasing.

It was unbearable. He broke into a run.

But his legs were blocks of wood. In no time at all Fishpool was upon him; he drew his sword. Archie reached for his own dagger, but it would not come free of its scabbard. Fishpool stabbed him in the back. Archie screamed and fell to his knees. Fishpool ran him through from behind, again and again, until at last a red geyser of blood shot out the top of his head.

"No," he told the doctor, "no dreams. None that I can remember."

According to Freud, or anyway according to Archie's reading of Freud, the typical homosexual felt too much love for his (too-loving) mother; but instead of giving in to that Oedipal urge, he denied it, clamping down on it so hard that he ended up convinced that he hated not only his own mother but all of womankind.

This story, however, did not exhaust the possibilities. The homosexual might alternatively devote himself so wholeheartedly to his loving mother that he found it necessary to shun all her (female) competitors. If the mother refused to conform to the pattern, giving too little instead of too much love to her son, the son simply developed a compensatory attachment to his father, and (through him) all fathers. If there was no father around to form an attachment to, the son could take one of two routes to homosexuality: he could, in the absence of a male role model, become effeminate and feminized; or he could develop a compensatory attachment to other father-figures—other men.

Each of these stories sounded plausible enough in isolation. The question was, how did anyone ever arrive at *heterosexuality*? Some boys must emerge, unscathed as it were, from the same conditions of family life that produced homosexuals. Growing up without a father (as Archie had) or being fond of your mother (as Archie supposed he was) were perhaps necessary causes, but not sufficient ones, surely.

Adler did not have much to say about the origin of homosexuality, but confined himself to describing "the most salient traits of the homo-sexual." These were "inordinate ambition" and "extraordinarily pronounced caution" (or "fear of life"): "The attitude of the homosexual toward life will always be a *hesitating one*."

Archie felt a sinking in his guts. He was nothing if not hesitating. Or was he? Perhaps he was only cautious. Was his caution really "extraordinarily pronounced"? He did not think so. Or did he?

It didn't matter: "Inordinate ambition" was even more incriminating. Did he not, after all, believe himself to be earmarked for greatness? Had he not often drifted into daydreams of what it would

be like to be recognized, famous, admired? Had he not already determined the library call number that his *Freykynd* would receive? And
homosexuals, according to Adler, utilized their "different experiences" to "give strength to the belief that they are different from
other children. This difference appears to them in the nature of a
distinction—a view-point that their ambition of course willingly
encourages." Archie thought this way every day! Deep down, he
treated the fact that he was not like all the other stupid and stuck-up
boys as cause for pride, not shame. If he was lousy at sports (forgetting for the moment tennis and swimming), it was because he was an
intellectual. If he had no friends (forgetting for the moment Lyle and
Clayton Fishpool), it was because his soul moved on a more elevated
plane. If he had never had any luck with girls (and taking the awkward kiss with his cousin Patricia fully into account), it was because
he was a gentleman, or because he was too choosy, or because ...
because ...?

"Hey Archer, you're literary aren't you?"

"What's that supposed to mean?"

"How do you spell 'persuasion'?"

Archie told him. "What are you writing?"

"An essay for Rhetoric." Rodney gathered up the pages, tapped
them into order on the desktop, and cleared his throat. "It's called:
'The Art of Persuasion.'"

Hollingsward, jackknifed over his bed in a posture of debilitating
boredom, lifted his head and cried, "That's the topic, and you don't
even know how to *spell* it? We're going to be here all night."

"I'm just putting the finishing touches on it. Hey Archer, how do
you spell 'subtle'?"

"Let me see that."

The Art of Persuasion
by Rodney de van der Mullens (III)

The art of persuasion tries to change the heart and mind and therefore is a powerful tool that can altar views. The art of persuasion can be a suttle or direct tool but either ways it plays on the emotions and the change of view resulting from the persuasion is usually long lasting. Persuasion is an art because it is every where in our environment and it effects the decisions that we make every day in our life. My trip to New York last summer also resulted out of persuasion. I was hesitant to go but persuasion occurred and through revealing the opportunity is now, guilting me to obligations, and highlighting all the benefits I was persuaded to go.

It was worse than he would have thought possible. To conceal his dismay, he let out a long dismayed whistle. "You'd better give me your pen."

As he began circling the solecisms and underlining the misspellings that appeared in the first sentence, Rodney grew uneasy.

"Some of that's a matter of taste though, right? Personal preference?"

"No." Archie put down the pen. "You're going to have to rewrite the whole thing."

Hollingsward let out a yelp.

"*My cock*," Rodney sighed. To Caulkins and Hollingsward he said, "Hell, you guys go on without me."

Hollingsward raised his eyebrows at Caulkins, who held up one index finger. When at last he opened his mouth, it was to belch the word *oligarchy*. Then he rose to his feet. "Works for me."

Hollingsward sprang to life and clapped Rodney on the shoulder. "We'll keep them warmed up for you."

"Where are you going?," Archie asked.

"Oh, just into town."

"Yes?"

"It's Thursday."

"And what happens on Thursday?"

"Are you kidding?" Rodney looked at him earnestly, as if deciding between pity and admiration. "Thursday's when Downsfield lets out, man."

"And nubile tarts are free to roam the earth," intoned Caulkins sacerdotally, "and seek out the hot young willing cock."

Hollingsward tugged at his arm. "Come on come on, Mullens said he'd catch up."

Archie looked at the essay on the desk. "I guess it would probably be easier for me to fix myself."

Rodney looked at him.

"I mean, I'd be doing most of the work myself anyway. There's no point in both of us ..."

"Now *that's* the ticket!" said Hollingsward, slapping Archie's shoulder.

Rodney took his hand and shook it, then seemed embarrassed by the gesture. "You're a good cock, Arch," he said, without meeting his eye.

"Go on," said Archie, feeling rather like the eunuch persuading the sultan to have a little fun for a change.

When they were gone, he wondered what had come over him. He hadn't wanted them to leave. He hadn't wanted to be left alone with his thoughts, which had been spinning around the same track for so long that they were making him nauseous. Was he hopelessly self-destructive, or did he just relish the role of martyr? He didn't think he did. But did he?

Perhaps he was playing a new part, trying it on for size: The lonely homosexual, unable to derive pleasure from the same coarse pursuits as his peers, stays home and distracts himself with his airy lucubrations …

Or perhaps he had not wanted to be left alone with Rodney? But that was ridiculous. Even if he *was* a homo, surely Rodney was not his type. Surely he would be attracted to someone like Clayton Fishpool, someone intelligent, and attractive, and—

"Those guys are dicks."

Archie blenched, as if his thoughts had been visible.

"Let's get this motherfucker done," said Rodney, almost shyly, from the doorway. "Then let's go into town and rustle up some quim."

"The thing about women," said Rodney astutely, "is that they act like they're in control, but what they really want is to be controlled."

Archie nodded, astutely sucking Cherry Coke through his straw. "They behave so cool and superior but meanwhile all they really need is somebody to take charge."

"It's biological basically," said Rodney. "Their *mode opérant* is basically nurturing. So it makes sense that they're looking for someone to protect them, someone to provide for them."

"Someone to bring home the bacon."

"Someone to slip them the salami."

Archie didn't know what to say to this. Earlier, when a pack of Downsfield girls had come into the diner and ordered malteds, Rodney had said, with something like sickened awe, "What I couldn't do with a pair of gazongas like that." This kind of statement always rendered Archie speechless. What *did* one do with a pair of gazongas? Or, for that matter, a nice set of legs or a smashing ass? He understood the sentiment behind such comments: "That girl is physically attractive to me." It was their peculiar figurative expression, half nonsensical, half obscene, that bemused him, as if Rodney were speaking in some kind of childish masonic code. And when he himself tried to speak this language it always rang false. He simply could not say things like "I wouldn't kick *her* out of bed" or "Now *there's* a can I could drink from" without feeling like an imposter, or a troll. Although, in fact, he felt that way—guilty, dirty, stupid— whenever he even looked at a pretty girl. No doubt some prehistoric part of him longed to subdue and degrade her, pull her by the hair back to his cave. Probably that was why the salacious words turned to ashes in his mouth: shame.

But most of the time, talking to Rodney was easy. Archie did not have to try so hard. Not that Rodney was stupid; he could not spell, perhaps, but he had life smarts. And the two of them had a lot in common. Rodney too was the only child of a widowed mother. He too had transferred to Pervcliffe, just last year. He too had hated it at first.

"One summer," Archie said, "when I was about thirteen, my mother got it into her head that I needed a tutor. Of course, you can't really blame her ..."

Rodney leaned back and nodded nonchalantly in the direction of the door. Two Downsfielders had just come in.

"Nice," Archie mumbled.

He recognized the brunette.

She was the one he sometimes saw in his vision, embracing him from behind on that lonesome desert road.

"Ask them to join us."

"Are you crazy?"

"Wait here."

Archie could not watch. He hung his head over his plate and stuffed cold french fries in his mouth.

"Hey, you haven't met my roommate Arch yet, have you? Ladies, this is Arch my roommate. Arch my roommate, this is Sandra. And this is Meagan, my future ex-wife."

The girls laughed obligingly, as if they had already heard this joke but were too polite to say so. Archie saw with horror that he had extended his hand in greeting; now it hung in the air above the table, unnoticed, unacknowledged, irrefutable proof of his awkwardness. Did one even shake hands with girls? He grasped the ketchup bottle, as if this had been his goal all along, just as the girl of his dreams held out her hand to him.

"Hi Arch his roommate, I'm Sandra his future ex-wife's future ex-roommate."

Archie rangily upended the bottle, insouciantly slapped half a pint of ketchup onto his plate, and grinned wisely up at the girl of his dreams. Through a mouthful of half-chewed french fries he said, "Peeaarreeaagghh." He tried again, this time with greater emphasis: "*Pee*aarree*agghh*." The girl furrowed her brow and leaned closer. He felt the sweat break out on his back. He looked wildly at Rodney, who looked wildly at him. The other girl eyed him with remote distaste, as if she had picked him up on the sole of her shoe on her way to a wedding. The mass of sodden potato in his mouth seemed, meanwhile, to have expanded, so that smiling rangily or insouciantly or in any other way was out of the question; the best that he could manage, by waggling his eyebrows and bringing his lips together, was a sour, maniacal moue. Recognizing that the only way out of this predicament was to chew, he abandoned all attempts at non-verbal communication and began madly to chew. Then he bit his tongue.

Why did he do that?

Why did one bite one's tongue? Presumably because one was afraid of what one was about to say. What had he been about to say? Something stupid and inadequate, no doubt. But if his secret motive had been to avoid looking stupid, he surely could not have hit upon a worse solution than screaming in agony, spewing bloody mush from his mouth, and galumphing out into the night. Either his unconscious was even stupider than he was, or his problems went deeper than he realized.

Perhaps it was not the girl he'd been afraid of, but himself. What would he have discovered if he'd allowed himself to spend even a few minutes in conversation with a pretty girl? That he didn't care? That he wasn't nervous? That he was afraid to be around girls not because he might make an ass of himself, but because it might not matter if he did? Maybe what he really felt around beautiful girls was not love, but terrifying, vertiginous indifference.

But that didn't make any sense either, because, by the doctor's logic, an indifference to the opposite sex would only point to a repressed attraction to them. But no: to qualify as a reaction-formation, wouldn't it have to be stronger than mere indifference, something more like active hatred or repugnance? Unless, of course, it was possible to form a reaction-formation *to* a reaction-formation. Perhaps he so loved women that the sight of a pretty girl crippled him; disgusted by this weakness, he clamped down on it so hard that his lust underwent a subterranean transformation into loathing; but, being even more ashamed of his loathing than he had been of his lust, he clamped down again, until his troll-like, rapacious, destructive urges were refined into commonplace lust and wretched infatuation ...

But if one could form a reaction-formation to a reaction-formation, what prevented one from forming a reaction-formation to a reaction-formation to a reaction-formation? What prevented infinite regress? And more importantly, how did one ever discover one's true feelings? A loop had no starting point.

All he knew for certain was that he had not *meant* to bite his tongue. His unconscious, apparently, did not want him talking to girls.

*

Archie returned to the library and to "A Song of Myself," which Clayton Fishpool had brought to his attention as one of the best poems ever written—"in the English language, at least." Archie had perceived its brilliance the first time he read it. To think that someone had thought to write such long, unrhymed lines as long ago as 1858! And he liked the idea of grass as the "beautiful uncut hair of graves." That was poetry, all right.

But his second reading left him discomfited. There was an awful lot of talk of men, for one thing. Men, to Archie's way of thinking, were (like automobiles, politics, and wheelbarrows) not quite proper subject matter for poetry. But Whitman gave them as much attention as women, perhaps more. And what could be made of lines like these?

> I am enamoured of growing outdoors,
> Of men that live among cattle or taste of the ocean or woods ...
> I can eat and sleep with them week in and week out.

On his first reading, he had chalked this sort of thing up to the innocence of earlier times: Whitman could not have known what people would one day mean when they said "sleep with" someone. But how did Whitman know what men tasted like? Was this just poetry—that is, saying what you didn't mean, not saying what you did mean—or was this something else?

Let's be blunt, he said to himself. *Let's cut to the chase. Let's not mince words.*

It was possible that Walt Whitman had been a homosexual. Many famous writers had been. (He could not at the moment think of any, aside from Oscar Wilde.) One could enjoy their works without being homosexual oneself. Though possibly it helped...

Was Clayton Fishpool a homosexual? Was that why he had befriended Archie, invited him to join the Literary Club? Because he had recognized in him a kindred spirit?

Just like the man in the wood outside Templeton.

But that was different. Archie had been, after all, in that wood on the edge of town near the public toilets, a known meeting place for homosexuals. The man could perhaps be forgiven his assumption.

Well, what if Clayton Fishpool had made a similar mistake?

From the stacks, Archie pulled every book by Lytton Strachey the library owned and returned with them to his carrel. He did not believe he would find what he was looking for. After all, it wasn't the sort of detail you could expect to find in a scholarly introduction or the biographical note on the dust jacket. He had already resigned himself to the futility of his task when he came upon, in *Lytton Strachey by Himself*, an autobiographical essay that quickly came to the point:

> Perhaps if I could have lain with Bunny ... And then I smiled to think of my romantic visions before coming of a recrudescence of that affair, under Duncan's nose—and of his dimness on my arrival, and of how very very little I wanted to lie with him now!

There could no be question of what "lie with" meant here—not with "romantic visions" and "that affair" in the same sentence. But he read on, just to be sure.

As the first flush of victory at having confirmed a wild hypothesis began to fade, it was replaced by an at first pleasurable, then disquieting, shock of recognition. For, in many ways, Strachey was exactly like him, he was exactly like Strachey: indecisive, self-doubting, filled with daydreams and velleities, addicted to introspection and to self-dramatization: "I imagined myself reading about myself in a novel by Tolstoy—reading quickly, and turning over the pages as fast as I could, in my excitement to know what would happen in the end."

But as he read on, the shock of recognition faded too, and with it the worry about what it might portend, what it might prove about Clayton Fishpool or about himself.

And then the vision of that young postman with the fair hair and lovely country complexion who had smiled at me and said 'Good evening, sir,' as he passed on his bicycle, flashed upon me. My scheme of meeting him in the long lane past the village recurred to me, and then I began embroidering romantic and only *just* possible adventures which might follow: the bedroom in the inn at Norwich, and all the rest. But there was the necessity of talking to him first; and I went once more through the calculations of time and place, and saw that my plan really might, if I had the nerve, come off …

He read quickly, turning over the pages as fast as he could, to find out what would happen next.

PART II

EAT THE RICH AND SHIT THE POOR

"You fiend!" exclaimed the Duchess. "How dare you kiss me!"

Such, if we may believe tradition, was the ideal first line proposed by a "psychologist" when asked to give an opening for a story that would grip attention and foster interest.

Here was a man who was trying to apply his knowledge of human nature. He knew that an exclamation gets attention. He knew that most people are interested in the nobility. He knew that everyone is interested in sex. He tried, successfully or not, to cram an appeal to all of these into one short sentence. He was an applied psychologist.

H.K. Nixon

MR. CUSTARD DROVE THE SPEED LIMIT. He was in no hurry. In fact, he had never felt less anxious in all his life.

He always stopped for hitchhikers, because driving bored him and he liked to have someone to talk to. He had in fact just come from Loyola (well, he'd been there a few days ago; he did not know what day it was now, exactly) but he saw no reason not to go back, if that was where circumstances conspired to take him. Francine had set up an appointment for him in Carbon, towards which he had more or less been heading, but he would have missed the meeting by now anyway, and he could always make it up later. He did not set great store by schedules or appointment-making like some people did, but preferred to arrive at places and events naturally, in the fullness of time. He was, in the lingo of Dr. Yard, "open to experience."

"Now what takes you ladies to Loyola?"

The one in the front with him, the skinny one, did not want to answer, but the one in the back had been raised with better manners.

"We missed our bus," she said.

"Going to meet someone," said the skinny one.

"Bad luck," said Mr. Custard, as if this were his professional diagnosis. "For you ladies, that is. Good luck for me!"

The skinny one made a derisive sound, and Mr. Custard realized that unflappable cheerfulness, which worked so well with middle-aged and older ladies, would have limited effectiveness with these two.

"Damn nasty old day to be stranded on the side of the road," he said, scowling at the dark patches of cloud hanging over the highway, which five minutes earlier he had been praising to the cashier at the filling station. He had been trying to get her to cash a cheque, but she'd insisted on calling the owner.

"What, you mean to tell me *you* don't own this place? A capable woman like you?"

She smacked her lips in distaste, though not at his flattery. "Wouldn't care to neither. Loses money hand over fist."

"Hand *under* fist," he quipped, and she pressed a thumb into the cheek opposite the telephone receiver to hide a smile.

They stood on opposite sides of the counter looking out the unwashed window at the sky. Mr. Custard sighed contentedly, giving the easy impression that he was not in any hurry.

"Those clouds look ugly," he said, "but, you know, they keep some of the heat off."

"He don't always answer on the first ring," she explained, rolling her eyes to indicate that this was a kind of understatement.

"You know what you need?" He slapped his hand on the counter. "A place like this?"

"What's that?"

"You need a 'Going Out of Business' sign."

She thumbed her cheek, rolled her eyes, and shook her head.

"I got a bunch of them in the car. Cheap."

"You sell 'Going Out of Business' signs?" She pulled the phone away to devote both ears to hearing what she was hearing.

He had not sold her any signs, but he could have. There came a point in every conversation when he knew he could sell someone something, borrow money off them, or pass a cheque on them. Technically, the signs were samples and he wasn't supposed to be selling them at all; it was the *idea* he was selling to the man up in

Carbon. But he could have sold her five signs, if he'd cared to. Same with the pump boy outside, who was still standing there gawping at Francine's old beater, which Mr. Custard had led him to believe once belonged to Bonnie and Clyde. After that, he could have sold him anything, the car or just about anything else. It wasn't a matter of pulling the wool over a person's eyes, but lifting the veil from them. Mr. Custard ushered people across the border of their everyday experience into a wider world, a larger-than-life world where heroes and villains still existed and marvelous things still happened—and might happen to *them*. For Mr. Custard, the joy of selling was in getting them to cross over; once that was accomplished, he often didn't bother to carry the deal to a conclusion. He hunted for sport, not for food. All the pleasure was in getting them on the hook.

He did not sell any signs or wait around for her to cash the cheque but left it with her, saying he would pick up the cash on his way back through in a day or two. In the meantime, as a "surety," he said, he took one packet of gum.

He popped a piece in his mouth now, without for a moment taking his eyes off the highway. He held the packet out to the skinny girl, who made a buzzing chirp of refusal, so he reached back over the seat until he felt a stick slide out of the wrapper. In lieu of thanks he received another grunt, but slightly longer and with a note of apology in it. He decided that the girl in front, the skinny one, thought she was the leader, but the one in back, the chubby one with eczema who was always cleaning her glasses, followed her lead only when it suited her. From the first second he'd seen them across the road he'd recognized that his job would be to get the skinny one alone—that is, to get rid of the chubby one. Practically speaking this would mean winning the skinny one over to his side while alienating the chubby one, a feat which would itself entail setting the girls against each other.

He had not even begun to imagine how all this might be accomplished, but this suited him down to the ground. He did not like planning ahead. He believed that he was at his best when forced to act spontaneously, without forethought or, indeed, thought. Besides, knowing what to do next was almost like already having done it. He had a weak mind's eye, and consequently no taste for fantasy: visualizing a future event was the surest way for him to lose all interest in it. He had cultivated the habit of thinking only of the obstacle or challenge directly before him, never of its probable consequence or outcome.

He'd figure something out. It was only a shame that so far the chubby one had shown herself more disposed to be friendly. Well, he had his work cut out for him. Dr. Yard shook his head wonderingly.

"What all're your ladies' names?" he asked, not too cheerfully. "I'm Custard."

Again, the skinny one hesitated, and the chubby one waited to take her cue.

"Melissa," said the skinny one at last.

"Connie," said the other.

"But folks call her 'Slim.'"

"They call *her* 'Missy.'"

"Well, folks call *me* Custard," said Mr. Custard diplomatically. "Sometimes Mr. Custard, sometimes Corporal Field Sergeant Custard. Sometimes Dr. Custard."

He chewed his gum energetically, snapping his mouth open after every bite, and waited for this information to settle—not all the way, just a little.

"Sometimes Damn You Custard," he chuckled, then made his face grim again when this got no response from the girls. "And how old're all you ladies?" he said, and immediately wished he hadn't asked.

"Nineteen," said the one called Missy, with a slight quaver, as though she were guessing someone's weight.

"Twenty," said the one called Slim, with a note of gloating.

He admired her pluck but could not encourage it. Addressing the skinny one, he said, "That's a fine age. Why, that's not only the age you can legally drink at, but the age you can legally marry at."

At this absurd notion, the girl made a noise that bore some resemblance to laughter.

Mr. Custard was gratified, but he was not born yesterday. He did not believe for a second that they were nineteen and twenty. He was pleased however that they had taken the trouble to lie. If they had come clean he would have had no choice but to not believe them. If they were as young as he thought they probably were—closer to half than to two-thirds his age—it might lead to trouble if he ever managed to get the skinny one alone like he hoped to. If they had told him the truth he would have had to claim that they'd acted older, or that he'd forgotten.

One of Mr. Custard's favorite pastimes was concocting defenses and alibis in advance. He rarely got to use them, however, which was unfortunate. The elaborate justifications that he constructed for his various acts were, in his own estimation, often as brilliant as the acts themselves. In his mind he laid out these excuses, with all the patience and skill of a bricklayer, before Dr. Yard, who in his imagination was always gradually, grudgingly won over.

Encouraged, Mr. Custard asked both of them, with a playful leer in his voice, "Are all you ladies *married?*"

They giggled in hiccups, like two sponges getting the bubbles squeezed out of them.

"Are all you ladies *drunk*?" cried Mr. Custard.

That did it. They split their sides. They giggled till they wheezed.

He wouldn't have to be so careful anymore, wouldn't have to scowl so much. They were on his side.

When they'd calmed down, the one perversely called Slim asked, "You reading all these here books?"

Mr. Custard smiled humbly and said, "I'm writing one."

The skinny one made a sound that might have indicated surprise or curiosity had she held it longer. As if translating this into English, the chubby one leaned forward and asked, "What's it about?"

"Psychology," he said.

He was no longer sure why he had taken the books; perhaps it had tickled him to imagine himself as a scholar, the sort of maverick genius who *would* steal books. In fact, he didn't care for reading, and hadn't glanced at so much as a newspaper since leaving high school. He sometimes boasted about this to Francine, who liked to proclaim that the magazines she fanned in front of her face were "bettering." He would then cite his own superior cleverness and long-time aliteracy as disproof, but the point was usually lost on her.

With most people he found it more useful to present himself as learned and widely read. After a few days in the hospital he had even borrowed a book from the floor nurse and let himself be seen with it in various contemplative poses about the ward and inner grounds. One day, shut up indoors due to rain and with Dr. Yard away for the afternoon, he had been driven by boredom to actually open the book and look inside it. He got as far as the first few words of Chapter One—"The Duke and the Duchess were …"—when across the activity room Harold, one of the resident schizos, began throwing a fit, pulling antennas out of his head and stomping on radio waves. Mr. Custard carefully closed the book on his forefinger and sauntered over to watch the orderlies subdue Harold. He liked to stand nearby, looking cheerful and reasonable and sane, whenever one of the inmates went off their nut. Sometimes he even offered the orderlies a helping hand. When Harold had been injected and dragged back to his room, Mr. Custard returned to his easy chair and to the book. But he found that his eyes would not focus on the text. His brain simply rejected it. He realized he did not care the slightest goddamn bit about some goddamn worthless duke and duchess. What the hell did they have to do with *him*? It came to him then quite vividly, in a clarifying surge of rage, that reading was a sustained act of voluntary madness. To read was to remove yourself from life, to absent yourself from reality, and was there a better definition of insanity? That night he burned the book, a page at a time, in one of his ward-mates' bedpans, with matches he'd acquired from Mitkin, one of several sympathetic orderlies who realized that Mr. Custard did not belong there.

The skinny one called Missy cleared her throat and after a pause asked as casually as she could, "So you're a doctor?"

In his mind, Dr. Yard crossed his arms, shook his head, and grumbled, *Saner than all of us put together.*

"You girls waiting on someone?"

Slim turned around, startled. The truck had crept over to them from the gas pumps, crunching gravel all the way, but so many vehicles had already passed by in either direction that they had become almost invisible to her, like the groundhogs scurrying around the high school baseball field.

In the truck were two boys, eighteen or twenty. The one closest to them, leaning out the passenger-side window, had shaggy brown hair and a sweet, knowing smile. Instinctively Slim took off her glasses and pretended to polish them, but before she could say how do you do, Missy, sitting with her back against one post of the giant GAS sign, growled up at them, "Not for you we ain't."

"Well, excuse us for sucking air."

Slim gave them a parting look that was grim but not unfriendly. As the truck lurched forward, its wheels churning up dust, she thought she heard the driver shout something shocking: two words, one an adjective and one a noun. She was stunned; then she replaced her glasses and murmured, just loud enough for Missy to hear if she chose to, "Adolescents."

Missy paid her no mind, and Slim wandered down the gravel shoulder to scratch her arm in privacy. She permitted herself seven seconds, with fingernails but through the sleeve, which seemed a minor enough lapse given the circumstances.

The adjective had been "fat." She was not yet ready to contemplate the noun.

Missy was not talking to her, but that suited Slim just fine. As far as she was concerned, Missy's silence was proof of a guilty conscience. She knew she'd caused them to miss the bus.

But Slim was damned if she was going to stoop to such adolescent behavior herself. She walked back, placed one hand on her hip and the other above her eyes (though the sun was in the other direction and almost behind the mountains now) and looked down the highway in the direction the truck had gone.

"Hell, I wonder if we shouldn't've *taken* that ride."

Missy issued a dismissive syllable through her nose. Missy preferred, whenever possible, to express her point of view non-verbally: she had found that sighs, grunts, and gasps were more difficult to refute than even the most eloquent arguments.

"Nothing we can do about it now," said Slim, and offered a few of her gramma's proverbs on the impossibility of undoing that which was already done and the inevitable improvement of a bad situation. She was afraid that if she did not make light of their predicament she would cry.

Missy ripped a blade of crabgrass in half and tore another one out of the ground.

"We'll have to take *some* ride," Slim hypothesized.

"Those goons would have raped us and left us in the ditch to die," said Missy, as though she relished the idea.

Slim shrugged and walked off down the shoulder. The sky was turning mauve above the pines, which swayed slightly in the cool windless air, as though drunk. Slim rubbed her arm for three seconds, under the sleeve but without fingernails.

"Adolescent" was one of her gramma's favorite epithets, but now that Slim had run away, she felt more kindly towards The Gramophone. She almost wished her gramma were here to see Missy now. For the longest time, The Gramophone had had a very low opinion of Slim's friend, and was always insinuating—through proverbs, homilies, and allegorical newspaper clippings—that Missy was a "bad influence." (This was another of her pet phrases; there were few people on the planet who escaped being a bad influence on someone or other at some time or another.) But after Missy "ran away from home" (her suitcase, Slim discovered, had contained little more than cigarettes and shampoo), The Gramophone had started treating her like a saint. It was no longer Missy but her mother, Mrs. Acorne, who was the bad influence. At the breakfast table (while Missy slept in) Slim's gramma now fulminated against not "peer pressure" but the creeping evil of "hereditary delinquency," and newspaper stories about roaming gangs of wayward youth were replaced by tales of bank-robbing families and orphan murderers. "I'm more of an orphan than *she* is," Slim protested, but her gramma seemed to think this clinched the matter: In her book, you were better off with two dead parents than an absent one. Divorce, in her book, was about the worst thing you could inflict on a child.

Slim might have been inclined to agree that Mrs. Acorne was bad, but you could hardly call her an influence. No matter how loudly or how often she shrieked at Missy to do this or harped at her to stop that, as far as Slim could tell it trickled in one ear and right out the other without leaving behind the slightest residue. Missy did as she pleased, when she pleased. This was the very characteristic that had made Slim fall in love with her in the first place. She desperately wanted to attain that same imperturbable state of grace; she dreamed of a day when her gramma's harangues would slide right off her like grease off a hot griddle.

Even here, however, miles from home, she could not block out The Gramophone's voice. It was still in her head, still stuck in the same old grooves.

Stop that scratching, it said.

Slim yanked down the sleeve. She had already scratched more today than she normally permitted herself in an entire week. If she kept it up she was going to break the skin. But it was not her fault; she was, she reminded herself, under some stress.

It was, beyond dispute, Missy who had made them miss the bus. On finding the toilet at the filling station locked, she'd gone off in search of another. Missy, of all people—with her air of world-weariness and her talk of going to live with her real father in the city—Missy did not know that sometimes you had to ask for the key! But Slim knew better than to make a federal case of it. Missy had, of course, when she'd come back and found the bus gone, given Slim a look of accusation, but even then she had not dared say anything. For she knew what Slim's reply would have been.

"You can't seriously expect me to hold up a busful of people just for the two of us?"

Missy could blame her all she wanted with her eyes, but Slim, who knew that she was in the right, did not have to say anything, and could thus savor both her righteousness and her restraint.

According to the woman inside, the next bus was not due till the same time tomorrow. The bus company would hold their bags at the depot, but the girls had no way of getting into the city, and no money to pay for a hotel room—if there even was a hotel around these parts. When Slim had asked the woman the name of this place so she could try to find it on her map, the woman had replied, "Highway 9." They were nowhere.

A semi-trailer hurtled by, about two feet away, and let out a blast of its horn. This shocked Slim no less than the vulgar insult had done, and she had to close her eyes tightly for a moment to muster her nerve.

When she turned around, Missy was no longer sitting under the sign but had moved to the edge of the road. She stood there sloppily, as if her torso had been dumped onto her legs, and stuck her thumb out at a passing car. The car stopped.

There were three people inside. Missy peered in and said, "Sorry, we thought you were someone else. We're waiting for our friends." The car drove off.

Slim rejoined her friend. "What're you doing?"

"What's it look like?"

Another car approached and Missy pointed her thumb at it, but this one drove past without slowing.

"What'd you tell them we were waiting for someone for?"

Missy hummed through her teeth. This was one of her all-purpose sounds, which she used in a variety of situations to express boredom or disdain. She stared at Slim with dulled compassion.

"I didn't like the look of them," she explained at last. "There was three of them."

Slim clucked her tongue vaguely.

"There's two of us," said Missy.

"No kidding."

"You want to get murdered and raped?"

This, like many of Missy's questions, could not be answered by anything but a blasé or violent non sequitur. "Christ on a stick," Slim grumbled, "I'd kill for a cigarette."

"No you wouldn't," said Missy. Because she had introduced Slim to smoking, she liked to treat her as a mere dabbler.

"You ladies in need of a ride?"

A car going in the wrong direction had pulled over on the opposite side of the road. The solitary driver, a man in a bright red T-shirt, was leaning out his window as though trying to climb through it.

Missy showed Slim her sardonic, unsurprised face, the one she used to say that she alone knew the answers to the questions that everyone else around her had not yet even formulated.

"Which way you heading?," Missy shouted back.

Slim was, despite herself, impressed by Missy's lackadaisical use of the word "heading," which would never have occurred to her. The sudden awareness of her own juvenility curdled her stomach.

The man seemed not to have heard her. "What's all your destination?"

"The city," drawled Missy, tilting her head in the direction he'd come from.

"Which one?"

"Loyola," drawled Slim, eager to break into the conversation.

"Shitfire," the man grinned. "Me too."

Before either girl could reply, he had ducked back inside the car and begun attacking the steering wheel. Through what appeared to be sheer strength alone, he managed to turn the car around and pull it across the highway—which luckily happened to be empty just then.

"Meet me at the pumps," he called to them through the cloud of black exhaust that the car belched into the air.

The girls watched him leap out of the car and confer with the pump boy. He made several expansive gestures towards his vehicle, then hustled inside the filling station.

"Well, there's only one of *him*," said Slim tartly.

"C'mon."

"You're crazy."

Missy looked around for her bag; remembering that it was already on its way to the city, she gave her look-around an air of sarcastic valediction, then launched herself towards the man's car like a novice swimmer kicking off from the side of a pool.

Slim chased after her. "But he lied! He was going in the opposite direction!"

"He's going our way now," she shrugged, but slowed her pace. "He probably turned back to get gas." She stopped altogether and crossed her arms as though waiting for Slim, who was right beside her, to catch up. "I like his *car*," she said at last through an impenetrable fog of sarcasm.

Slim looked at the car. It may have been a color once, but all the paintable surfaces had long ago been overrun by rust. There was a deep and complex dent near the back end which prevented the trunk from shutting properly. Over all of this—rust and dent and windows and tires—the entire vehicle was coated in a thin, even layer of dirt, like a rum ball that had been rolled in cocoa powder.

"It's a hunk of junk," Slim said. She noticed that the pump boy had come no nearer, but stood there still contemplating the car, or the vision of it that the man in the red T-shirt had conjured for him.

Missy made the sort of sound that an heiress might make at the sight of squalor. "Would a rapist drive around in that hunk of junk?"

Slim knew little of the automotive preferences of rapists, and doubted Missy knew more. But her question, as usual, was rhetorical, and did not admit much scope for reply. Slim responded with a sigh of expostulation, as if Missy had been twisting her words; but the argument was already lost.

The man came out of the filling station and waved energetically, like someone in a crowd. He half strode, half jogged back to the car, clapped the pump boy (who had done nothing more than remove the squeegee from its bucket) on the back and pressed a coin into his palm. "Thanks, buster." Then he threw open the car door and called to the girls, "Hop in, ladies!"

"C'mon," said Missy.

Slim, to deny that she had been coerced, made sure to reach the car first.

"There's a dog back here," she said. The dog looked up at her without raising its knobby, triangular head from its paws. Slim thought she probably hated dogs.

"That's Good Dog," said the man from the front seat. "He's a good dog."

Missy opened the front passenger door.

"What're you doing," Slim hissed at her over the roof of the car.

Missy made her eyes round and reproving, as if this were something they'd already discussed. "It'd be rude for us to *both* sit in back," she whispered, and climbed in.

The man started the car. Slim went around to the other side, where the seat was covered in books and papers and cardboard signs.

The pump boy watched the car till it was out of sight. "Didn't look like much," he muttered, and dropped the squeegee back in the bucket of dirty water. He hitched up his overalls by the pockets and trudged back inside. The highway, for a moment, was silent. The sun had gone down behind the mountains and the pines shivered in the windless air, as if chilled.

Mr. Custard told the girls about himself. This was as great a pleasure for him as it was for his audience, for he no more knew than they did what he was going to say. To his satisfaction, he learned that he had been born in Hawaii (which explained the T-shirt), had been raised amid six siblings by a stern saint of a mother, had rather listlessly excelled in his studies, had volunteered for the army and fought in "the war" (the horrors of which he left to their imaginations), had rambled around the country for a time, had boxed professionally (winning, he humbly implied, every fight), and had finally fulfilled his lifelong dream by becoming a psychologist. He was at first vague about his career, but the more he talked, the more he warmed to the topic.

"I'm a sane man working with insane men, that's all," he said. "But let me ask you: Ain't that the description of every sane man that walks the earth? Let me tell you all a little secret. When I was all your age, maybe younger, folks around thought *I* was nuts." He shook his head, sharing their disbelief. "I know, but it's true. Even my own dear mama—who had the kindest, most generous soul of any woman that ever lived—even my own mama thought I was a bit, well, let's say 'different.' I didn't fit the mold. They didn't have the word back then and she wouldn't've known it if they did, but she thought I was *autistic*. That word comes from 'auto,' which is Latin by way of Greek for 'yourself.' Like 'automobile,' which is a 'yourself-mobile,' yourself *mo*-bile, that is, a thing you drive yourself around in. Well," he chuckled, "that's enough of my showing off. Another word for it is 'selfish.' That's the word my mama used, as a matter of fact. She used to say I had no feelings for no one but myself. She used to say it was like nobody but myself existed. Harsh words! Now let me tell you the secret. You ever lied staring up at some clouds? Shitfire—course you have. You ever notice how it starts to feel it's not *them* that's moving, but *you*? Well, that's what it's like in the world these days for a sane man. It's *everyone else* that's nutty as a goddamn fruitcake but it's *you* that starts to feel crazy! Eventually I figured it out, that feeling crazy is about the sanest way to feel in this world. *Crazy* people don't feel crazy! Let me tell you, I got patients who think God is sending them private messages on invisible rainbows tied to their—well, certain parts of their bodies, let's just say. And *those* sons of bitches are convinced, I mean dead positive, that they're the sanest thing going. You tell them they're mad as a hopping June bug making love to a March hare and they just smile and say 'Pass the potatoes.' So a psychologist's job ain't so different from the average person's. Ain't we all surrounded by sickos and loonies who think there's something wrong with *us*? I mean, holy coyote: my own mama!"

Mr. Custard lapsed into a brief silence, mentally replaying with satisfaction his speech. Up ahead, an orange glow rose above the black pines and the blue highway—and for a moment his heart kicked excitedly. Then he realized it was just a town.

"Are all you ladies hungry? You all eat lately?"

The skinny one made a sound suggesting that she would never do such a thing, while the chubby one in the back, eager to accommodate, said that she was ravenous, but could wait.

Mr. Custard was not hungry himself. He never got hungry, really. He ate to pass the time or to make it with waitresses. At the moment he was tired of driving and felt the need to stretch his legs.

He knew the town. Hadn't he been here just last night? He grappled with the temptation to pull in again at Rosie's Roadhouse. He liked retracing his steps, enjoyed being recognized. These returns lent his days a harmony that he found almost irresistible, as he supposed the great poet Shakespeare must have found a rhyme irresistible. But as much as he would have enjoyed a scene with the platinum-blonde waitress, whose dog and books were in the back seat of his car, he could not see any way to turn that reunion to his simultaneous advantage with the girls. He was open to experience and welcomed complications for their entertainment value, but he understood in an abstract way that many people did not.

Sometimes the impossibility of doing everything at once gave him an almost physical pang of frustration. He had a poor memory and was averse to foresight, so to a great extent his life was circumscribed by last night's and this night's sleep. This confinement gave him leave to enjoy himself as best he could, but it also deprived him of the joys of anticipation and reminiscence. The future was whatever at that moment he wanted, and the past was whatever he said it was. The present was all that really existed. Whatever he wasn't doing right now could never be done.

"A joy postponed," he muttered, "is a joy forgone."

"Who said that?" asked the one called Slim.

"Shakespeare," said Mr. Custard. He always attributed anything epigrammatic to Shakespeare—or sometimes, lately, to Freud, whom he respectfully called "Dr. Freud."

He pulled up under a neon sign that buzzed polyphonically, like a horde of mosquitoes. "Here we are!" he cried, smacking the steering wheel. The skinny one hugged herself and looked out the windshield skeptically, so he improvised an explanation for his enthusiasm: "Best goddamn steak sandwich in a fifty-mile radius."

They got out of the car and Mr. Custard sniffed the air.

"This here dog ..." began Slim, holding her door open uncertainly.

"That's a good dog," said Mr. Custard automatically. The waitress last night had yelled "Bad dog!" every time it jumped up on Mr. Custard. For some reason, dogs loved him. As a joke, he'd stolen this one and rechristened it Good Dog, but since then he had not given it much thought. Animals bored him.

"Slim's a *vegetarian*," said Missy, working extra syllables into the strange word.

"I am not," said Slim, slamming the car door and hurrying after them. "I mean, not anymore. I eat meat sometimes."

A waitress came forward with three menus.

"We want ... a booth," said Mr. Custard with tentative zeal, as if choosing his favorite of many favorite colors. "By the window. We won't need those," he said, waving away the menus as they were seated, the girls across from him. "Three steak sandwiches."

"We don't got steak sandwich," said the waitress.

"You all got steak?" asked Mr. Custard, by no means dismayed.

"It's on the menu," said the waitress, with a meaningful glance at the menus.

"You all got toast?"

"It's on the menu too."

"You all got gravy?"

She sighed wistfully, thinking of other, better-paying jobs. "Ten cents extra with your choice of tater."

But Mr. Custard abruptly abandoned his leading questions and asked the girls what they wanted. They were unable to resist the urge to pick up and peruse the menus.

"I'll come back for all your orders."

"Hold on a second, sister," said Mr. Custard. "What's the special?"

She looked at him distantly. "There ain't no special. It's all special."

Mr. Custard had a rich, fruity, irresistible laugh that seemed to touch several notes at once, like a chord strummed on a guitar. The waitress and the girls were swept up into his laughter as into a street dance.

"It's all special. I like that." He put his elbows on the table. "Tell me though now: What's *good?*"

The waitress whistled and seemed to shrink a couple of inches. "I don't know if I'm the one to ask."

"You don't eat here?"

"Can't afford to."

Mr. Custard placed his hands palm-down on the table, closed his eyes, and said, "They *charge* you?"

"Not even a discount."

"But you work here!"

She gave him a look like she felt a little sorry for anyone so naive.

Mr. Custard tried a different tack. He whispered, "How's the cook?"

"Aw, Clem's all right. Clean and all. Not like some of them."

"What's *safe?*" asked Mr. Custard.

She stared blankly out the window for a few seconds, then decided to give his question some thought. "The chicken wings come frozen in a big box," she offered at last.

"Then we'll have the wings," said Mr. Custard grandiosely, to please her.

"Three?"

The skinny one grunted. The chubby one looked up from her menu and asked, "You got french fries?"

The waitress scribbled on her pad with a pencil.

"And bring us some bread," said Mr. Custard.

"Just bread?"

"For an appetizer."

"Something to drink?"

"Yes. Water. Coffee. No, beer. You ladies want something to drink? These ladies are nineteen and twenty," added Mr. Custard with subdued pride.

"Naw," said the skinny one.

"No thank you," said the chubby one.

The waitress carried their order to the kitchen as though it were a disagreeable burden. Mr. Custard, who did not believe he had quite won her over, felt a strong urge to follow her. Instead, he pulled on his fingers till each of his knuckles popped, then looked at the girls slyly, as if he'd just performed a cartwheel.

"Hot in here, ain't it?" he sighed.

The waitress dropped their drinks and a bowl of bread onto the table.

"I heard you had some excitement round here the other day ago," said Mr. Custard.

"Who told you *that*?" She looked prepared to search out the source and set them straight.

"No one. I was just passing through. I'm a salesman," he explained.

"Well there ain't no excitement round here since *I* was born," said the waitress, and stalked off.

The girls looked at him quizzically. He smiled, unruffled. So they'd discovered he was a salesman as well as a psychologist. So what?

He stood and stretched, lifting his arms and twisting from side to side like he was wringing out a rag. "Excuse me," he winked, "nature calls." He made a friendly circuit of the entire room before exiting through the hallway that led to the toilets. He'd never had to piss so bad in all his life.

Missy had never met a psychologist before. The men she knew in Delyle, the men who'd been coming up to talk to her in Soda's like they were renewing an old acquaintance since she was twelve, were all loggers and mechanics and mill workers. They all had the same cagey, distrustful, seagull strut, as if whatever direction they happened to be walking was just the long way round to what they really meant to get at. They all looked at you with the same beady, sideways squint, as if you were a bear too stupid to realize they had a shotgun behind their back.

Mr. Custard, on the other hand, had an honest gaze; he saw only what he looked at, and then he saw it completely. He had a face like a hatchet: pointed, probing, and sharp. His profile was normal, all his features in the right proportions (though perhaps his nose was a bit longer than most), but when looked at straight on, his head was shockingly narrow. His gaze, however, more than the shape of his head, gave her the impression of a hatchet. He swung his eyes about like a woodsman swinging an axe, lodging it to the hilt in one object after another. Whoosh-*chop*, he sank his gaze into her; whoosh-*chop*, into Slim; whoosh-*chop*, into the waitress. His eyes were a luminous light brown, with fanning rays of grey and blue. She had never seen such clear, such finely detailed eyes. They seemed to be in sharper focus than the rest of his face.

The girls sat there, each staring straight ahead, startled by the silence that Mr. Custard had left in his wake, like the ringing in one's ears after a loud noise. Deprived of its object and focus, the competitive animosity that had been growing between them was suddenly laid bare, and neither would look at or acknowledge it.

Missy was convinced that Slim's inane friendliness was an assault on her own policy of laconic aloofness. In her experience with men, she'd found that acting cold and uninterested—even if she was genuinely cold and uninterested—was the most effective way to inflame their ardor. She believed that this tactic was succeeding with Mr. Custard and that Slim was only making a fool of herself, but she resented the distraction of Slim's stupid, stubborn presence, which prevented him from proceeding in the usual manner.

In the car, listening to him talk, Missy had felt a strong urge to abandon her policy and tell him everything. Here was a man who understood people. Here was a man she could talk to! The only thing stopping her was Slim. Anything she might have said would have sounded ridiculous in front of her friend. Why, thought Missy miserably, had she brought her along?

Slim would never have dared to run away if Missy hadn't done it first. Indeed, Slim seemed compelled to mimic Missy's every act and attitude. At first she had found this flattering, but lately it had begun to annoy her that Slim had no personality, no substance of her own. To be reflected in an empty mirror was no honor.

The most aggravating of all Slim's homages was her affectation of hating Mrs. Ludlow, her grandmother. If Missy hated her own mother it was for good reason: because Maude didn't give a howling damn about her. Screaming at you was only a habit of hers. She'd screamed at Mike and Ted, too, and it had about as much to do with anything you'd done or said as with the weather. Missy only played hooky or stayed out all night to give her mother's shrieking condemnations an occasional justification. Slim, on the other hand, played hooky and stayed out all night to get a rise out of her grandmother, whom she then despised for chastising her. And she seemed to despise her praise as much as her criticism. Once, Mrs. Ludlow had been telling Missy a story about Slim as a kid. "She was such a *clever* girl," she was saying, when Slim sprang up from the table and grabbed a lumpen clay ashtray that she had made for Mrs. Ludlow when she was six or seven. (Missy had made just such an ashtray herself, though she could not remember what had become of it.) "Why do you even *keep* this hideous thing?," Slim had screamed. "You don't even smoke!" Then she'd smashed it on the floor and stomped out of the room like she was stepping on the devil's face. A week or so later Missy noticed that the ashtray was back in place on its shelf: Mrs. Ludlow had glued it back together.

The waitress brought three plates of wings, two of them balanced on the inside of her arm, and a basket of french fries.

"Your friend, he all right?" she asked, as if it wasn't any of her business.

Missy made a sound of indifference. Slim said, "He just went to the, you know—nature calls."

When the waitress had gone, Slim moved around to the other side of the booth and looked out the window.

"His car's gone," she said.

Missy refused even to be surprised. With a minute mental adjustment, she corrected her mistake and accepted that Mr. Custard was, in fact, after all, no different from any of the men in Delyle.

"He said he was a salesman," she murmured, poking at a chicken wing. It was red, pimply, and slimy, and she could imagine it being torn off a real chicken.

"He said he was writing a book," said Slim. "But the books he had—" She shook her head. "*A Dictionary of English Surnames*, that was one."

"That T-shirt," said Missy. "My uncle Lewis had one. A blue one, but the same coconuts and trees on it and things."

Slim nodded. "That dog," she said.

Missy pursed her lips in agreement. "Nobody calls their dog 'Good Dog.'"

Slim held up a french fry, peered at it skeptically, then laid it back among the others.

"We can't pay for this," said Missy suddenly, as it occurred to her.

"We got no money," Slim agreed.

"Shitfire," said Missy.

"Holy coyote," said Slim.

"Eat the rich and shit the poor," they drawled in unison.

The girls' eyes met briefly, then glanced away.

With both hands, Missy lifted Mr. Custard's untouched glass of beer to her lips. It tasted sour and grainy—not at all what she had expected. She masked her surprise with a grimace of satisfaction.

"Helps me think," she confided, sliding the glass back to its original position.

Slim nodded and pulled the glass to herself. She sniffed it a little before sipping, Missy thought, but otherwise betrayed no lack of familiarity with the beverage.

They drank the beer surreptitiously, watching out for the waitress and returning the glass to the same spot after each swallow. Missy felt that, in some small way, justice was being done: if they had eaten the food *they* had ordered, it would be stealing; but drinking Mr. Custard's beer was making *him* the thief, which was just what he deserved.

A family of three came in, turning their bewildered heads in every direction as if trying to figure out where the food was. The waitress led them to a table.

"When she takes that order," Missy whispered.

"She'll have her back to us," Slim finished.

The waitress hung back, looking their way occasionally. Then the man with his family beckoned.

"Now," Missy mouthed.

The door chimed incriminatingly, but no one shouted at them to stop; and then they were outside and running, first from nervousness and fear, then for pleasure. Missy felt that all the blood in her body had gone to her head and was churning around in her brain like water in a washing machine. Behind her, Slim let out a whoop that echoed down the silent street.

The sky had gone from blue to purple and black. The town was even smaller and dingier than Delyle. On one side of the road was a line of dusty shops, all dark and closed; on the other was a sparse copse of pines. A car turned onto the road, its headlights stretching the girls' shadows out from their feet, and they slowed to a brisk, skipping walk as it passed. Missy felt like laughing, but she funneled the impulse down into her limbs, swinging her arms and kicking her feet as she walked.

Soon the cold of the night had pinched off even this lingering energy. She put on her coat and hugged herself, trying to hold on to the warm glow from the beer and the triumph of their escape. She had begun to recognize, as an abstract proposition, that they were stranded here, in the middle of nowhere, with the cold of night settling in, without a ride or any money or any hope of finding a place to sleep, when Slim drew up short and grabbed her arm.

"That's his car."

It was parked, roughly speaking, in front of another diner. The girls approached without hesitation, as if it were their own. Indeed, Missy felt an impulse to throw open the door and crawl inside and wait for Mr. Custard as if nothing had happened. At first sight of the car, she had felt simple relief; but as this hardly seemed adequate in the circumstances, she clenched her teeth and tried to feel angry.

"We should cut his tires," she said experimentally.

"We should … steal his dog," said Slim, scratching at her eczema.

The dog, still in back, lifted its head as their shadows passed over the windows.

Grinning and shivering, they stared at the diner, which gave off a provokingly warm and soft light.

Missy articulated a new grunt, one comprised of promise, threat, and resolve.

"C'mon," she said.

They strode side by side across the parking lot; but when they reached the entrance, Missy held the door for Slim, who was left no choice but to go first.

The wind picked up and across the road the pines shuffled restlessly. In the car, the dog cracked its lips in a squeaking yawn, then fussily laid its head back on the seat.

When Slim awoke, she was alone in the car—even the dog was gone. Through the windows she could see nothing but vertical bars of blackness against granular swaths of grey. Trees and snow. She was shivering and had the feeling that she had been doing so for some time.

She remembered falling asleep. Anyway, she remembered the warmth of the car, the headlights scrubbing the highway clean before them, and the reassuring flow of speech from Mr. Custard beside her. As long as he went on talking she could keep an eye on him, as it were, even with her eyes closed. He'd been telling them about his first fight, the first moment he realized that he had a rare gift for knocking people down. It had not been a violent story. He had spoken almost lovingly of his opponent, a big, dull-witted boy three years older than him. The way Mr. Custard told it, the fight had been nothing but a dance followed by a sleep.

Where was she? She quickly corrected the pronoun in her mind (she would not yet face the fact that she was alone): *Where are we?*

She did not remember turning off the highway, though she thought she recalled the gramophone-like crackle of gravel beneath the car's wheels. She remembered, she thought, waking briefly, and asking him where they were going. "To get gas," hadn't he said? She'd fallen back asleep.

A thought, or the prospect of one, blinked on in her mind, like the status light on the radio at home that came on when it had warmed up and was ready to be played. She ignored it, scratching her arm instead.

The inside of her head felt hot and sticky, like a feverish mouth. She could not peel apart individual ideas. The seeping cold, the black bars of pines, Missy's absence, and the matter of how she—*they*—had come to be here, all had to be taken together, in one unmanageable clot.

She remembered walking towards Rosie's Roadhouse with Missy, feeling quite sure of themselves. Then Missy held the door for her, and Slim hesitated, realizing that her friend did not, after all, know what they were going to do, what they were going to say.

He was at the counter with his back to the door, talking to two waitresses.

"'War hero'?" he said, shaking his head with slow, measured scorn. "No, I don't think I care for the term. After all, what's a hero? How's it defined, that's what I want to know—and who's defining it? A person of exceptional powers or extraordinary abilities? Exceptional compared to what? Extraordinary compared to who? Once you realize most folks are monkeys or crazy you realize it don't take much to be a hero and won't thank no son of a bitch for calling you one. Shitfire. And never mind what's a hero—what's a *war*?"

Slim sat down two stools to his right, leaving a space for Missy. But Missy did not take it, sitting instead on Slim's right. That, then, was how it was going to be: Missy was going to just go on holding the door for Slim.

Well, to hell with that.

"Howdy," she said. Her voice was calm, but she realized she was scratching her arm. She took off her glasses and began to wipe them with a napkin.

"Get you girls something?" asked one of the waitresses, leaning against the refrigerator like she was keeping it upright.

"Why, these here ladies are my nieces!" cried Mr. Custard, slapping the counter with unfeigned joy. "Ladies, these here are Lorna and Lola, friends of a friend of mine and therefore friends of mine and friends of my friends."

"How *do* you know Irene anyhow?" asked the other waitress, slumped over the counter and peering sideways at Mr. Custard as if he were some clever, skittish animal in the zoo.

"I come in here all the time," he said.

"Then how come I never seen you," she demanded, charmed by his furtiveness.

Mr. Custard turned to Slim. His gaze went into her and she felt for a moment, till she tore her eyes away, that she had never seen anyone so happy to see her in all her life. He was not in the least alarmed or embarrassed by their arrival.

"You ladies want something to eat?" he asked. "They got the best damn burger in town here. In fact, I'll have one of them fellas myself. But hold the mushrooms."

The waitress leaning against the fridge said, "Our burgers don't ordinarily come *with* mushrooms."

"They're extra," said the other.

"Then I'll have mine *with* mushrooms. Make it *double* mushrooms." He turned to Slim and cupped a hand to his mouth in a mock whisper. "That way they got to make it fresh."

"We make everything fresh!" cried the one slumped over the counter, pleasantly scandalized.

"I'll have the same," said Slim, blushing in anticipation of their laughter, "... but hold the burger."

They didn't laugh, so she kept her face straight and pretended it hadn't been a joke.

"Something for you, honey?"

Missy grunted, then grunted again, annoyed that the first grunt had not carried her meaning. "The same," she clarified.

"Same as him or same as your friend?"

"As him," she said, with a grunt of impatience.

Slim emitted a grunt of her own. They had come in here allied against him, but now it seemed that Missy had abandoned both their alliance and their grievance. For a moment she keenly hated both of them, Missy and Mr. Custard. She wanted to crush something, but had nothing to crush but her own feelings, her own desire to crush something. She lashed out by lashing inwards, and did the last thing she wanted to do, which was stay put and smile, and said the last thing that would normally have entered her head: "And I'll have one of *those*," she said, pointing her finger like a gun at Mr. Custard's half-finished beer. "Same as him."

"You old enough for that, sugar?"

"Eat the rich and shit the poor," said Mr. Custard with placid indignation, "these ladies are my *nieces*. They're nineteen and twenty years old. Old enough to drink, old enough to get married, by God."

"What about you, angel?"

Missy glumly shook her head, and Slim felt a flush of triumph.

They ate and drank and Mr. Custard, through an ever-present mouthful of half-chewed burger, regaled them with tales of his childhood. It took all of Slim's attention and ingenuity to correlate what he was saying now with what he had told them in the car. Now he had only five siblings—but she reasoned that earlier he had been counting himself. Now his family lived on a milk farm—but she supposed they must have milk farms in Hawaii too. Again the most salient figure of his youth was his mother, but it was not easy to reconcile the woman as he described her now with the one who had called him "selfish." Now he said that she had been dissatisfied with all her children except for the youngest—namely, Mr. Custard himself. He never came right out and said that he had been her favorite, but he was conspicuously absent from the litany of disappointments she had suffered at the hands of her offspring. One had died in the war; one had died in childbirth; one had married the wrong kind of man; one had dropped out of high school and run away from home; one had been arrested on charges of "unmotivated assault"; one had ended up in the booby hatch. There were more sins than there were children—but Slim figured that some of his siblings may have committed more than one.

That he might be lying occurred to her only fleetingly and abstractly. He showed none of the hesitation or embarrassment of a liar, and the details he furnished were too richly embellished to be the product of anyone's mere imagination. She supposed that some facts had possibly become garbled or confused with the passage of time and through numerous retellings, but she did not seriously doubt that the stories he told had a firm foundation in his own personal experience. Where else could they have come from?

And unlike any liar she had ever known, he did not seem at all concerned that you believe him. He did not swear, or repeat himself, or say "honest." He contradicted himself and neither blushed nor took any pains to resolve these contradictions. The fact that he didn't even bother to be consistent proved that he wasn't lying; the stories he told must be, in some fundamental way, true. She even began to question her earlier doubts. Wasn't it possible that he might need a dictionary of names to write a book on psychology? Wasn't it possible that he was both a psychologist and a salesman? Maybe he sold psychological supplies; or maybe he drove around recruiting new patients, and it was just easier to say "salesman" to a simple-minded waitress than to explain.

But then he did lie. After they finished eating he patted his belly, then his pockets, and told the waitresses that his cheques were in the car. He asked Slim and Missy to help him bring the books in for their friend. But when they were outside, he told them to hop in. Then he'd driven off without a word.

So she knew what he looked like when he lied. He looked the same. Nothing changed. They were miles down the highway before she even realized that they weren't going back.

"We didn't pay," she said.

"You girls have any money?" asked Mr. Custard. "Didn't think so! So you see, we *couldn't've* paid, even if we wanted to."

There was none of the exultation that she'd felt when she and Missy had run out of the first diner. She felt now only a sucking emptiness in her chest. She felt like a cheat.

"Is that why you ditched us? You didn't have any money?"

He nodded deeply, like someone making a long-overdue confession. "Of course," he said thoughtfully, "even if that wasn't why, I'd probably say it was. But it was," he added quickly, "it was."

In the back seat Missy made a perturbed sound, and added the gloss: "Why *don't* you have any money?"

Mr. Custard shook his head slowly and sadly. "My hospital."

Missy made a sound indicative of the inadequacy of this reply.

For a long time he stared out the windshield at the rolling highway.

"It burned down," he said at last.

Slim had felt better as soon as he opened his mouth; it was some time before his meaning caught up with her relief. She realized now that it hadn't mattered what he'd said, only that he'd said something. He'd taken the trouble to justify himself. It was like the answers her teachers had offered to so many of her questions about the universe: she was happy to accept just about any answer other than "I don't know" or "Because." To be told that atoms were composed of sub-atoms or that things fell because of something called gravity was satisfying because these *were* explanations, because they were answers. Knowing that her questions had answers was enough. The only insupportable universe was a universe in which things happened for no reason.

"Is that true?" she asked softly, naively imploring him to reassure her, even though she knew what he himself had admitted: that his answer would be the same whether he told the truth or not.

She had seen him lie to those waitresses. Had she seen him, at any time, tell the truth?

The outline of the thought that had blinked on in her mind now returned, and this time she looked at it. Her gramma was going to kill her—because Mr. Custard was going to kill them both. This realization came to her in her gramma's voice: *He's a psycho.*

He was not a psychologist. Those were not his books. This was probably not his car. He had taken her and Missy out into the backwoods in the middle of the night. Missy was already gone. He would come for her next. He would have a knife or, what was somehow worse, a rope, and someone opened the car door and she screamed.

"Jumping Jesus, what the hell, I thought you were sleeping," cried Missy, startled into loquacity.

Slim jumped out of the car, holding her hands up like blades. "Where is he?"

Missy groaned at Slim's ignorance. "Went to find gas," she said at last, getting into the seat that Slim had vacated. "Thing's below E already."

"This ain't a filling station. This ain't nowhere."

Missy hunched her shoulders for warmth. "He went to siphon some out of some goddamn tractor or something I guess. He had a, you know, a gas can."

They could see their breath in the yellow light that spilled from the car onto the snowy gravel. Slim wanted a cigarette, then felt dizzy at the returning thought: Gramma would kill her.

There was a sound in the distance, a sharp crack like a branch snapping in the wind.

Had he shot the dog?

"Get out the car," Slim said.

"You're crazy."

Slim knew she was not being reasonable. He'd only stopped to find gas, she told herself; he'd gone off with a jerrycan, not a gun. But it was no use. The certain dread she'd felt moments ago had not had time to dissipate, and was still being pumped around inside her by her heart.

Slim heard his footsteps, quick little crunches like a mouse gnawing at a wall, before she saw him. He was running towards them, clucking to himself like a hen, and every so often bubbling over into some shout of jubilation: "Oodilolly!" or "Holy coyote!" He was not carrying a jerrycan. Slim took a step back from the car.

Before he could reach them, a black shape came bounding out of the woods and attached itself to his leg. It was the dog. Mr. Custard let out a scream—not of pain or even anger but sheer incredulity. He whipped and thrashed his leg madly, and with a whimper the black shape came loose and fell skidding to the ground. Almost without breaking stride, Mr. Custard lunged and kicked the dog with all his might, then threw himself into the car, started the engine, and slammed it into gear. Slim jumped back, shielding her face from the spray of gravel and ice. Missy, who had had one foot out the door, shouted incoherently, perhaps to Slim. Then, to keep herself from falling out, she had to pull the door shut—and just in time, as the car fishtailed, shot down the road, and disappeared into the pines.

Slim stood listening to the roar of her own heart; then, as her pulse subsided, she could make out another sound in the distance, a drawn-out rasping sound, like someone continuously sliding open a window that had not been opened in a long time.

She went to the dog, and was at first relieved, then only doubly frightened, to hear it whining. If it was hurt, if it was dying, she would have to do something.

She crouched and placed a hand on its lumpy skull until the animal stopped growling.

The moon was overhead, but, in the direction from which Mr. Custard had come running, a dim orange glow had appeared above the black outline of the trees. She walked towards it. The dog followed, at a distance.

The road curved and began to widen, the gravel gave way to deep tracks of frozen mud, and the pines parted to reveal a farmyard, littered with hulks of machinery and tufts of grass, all bathed in the same undulating orange light. The rasping sound grew louder until it became a crackling roar. She rounded the farmhouse and saw the fire.

It was a barn, or had been. The fire had consumed all the structure's details in the brilliance of its blaze, so that it looked like a child's drawing of a barn: thick black lines for walls, a gaping black opening for a door, and clumsy black triangles for rafters, which had already begun to sag. Shivering, Slim walked towards it, and imagined she could feel its heat.

A man stood motionless, as if suspended in gelatin, halfway between the house and the conflagration. A stick lay in his out-stretched arms like a dead thing that he was afraid to touch. As Slim came nearer she saw that it was a gun.

He looked at her, and at the house, and at the barn. His eyes were wild and unseeing, as if he'd just been struck blind.

"What happened?"

"Burnt my barn," he said thickly. "Burnt my goddamn barn."

"Why?"

He peered at her then, flames in his eyes. "Who're you? Where do you come from? What do you want here?"

She opened her mouth but nothing would come out. She shook her head and looked around dismally.

"My dog," she blurted at last, scratching her arms till they bled. "My dog's hurt."

Dr. Yard was talking to him but Mr. Custard was finding it difficult to concentrate. He had never felt so sleepy in all his life. There was a prickly pain in his leg where the dog had bit him, and a clenching pain in his shoulder where he supposed the crazy man had shot him—actually *shot* him!—shot *him*! He'd never been shot at before, not in his entire life! He hadn't felt anything at the time but a cold wet sting, neither pleasure nor pain; but now it felt as if his stomach had relocated to his shoulder and begun digesting itself. His blood, too, was everywhere. He was surprised at how dark and rich and thick it was, almost like oil. He was disappointed to find that it tasted like salt, only salt.

The girl had her face pressed against the window like she was trying to draw air through it. Everything was slowing down, time was coming in drops—the better to help him register the situation's novelty. But every so often the highway snapped its neck suddenly to one side as if trying to buck him off. Dr. Yard was talking to him—not, he thought, altogether without approval—but he could not distinguish the words.

The same thing had happened at the hospital. Whenever Dr. Yard spoke to him at any length, his words dissolved into mere gabble, strings of isolated syllables more like Morse code than human speech; and even his face, as Mr. Custard watched, would gradually fragment into its constituent features, so that he found he could attend to the man's spongy nose, or to the scraping of his eyelids over his flat grey eyes, or to the flapping of the dewlap beneath his chin, or to the slick, darting movements of his wet tongue, or to the flecks of spittle collecting in the corners of his mouth; but he could never attend to all of them at once. The harder he tried to make the sounds fit together into words or the words into sentences, the more they disintegrated, and it was the same with the face. Two eyes plus one mouth plus one nose equals one face, he assured himself. But it wasn't true. Two eyes, a nose, and a mouth did not make a face. Something was missing.

The car was almost out of gas. He was amazed that it hadn't run out already. What would he do when it stopped? He didn't know, and the not-knowing excited him. Anything could happen! He was open to experience. His mother called it "selfish," but Dr. Yard, a professional psychologist, had called it being "open to experience."

But Dr. Yard had been wrong about his mother. She *had* been a saint. She would never have let him be thrown in jail for hanging a few lousy bucks' worth of paper! And if he had never been put in, he would never have had to pretend he was nuts in order to get out. She had always taken good care of him; he was her baby. But Dr. Yard didn't like that story, so Mr. Custard told him another one.

The thought of his mother made him think of Francine. Would she be angry at him for missing his appointment? Well, she'd certainly forgive him when she saw the blood. She would clean him up, put him to bed. He would cry a little; that would help.

The scene suddenly bored him; it had happened just like that hundreds of times. Francine in her nightgown, screaming at him, then comforting him; slapping his face, then holding his head to her freckled chest. Francine with her young body and her old face, the skin that seemed to have slipped half an inch down her skull. No, he couldn't go home. Anyway, it didn't matter. He'd never make it. He was almost out of gas.

But that had happened before too, plenty of times. He could see it now, unfortunately; the not-knowing was gone. He would wait, preferably for a woman, or else a family, and would hitch a ride into the nearest town. He would tell them a story and borrow five bucks. He would pass a cheque at a filling station. He would go to a restaurant and pick up a waitress. He would go back for the car, or he would call up Francine collect and he would cry and she would come get him.

He yawned. He was sleepier than ever. The ditches on either side of the road yawned with him. The highway bridled, trying to shake him. Dr. Yard smiled grudgingly, shook his head in admiration. "Get some rest," he advised. "You've earned it."

He was talking about the fire. It had been a good fire.

Mr. Custard stomped on the gas pedal. The highway straightened out, momentarily subdued.

"Hey, slow down," pleaded the doctor—or perhaps it was the girl, the skinny one. Perhaps it was she who had been talking to him all along. He realized he'd gotten her alone. He'd won. The thought gave him no pleasure. She was not, after all, very pretty.

Mr. Custard had made something beautiful, and while he'd been standing there admiring it, he'd been shot at by a crazy person.

"Life!" he muttered, almost tenderly.

A pair of headlights appeared on the horizon. He went towards them in slow motion.

Here, he thought, was something new.

PART III

PADDLING AN ICEBERG

"Fiction is *psychology; psychology* is *fiction!*
Jim Bird

SUNDAY.

HI **THERE, SHE THOUGHT,** *I'm Margo Penn-Jennings (inquisitive pause) and I'm here for the (sardonic pause) self-help seminar.*

She did not like the sound of this in her head. The tone of her inner voice was prim, nasal, and superior. As she crossed the hotel lobby and approached the check-in table, with its giant HEALTHY SELF banner hiding the legs of the women who sat behind it, Margo resolved that she would not say anything like this, but instead, simply, whatever popped into her head.

"Hi there," Margo heard herself say, "I'm Margo Penn-Jennings and I'm here for the self-help … thing. Ha."

You're an idiot, her mind told her.

The women behind the table, in a flurry of uncoordinated activity, located her name on their list, had her sign in, produced a bundle of pamphlets and booklets held together with elastic bands which they called "the material," and scolded her affectionately for being late. "You almost missed Jim Bird's opening learning." They said the man's name like it was a single word, like he was a kind of bird—a jimbird.

"But …" She began rummaging in her purse for the timetable that would exonerate her. "The seminar doesn't start till tomorrow I thought."

"Oh no," said one of the women, "this is a spontaneous event." She uttered these last two words with so little emphasis that they

101

sounded capitalized, as if "Spontaneous Event" were one of the fundamental kinds of stuff in the universe. "You can leave your bags."

Margo entered the already hushed convention room and, with her dogged instinct for thrift, took a seat among the "better" ones near the front. There were many chairs still vacant. Evidently she was not the only one to arrive late.

The portable stage was also empty, and remained that way for ten more minutes. The audience did not seem to mind. Their coughs were politely muffled; their chairs creaked softly, as if they were only settling more deeply into them; no one spoke. Margo turned and looked around the room, smiling when others' eyes met hers. They all looked disgustingly normal.

At last a man got up on the stage, apparently to inspect the microphone. With a shiver of pleasant indignation, Margo felt sure that they were about to be told that the spontaneous event had been spontaneously cancelled.

"You've all made a mistake," the man said, his amplified voice booming at them from every direction, making Margo jump. "You shouldn't have come. There's nothing wrong with any of you. Acknowledging you have a problem isn't the first step towards fixing the problem—it *is* the problem."

The man on stage, Margo realized, was none other than the jim-bird himself.

Pay attention, she told her mind.

You shut up, said her mind, *I'm trying to listen.*

"You will become what you are."

At nineteen, Jim Bird read these words and found a bitter solace in them.

He was, at that time, grappling with free will. This was, to him, no airy philosophical inquiry, but as pertinent as a speeding ticket.

He had treated a girl badly, and the question that weighed on him was whether or not he was to blame for his behavior—whether or not he was to blame for *who he was*, for he knew deep down that in his dealings with the girl he had acted only in accordance with his own wishes. The question was, therefore: Could he have wished otherwise? Could he someday *want* to do right, or was he doomed by a shabby character to act always in perfect self-interest? He hated himself for the way he'd treated the girl; but if he could not have acted differently, then surely it was pointless to hate himself.

Could he change himself? Could he choose who to be, or was his character immutable?

He found the answer he was looking for in Nietzsche.

The individual is, in his future and in his past, a piece of fate, one law more, one necessity more in everything that is and everything that will be. To say to him "change yourself" means to demand that everything should change, even in the past.

Because human beings take themselves to be free, they feel regret and pangs of conscience. But no one is responsible for his actions, no one for his nature. Judging is the same as being unjust. This holds equally true when the individual judges himself.

The sting of conscience is, like a snake stinging a stone, a piece of stupidity. Never yield to remorse, but at once tell yourself: Remorse would simply mean adding to the first act of stupidity a second.

Though this wisdom did not permit Jim to forgive himself or even stop hating himself, it did make him feel better. It was a kind of relief to establish, once and for all, that he would never be a better person, that he would never be able to rise above his despicable nature. In fact, admitting his worthlessness gave him a kind of intoxicating satisfaction. He had begun to *like* hating himself. "Whoever despises himself," as Nietzsche said, "still respects himself as one who despises." This may seem paradoxical, but it is the nature of hatred: One always loves oneself for hating. It is *good* to hate evil, and that which we hate is always, *ipso facto*, evil. I have always thought "righteous indignation" to be a tautology, for the greater the indignation, the greater the sense of righteousness. As humans we may love, but it is only as angels that we hate.

This is why hatred is such a pernicious pleasure. The more despicable we make the object of our hatred out to be, the more saint-like we feel ourselves to be by comparison. Sometimes, to savor our righteous indignation even more piquantly, we will actually cooperate with our tormentors, and stick our neck under their bootheel. I met a woman once who, feeling she was being cheated by a shopkeeper, in a fit of rage threw down twice as much money as her bandit was actually demanding and stormed out triumphantly. She liked this story, which she told again and again with bitter satisfaction, not because it showed she had done anything particularly wise, but because it showed she had been *wronged*—gloriously, angelically wronged.

Hatred is as much self-aggrandizement as it is other-deprecation; and the strange paradox of self-loathing is that it engenders such self-respect.

This can operate the other way, too. Margo, attending Jim Bird's Healthy Self seminar years later, would write in her journal, "Of COURSE I hate myself. What self-respecting person doesn't hate herself?" If nobody's perfect, if all of us are flawed, then liking yourself can only be the most obscene arrogance. Whoever respects himself must despise himself as one who respects.

Jim Bird, at nineteen, felt that he had, as Nietzsche promised, become what he was. He was (as the girl he had wronged had told him) "a real shit."

It was only years later, when his wife left him, that Jim Bird was at last able to stop hating himself.

"It's not about you," she assured him with maddening benevolence. "I am the only one responsible for my own happiness. I have to *choose me.*"

She had just returned from a self-help seminar.

She removed her belongings from the apartment with the precision of a surgeon excising a tumor, without disturbing any of his things—thus dispelling the illusion that their lives had become intertwined. He saw not respect but contempt in the way she left his things so fastidiously untouched. Even his books stood uncannily upright on the shelves, none toppling over into the vacated spaces.

But she had, he discovered, left behind (accidentally?) a few of her self-help books.

Instead of ripping them in half or throwing them out the window, he read them—and this, through the ravaging haze of his hatred, felt like the more destructive act.

Smile, they said. This was the pith of their wisdom. Smiling was the panacea. The way to be happy was simply to *be happy.* We aren't unhappy because bad things happen to us—oh no. We're unhappy because we frown. So instead of frowning when bad things happen—smile!

Citing everyone from Milton to Emerson (but especially Emerson), these self-help gurus asserted that we only ever experience the world through our own consciousness. A man does not enjoy Paris, he *enjoys himself* in Paris. If the world seems gloomy to you, it is because *you* are gloomy. Events and circumstances are in and of themselves neutral; how else explain the commonplace fact that the same event or circumstance can make one man happy and another sad? Therefore it

is pointless trying to change the world. In order to achieve contentment, you have only to change your *response* to the world. When
"bad" things happen, call them "good." When life gives you lemons,
visualize lemonade. When the world frowns, just smile.

Even if you didn't believe you were happy, you should go
through the motions, act like you were, and eventually happiness
would come to you. How this would happen was left mysterious,
but often the faith was couched in a sort of magical thinking of the
like-attracts-like variety: Happy people attract happy people, happy
thoughts attract happy outcomes. This was the power of positive
thinking, of mind over matter, of dreams over reality: If you only
imagined it vividly enough, if you only desired it strongly enough,
it would be yours.

And this kind of thing, Jim realized with growing horror, was
infiltrating popular consciousness in countless ways. It was now considered bad manners to be or even to look unhappy, because it was
supposedly within your power to be otherwise. Colleagues, students,
and complete strangers had come up to him and told him to smile.
"It takes less muscles to smile than to frown," they informed him
(thereby exhibiting in a single sentence (1) the egoistic conviction
that personal happiness was the highest goal of human life, (2) the
slothful belief that what was *easy* was always preferable to what was
hard, and (3) further evidence of the inexorable degradation of the
English language: they should, of course, have said "It takes fewer
muscles to smile"). Athletes in interviews no longer attributed their
successes to practice or talent, or their failures to bad luck or inferior
skill; nowadays, it seemed, the winners were always those who had
wanted it more. "We just went out there and gave 110 percent," they
shrugged, with the implication that the other guys must have given
109 percent or less. Even Bird's students lately seemed to believe that
their grades should reflect not their performance but their desire or

the degree of their commitment. "But I'm *not* a B-student," they'd say, after putting in what they felt was an A-student's effort; or, even more bluntly: "I really *need* this A," by which they meant, of course, that they really wanted it—and wasn't wanting something badly enough the necessary and sufficient condition of getting it?

But the philosophy of self-help was not just silly, it was potentially dangerous. Self-help, it seemed to him, could actually do harm. It did this in two ways: it put too much emphasis on the "self," and too much emphasis on the "help."

By telling you repeatedly that (he recalled his wife's words) *you* were the only one responsible for your own happiness, self-help also implied conversely that your unhappiness was *your* fault alone. Never mind that your children were ungrateful or your boss an insufferable prick: if you were unhappy at home or at work, that was your choice—you were doing it to yourself. This was victim-blaming at its most flagrant. Now, instead of just being miserable at work, you were made to feel additionally miserable for *feeling* miserable. Furthermore, the absolute emphasis placed on "self" could only encourage meekness and docility. Don't rock the boat—it's not the boat's fault you're unhappy! This was, as Henry James said of stoicism, a philosophy fit only for slaves, for it taught men to embrace the status quo. But what if the status quo really were to blame? Self-helpers were told, when faced with injustice, to find inner contentment; but when confronted with a genuine evil, was it not suicidal to pretend that everything was fine?

"It is important to eliminate from conversations all negative ideas," said Norman Vincent Peale, arch-prophet of positive thinking,

for they tend to produce tension and annoyance inwardly. For example, when you are with a group of people at luncheon, do not comment that the 'Communists will soon take over the country.' In the first place, Communists are not going to take over the country, and by so asserting you create a depressing reaction in the minds of others. It undoubtedly affects digestion adversely.

It would only have been necessary to replace "Communists" with "rampant militarization" or "the attenuation of civil rights" or "the exploding gulf between rich and poor" to update this advice to the era and milieu in which Jim Bird read these words. There were times, surely, when a little dyspepsia was justified?

Then there was the emphasis put on "help." A cure always implied a disease. The incredible proliferation of self-help manuals over the past fifty years sent at least one clear message: *You need help.* "Ask yourself whether you are happy, and you cease to be so"; with so many books and magazines and television shows shrilly asking you, again and again, "Are *you* happy? Are you happy *enough?*" was it any wonder that people began to doubt that they *were* happy, or happy enough? With so many medicines being offered, how could one feel healthy? The solutions being offered were themselves the problem. No one ever acquired happiness by grasping at it.

Bird catalogued his criticisms methodically, as though it were his job. For indeed, the idea for a new project had begun to take form. He would write a book, scholarly and caustic, condemning the self-help industry. He needed a new project. It was five years since his first book had been published. An analysis of Nietzsche's conception of the will, the book was more successful than it should have been, for it had appeared at a propitious time. Nietzsche had been prophetic in many areas, but his belief that volition was an illusion, merely the subjective experience of a system of semi-independent urges blindly colliding like chemicals in a beaker—this view of the mind seemed tailor-made for the so-called "Decade of the Brain," when neuroscientists and psychologists alike strove to map all the parts of the personality onto sections of grey matter, hoping thereby to prove that we are nothing but our brains and therefore as much in thrall to the rigid laws of cause and effect as any other physical system. One of the lions of this movement, a famous philosopher who wrote popular books on materialistic determinism (as it was called), even provided Bird's book with a lengthy introduction, in which he generously (if somewhat anachronistically) indicated the ways in which Nietzsche's views echoed his, the philosopher's, own: "The will, as Nietzsche would be the first to admit, is, like consciousness itself, an illusion. What we call 'will' is just the shorthand employed by a complex machine to signify what I have elsewhere called 'self-referential subroutines' …" etc., etc. Bird's own name was not mentioned in this introduction, nor indeed were the ideas he presented in the text; Bird was not sure the famous philosopher had even read his book. Nevertheless, for this service, the philosopher's name appeared on the cover in a font that Bird (with a ruler) determined to be only two point sizes smaller than his own. But the book sold well, and Bird's academic future was assured.

The Decade of the Brain, however, had come and gone, and whether or not it had achieved its objectives, Bird knew that he wanted nothing more to do with anything that might appeal to neuroscientists, psychologists, or famous philosophers. He wanted to do something different. Here, at last, in self-help, he had found something different.

But he was afraid that to write this attack on self-help as a philosopher, to write this book as a piece of scholarly and caustic social criticism, would be to write over the heads of the very masses who consumed the stuff. An academic treatise would be "academic" in the worst sense of the word: detached, theoretical, dry—"merely academic." You could not denounce the populace from an ivory tower; you had to descend to the streets, like Zarathustra. Bird wanted, more than anything, to address his attack to self-help's adherents. He wanted to write something that his wife might read.

The only way to do that was to speak in their idiom, to adopt the language of the self-help books themselves.

He would write a self-help book to end all self-help books—an anti-self-help book. He would write a satire.

The writing came easily. Almost too easily—for, as Nietzsche said, "The sum of the inner movements which a man *finds easy,* and as a consequence performs gracefully and with pleasure, one calls his soul." Till now, Bird had taken it as axiomatic that writing was like giving birth: there had to be labor pains. In the past he had never been able to produce more than four or five hundred words a day, for he could not commit a single sentence to paper without becoming paralyzed by the thought that this one idea could be written a million different ways. Nietzsche said that the great writer could be recognized by how skillfully he avoided the words that every mediocre writer would have hit upon to express the same thing. Bird, who wanted only to be understood, would struggle desperately to hit upon those mediocre words; but everything he produced looked awkward, unnatural, flamboyantly recherché. Now, for the first time, the words suggested themselves. He turned out a thousand, fifteen hundred, two thousand words a day. He felt himself almost physically taken over by the project—much the same way (or so he imagined) that Nietzsche had been taken over by the writing of *Thus Spoke Zarathustra.* It was as if this was what, and how, he had been meant to write all his life; and this thought, so damaging to his scholar's ego, was the only dark spot on the otherwise ecstatic joy of composition.

He found that he could mimic the self-help books' conventions almost effortlessly, and indeed with pleasure, for in this medium that he had no respect for he could let himself go completely. Like a patient playing a villain in a psychodrama, he was free to say and do things he would never have said or done in his own person. It was downright cathartic.

He easily mastered the loose (i.e., ungrammatical), chatty (i.e., slangy), chummy (i.e., badgering) prose style, and had a knack for turning out phrases that could have been self-help boilerplate: "If you don't give in to your true self, your true self will give in to you." "Smiling is not a panacea—but it is a good cure for a frown." He managed to sustain the requisite tone of manic enthusiasm for over 300 pages through an unending barrage of italics, underscoring, boldface, capital letters, funny fonts, and other typographical tricks for signaling emphasis. He disguised his extended sermon as an interactive dialogue by putting a lot of obtuse questions into his reader's mouth ("I know, I know, you're thinking: But does this really apply to me?") and then answering them ("You bet it does, buster! It applies to *everyone*"). He borrowed the authority of great thinkers of the past, quoting everyone from Milton to Emerson (especially Emerson). He capitalized dubious concepts and gave them Unnecessary But Impressive Abbreviations (e.g., UBIAs). He manufactured supportive anecdotes and testimonials as needed. He employed a sort of pietistic scientism, citing "recent scientific studies" to demonstrate anything he wanted to demonstrate. He adopted at times a plodding conscientiousness, making clear what was already clear, defining terms in no need of defining, providing several synonyms for commonplace words, as if combating not just the reader's skepticism but their unfamiliarity with the English language. He was shamelessly repetitive, writing the same sentence several times in a single chapter, often verbatim. He summarized chapters in forewords and again in afterwords. He filled entire pages with synoptic tables and lists. (Self-help authors loved lists, especially lists with seven or ten items.) He created an outrageously transparent self-quiz which claimed to help the reader measure their "striving index," that is, the degree to which they overexerted themselves. (Question number 47:

"Do you exert yourself excessively? Never. Rarely. Sometimes. Often. Always. (Circle one.)" Question number 89: "Are you the kind of person who 'overdoes' it? Never. Rarely. Sometimes. Often. Always. (Circle one.)") He drew beautifully absurd diagrams of abstract ideas or psychological entities that were simply not susceptible to pictorial representation, and chuckled happily over them:

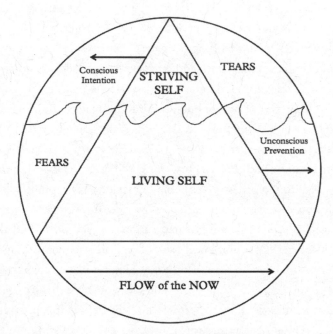

So (some of my readers may be forgiven for wondering), if *Letting Go* was written as a parody, a joke—then Jim Bird is a fraud? All his bestselling books, and the lucrative seminars spun off from them, are just a big hoax?

Not so fast, buster.

It is true that, soon after Bird sent the manuscript off to his agent, the joyous inspiration of composition faded and he ceased to think very highly of the project. It had been a distraction when he had needed one. It had siphoned off some of the anger he felt towards his wife. It had been, he supposed, a kind of primal-scream therapy. But now, in the deafening silence with which his agent received the manuscript, Bird felt acutely embarrassed by his cathartic howls. A person's respect for their own accomplishments is usually proportionate to their efforts; because Bird had not experienced any labor pains, he could not feel as though he had given birth. The manuscript was not his child, but something he had sloughed off. He had produced it as he grew hair, and once one's hair becomes detached from one's head, one tends to view it with disgust.

His agent, a broker of scholarly monographs to university presses, understandably did not know what to make of the manuscript. Whether or not it was intended as a joke, she did not think it was likely to help her client's academic career. So she sat on it, and did nothing. When, a year later, Bird wrote to ask if he could shop it around to publishers himself, she readily consented. (Later still, when the book appeared and soon shot to the #1 spot on the *New York Times* "advice" bestseller list, where it would stay for seventeen weeks, she casually consulted her lawyer to find out if she might still be contractually entitled to some of the royalties. She was told that it would depend on whether or not Bird had kept a copy of her consenting letter. The agent decided not to pursue the matter; instead, to savor the delicious sense of having been wronged, she annulled her contract with Bird herself.)

For a year, Bird was content to leave the book alone. But when he finally picked it up and read through it again, he was surprised. Because he had had time to forget much of it, and because it was not written in his usual labored style, he found that he could almost read it as the work of someone else—which is, of course, the best possible way to read one's own work.

It was undeniably silly, and dumb, and sloppily written—but then, he thought, so were all self-help books. And this *was* undeniably a self-help book.

But this one was different. This one said something he agreed with. This author, he felt, had gotten something right.

> You are (this author wrote) a piece of fate. Your body and your mind are governed by physical laws and necessities. That means you yourself are a law and a necessity. To improve yourself—to *change* yourself—it would be necessary to change the laws and necessities of the physical universe!
>
> Because you think you should be able to improve yourself, you feel pain and anguish when you fail to do so. You beat yourself up for not being better, for not being different. But NO ONE is to blame for who they are or who they are not!
>
> Hating yourself for not being someone else is like hating a rock for being a rock. It's not *being you* that makes you unhappy, it's *wanting to be someone else.*
>
> You are who you are. You can't be anyone else. Why would you want to be?

This, to Jim Bird, sounded familiar, and true. He had, it seemed, almost despite himself, written something of value. It was not a spoof, but an antidote.

When he sent the manuscript to several of the most prominent publishers of self-help books, he did so with some lingering shame (which was not much alleviated by signing his cover letters "Jim Bird" instead of "James R. Bird, Ph.D."). He still feared, at this point, that someone would see through him, would see that he was only joking. This fear finally began to diminish when the book was enthusiastically accepted by a large and powerful publishing house. It diminished further when the book was launched, and still further when it began to sell in astounding numbers. No one called him a fraud. No one said, "But you're just a philosophy professor at a cut-rate university. What do *you* know?" On the contrary, letters began to pour in from across the country assuring him that he had said something true, something of value. He began, naturally enough, to believe it. He resigned his tenure at the university. He began to receive, and then to accept invitations to speak in public, to sign books, to be interviewed on television. He started to plan a second book, one that would rectify the flaws of the first, clear up some of his readers' misconceptions, and forestall further misreadings. By the time his ex-wife accosted him after one of his sold-out lectures, the feeling that he would be exposed as a sham had been almost completely extinguished.

"You're looking well," he said, sincerely and with a lack of malice that astonished himself. He noticed that she wasn't holding a copy of his book.

"You," she said, "are looking like you're making a tremendous fool of yourself."

After that, the self-help guru took his new career very seriously indeed.

MONDAY.

"Hi everybody, I'm—"

"Could you stand up for us?"

The girl stood awkwardly. "Well, I'm Sonja, and one thing about me is that I'm a waitress and a single mom." She got it out in one breath and sat back down. Margo smiled and clapped softly, but no one joined in.

Be quiet, she told herself.

"Now Sonja," said Ethan, pressing the tips of his index fingers against his lower lip, "is waitressing something you *are*, or something you *do*?"

Not sure whether to stand again to answer, she hovered briefly, half-crouched, above her chair. "Something I do?"

And so it went. "Tell us, John, are your grandchildren something you *are*, or something you *have*?" "Now Lottie, do you think jogging is something you *are*, or something you *like*?" Everyone sheepishly agreed that what they'd thought they *were* was actually just something they did or had or felt or liked.

At first Margo didn't understand; surely "single mom" was not just something you *did*? But then she was reminded of an activity they'd done at Personal Pursuit, the "rock-bottoming" exercise. The instructor kept asking variations on the same question; the idea was to dig deeper, to evaluate your stock responses, to unearth what you really meant or really felt about something. This in turn reminded her of the Martian exercise they'd done at Best You: "I'm sorry, I'm from Mars, what do you mean by 'single mom'? … What do you mean by 'not married'? … What do you mean by 'relationship'?" There, the point had been to peel away the layers of assumptions and conventions, to strip away the veneer of the self you presented to the world, and reveal the precious, if perhaps unlovely, self as *you* saw it. Maybe this was like that.

By the time Ethan pointed his praying hands at her, Margo had prepared and mentally recited what she felt was an unobjectionable introduction.

"Well Ethan, and everybody, *hi*. I'm Margo, though mostly folk call me Mar. In order of personal importance, I *am* … the proud mother of two wonderful and successful grown daughters, I *am* the co-owner and part-time manager of a flower arrangement and delivery business, I *am* an actor and a playwright, I *am* a novice watercolor painter, I *am* a hobby gardener, I *am* a former—"

Ethan cut her off: "Now, Margo, is painting something you *are*, or something you *do*?"

She'd known it was coming, but still the question perplexed her. "Well Ethan, *painting* is certainly something I do, but *painter*, I think, is something I *am* ..."

"Are you a painter, or someone who paints?"

She saw his point, or thought she did: she was just a dabbler. But she hadn't claimed to be a professional. "Someone who paints, I guess."

He accepted this as conclusively damning and shifted his attention to the next woman.

"Wait a second," she said. (*Shut up,* her mind barked at her.) "Isn't what you *do* part of what makes you who you *are*?" She looked around the room for support, and found it: everyone was smiling mildly and nodding at her.

"Let me turn that around and give the question back to you, Margo. If driving home one night you—God forbid—ran someone over, would that make you a 'murderer'?"

She was too flabbergasted to say anything more than "I guess not." After a moment's reflection she wanted to ask if she'd run over this person on purpose, then realized that this was not the crux of the matter. Yes, she thought, if I killed someone, that *would* make me a killer—wouldn't it? But it was too late to argue. Everyone was already smiling and nodding at the woman next to her, whose name Margo had missed.

TUESDAY.

He was fortyish, he smelled good, and his name was Bread.

She smiled her two-thirds amused smile. "Bread?"

"Bread," he repeated.

She felt the smile going stale. "*Brett?*"

"Bread," he said. "With a D."

Finally it dawned on her. He had an *accent.*

"Oh, *Brad!*" she almost shouted, then felt stupid: she sounded like she was correcting his pronunciation of his own name.

"Two minutes," called Ethan, "starting … *now.*"

She had offered to go first. So she started talking.

One of the problems with self-help books is their smug, apodictic tone—the way they make sweeping declarations, as if these were established facts applicable to everyone at all times. But anyone who has cultivated the moral belief that we are all unique individuals with unique needs will bridle at the notion that one size of advice fits all. Reading these books' prescriptions, we quite naturally and instinctively start to imagine scenarios in which, or people for whom, this advice would be laughably inappropriate— or even disastrous. For example, I found myself, when reading John Gray's really quite harmless "101 ways to score points with a woman," picturing all the women I knew who would be somewhat less than swept off their feet by your "offering to sharpen her knives in the kitchen" (#63), showing her that you are interested in what she is saying "by making little noises like ah ha, uh-huh, oh, mm-huh, and hmmmm" (#80), or "letting her know when you are planning to take a nap" (#23). It was also good cynical fun to dream up men for whom "treating her in ways you did at the beginning of the relationship" (#61) or "touching her with your hand sometimes when you talk to her" (#78) would be bad advice. Try it yourself.

This is just what William Gaddis does in his novel, *The Recognitions.* He lampoons the cult of Carnegie through one overearnest disciple, Mr. Pivner, who applies the principles of winning friends and influencing people even when being accosted by a crazy man on a New York City bus. Even "at this critical instant," his training does not fail him: he recalls chapter six, "How to Make

People Like You Instantly," which advises him to find something about the other person that he can honestly admire.

> —What a wonderful head of hair you have, said Mr. Pivner. The man beside him looked at the thin hair on Mr. Pivner's head, and then clutched a handful of his own. —Lotsa people like it, he said. Then he sat back and looked at Mr. Pivner carefully. —Say what is this, are you a queer or something?
>
> Mr. Pivner's eyes widened. —I ... I ...

This is funny, if not exactly convincing. Why, for instance, does Mr. Pivner want to make *this* man like him instantly? To blame Dale Carnegie or his book for this silly exchange is not quite fair.

Most of the criticisms of Jim Bird suffer from the same sort of straw-man irrelevance. It is all too easy to imagine people (serial killers and pedophiles are most commonly adduced) who perhaps should *not* be encouraged to accept themselves, or to stop striving to change who they are. But what about the average person? What does someone of average intelligence with average-sized problems get, or not get, out of a Healthy Self seminar?

What Margo had hoped to get was a little inspiration. This was her fourth self-improvement seminar. The first one, which she had attended nearly ten years ago, had helped her get over, or "get past," her husband Bill's death. The second one had given her the courage to change careers—to give up acting. The third one, three years ago, had revealed to her that her daughters no longer depended on her and that she had the right to pursue her own happiness; that is, it had helped her to move out and remarry without guilt. Now, having left Bertie, her second husband, and moved back home, she knew only that she needed to change her life again. She was 55 and didn't know who she was or what she should be doing. She felt as though she had forgotten her lines, misplaced her script. At night, in bed, she couldn't sleep, because she didn't know what to do with her teeth: if she held them together, she felt as though she were clenching her jaw; if she held them apart, she felt as though she were gawping. Nothing felt natural anymore. Nothing felt normal.

She told some of this to Brad, but found it difficult to concentrate with him staring at her. When it was his turn to speak, she found it even more difficult to listen. They were sitting, as instructed, facing each other, with feet flat on the floor, hands on knees, and backs straight. This posture did not make her feel "open," "receptive," or "attentive," but stiff and ridiculous, and this sense of her own ridiculousness acted as a far greater barrier to receptivity than crossed arms or slouching ever could have. She was also not supposed to speak while he talked, but it took a conscious effort of will to suppress every syllable of encouragement or simple acknowledgement—every ah ha, uh-huh, oh, mm-huh, and hmmmm. But the worst was the enforced eye contact. It was simply not natural to stare steadily into someone's eyes while you talked at them. It was faintly aggressive, a sort of challenge: What do you think of *this*, hey?

You dummy, she told herself. This was surely the point of the whole exercise. This was what they were supposed to discover: that communication was a two-way street, that listening was not passive but active, that body language was half the message, that trying too hard to listen was precisely what prevented you from hearing—that, in Jim Bird's terms, *striving* was what kept you from *living*. Of course! She smiled, then blushed, afraid that Brad would misconstrue her smile. He too, she now saw, was grappling with the eye contact: the effort of not looking away was draining his face and his voice of all expression. What he seemed to be telling her—with eerie, almost sinister dispassion—was that he was tired of hurting women.

"Time's up! Now who wants to share their insights on this learning?"

As usual, no one put up their hand right away. Margo, having solved the lesson, did not want to deprive the others of a chance to figure it out, and stayed silent.

Eventually they began cautiously to lift their arms, and Ethan lowered his prayer-clasped hands and pointed to them one by one.

"I really enjoyed that."

"Me too."

"Excellent," said Ethan. "Can you tell me why?"

"I don't know. It was different?"

Ethan nodded, grimly encouraging, like a physiotherapist watching a car crash victim take their first painful steps. "*How* was it different—anyone?"

"It was more natural."

"I felt that by not interrupting all the time I could really *hear* my partner."

There was a general murmur of agreement.

"I felt that when I was *talking* I was really paying attention to what I was *saying*. I was worried I wouldn't know what to say, but by looking Lottie in the eyes, I was able to concentrate—and it just came to me."

Ethan beamed. "Because your underself—your *true* self—was doing most of the work." His gaze, like a camera zooming out, diffused itself across everyone in the room equally. "By not looking at the outfield or the dugout but keeping our eyes firmly on the ball, by not pushing ourselves towards anything or pulling anything towards ourselves, by not fighting the stream of the now but letting it carry us, we are able to *flow*—to *let go*—to *let it happen*. Excellent! Anyone else?"

"But I didn't get that at all," Margo sputtered.

"Hands before 'ands,' please."

Annoyed, she lifted her hand minimally from her lap, then threw it up over her head, but Ethan only went on staring at her expectantly.

"By focusing so hard," she said slowly, aware that she was plucking her words from nowhere, "by trying so hard to listen, to pay attention, I just … drowned myself out."

There was another general murmur of agreement, identical to the first.

"Aha." Ethan smiled imperturbably. "I think we're up against the difference between effort*ful* focus and effort*less* focus. Being in the now with your partner is not about *trying* to *listen*. It is … about … *listening* to *try*. Next time," he said lightly, as if it were the easiest thing in the world, "relax."

Already, by the end of the second day, Margo realized that she was at the wrong seminar. She had not, on Sunday night, believed Jim Bird when he had said as much, for that, she assumed, was just a piece of rhetoric. It was like when spies in movies said, *Don't trust anyone—not even me.* Their bluntness, of course, was calculated to win your trust.

But now, alone in her hotel room, some of what he had been saying came back to her, with troubling implications.

"The only possible kind of happiness is happiness with who you *are*."

"You can't *change* yourself—your *self* is a *self*, after all! You can only *be* yourself."

But that was nonsense. She'd changed herself radically, and often. She was who she chose to be. Her self was what she made it.

She picked up the phone, then put it down. She ran a bath, but let it grow cold. She looked out her window and felt sad. She stood at the window in the hotel bathrobe and looked out at the sky growing dark over the city's lights and in her mind's eye saw herself standing at a window in a hotel bathrobe looking out at a dark sky above a city's lights, and she felt sad. Brad and a few others were having drinks downstairs in the bar but she did not feel like talking to anyone. Her face needed a rest.

She sat on the bed and flipped through the seminar "material" and, for the first time, the Jim Bird books that Danielle had found at the library for her. (As a joke, Margo supposed, Danielle had also brought home *The Will and The Won't*, Bird's old book on Nietzsche; but this Margo had left behind—not so much because she believed Nietzsche had been a misogynist and proto-Nazi (which she did), but because she found it stuffy and unreadable.)

"The drive towards self-improvement," she now read,

is a disease born out of self-hatred. You can't desire to improve yourself without desiring to change yourself, and you can't want to change yourself without hating the way you are. But what does it mean to hate yourself? It means one part of you hates another part of you. In other words, it means you're divided. And as everyone knows, it's united we stand, divided we fall.

NONSENSE, she wrote in the margin (in pencil—it *was* a library book). Then she pulled out her notebook and opened it to a clean page.

"Of COURSE I hate myself," she wrote. "What self-respecting person doesn't hate herself? Self-improvement is *achieved* through self-hatred. As a child, you reached for a hot stove and your mother slapped your hand. And quite right. But if your mother was not around, your body provided its own slap, maybe even more effective: the pain of burning yourself.

"This is how we learn: through pain, through remorse. When we do or say something stupid, or mean, or *wrong*, we mentally slap ourselves. Or anyway we *should*. We *should* hate ourselves, because none of us is perfect. (No, not even little old ME.)"

She put aside her notebook and called home. Luckily, Danielle was still pretending to be non-judgmental about the seminar, so Margo was able to complain without losing face.

"You don't even *get* Jim Bird," she said. "They break us up into 'connect groups' and stick us with a 'connect leader' all week."

"I hate it when people use verbs as nouns," said Danielle.

"I mean, there *are* three hundred of us, but for twenty-five hundred bucks you sort of feel entitled to—you know."

"The guy on TV."

Margo consulted her notebook, where she had jotted down some observations and criticisms that she thought Danielle might find amusing. "Our leader, though, this guy named Ethan. Must be all of thirty years old. He's very *casual*. In fact you get the impression he's playing a not very high-caliber game of Adverbs, and his word is 'casually.'"

"Artfully disheveled hair?"

"Check. And 'wild' eyebrows that he must comb backwards. And he always wears his shirt unbuttoned to the navel. But it's not very convincing. It's a very theatersportsy portrayal of casualness. You don't wear your shirt or your hair like that if you don't care how you wear your shirt or your hair—only if you want people to *think* you don't care how you wear your shirt or your hair."

"Wait—to the *navel?*"

"Well he wears a T-shirt underneath."

"Oh. Thank God. I had this image ..."

Margo lay back on the bed and looked up at the ceiling. "I don't even know what I'm doing here."

"Oh, you always hate it at first."

"What? No I don't."

"The first couple of days you don't know why you came, but by the end of the week it's the best thing to ever happen to you, it's changed your life, you've turned over a new— Sorry. But it's true."

"That's ridiculous," she said, but was vaguely troubled.

After she hung up, she turned on her laptop and opened her Resolutions file of three years ago. At about the time she had attended the Personal Pursuit seminar, her resolutions had been:

1. Write letter to Bertie
2. Learn Spanish
3. Wake up ten minutes earlier (weekdays)
4. Keep hands out of pockets (looks dowdy)
5. LOOK UP new words
6. More quality time with the daughters
7. Be goofier (take self less seriously)
8. Look in mirrors less
9. Exercise exercise exercise! (jogging?)
10. Floss (~3x week MIN.)

She read the list with dismay. Most of these resolutions could have been made last week. In fact, #6 was virtually identical to the #3 of today, and #10 had been upgraded to #7 (though now its demand had been decreased to twice a week). Spanish had been replaced by Norwegian—she had the crazy idea that she was going to translate Ibsen in her retirement—but she had, to date, learned nothing of either language. In fact she had made little progress with any of her old resolutions. She still battled with the snooze button most mornings, pulling herself out of bed at the last possible minute (she'd even tried setting the clock ahead, but, of course, *knowing* it was ahead, she counted on the extra time). She still had never jogged a day in her life (perhaps that needed to go back on the list?). She still gazed at herself in mirrors as often as ever, which probably only exacerbated her self-consciousness. But if she had been fighting self-consciousness, what about #4? She did not know if she still stuck her hands in her pockets more than she should, but it seemed a ridiculous thing to resolve not to do. But was her current #9 ("Smile with teeth") any better? She felt an urge to add a new resolution to her list: "Stop making stupid, petty, vain resolutions!"

There was however one significant difference between her list of three years ago and her list of today. Back then her #1 resolution had been "Write letter to Bertie." Now, of course, it was "Do not call Bertie."

So she *had* changed, in at least one very striking way. That was reassuring.

It was funny, though. She could not recall what sort of letter she had been going to write.

Well, she always hated writing letters, so perhaps it had only been something quite inconsequential. A thank-you note for some gift, maybe.

But why had it been #1?

WEDNESDAY.

They crumpled their pieces of paper into balls with the enthusiasm of kindergartners. Ethan drew a line on the floor with his toe and pointed at the garbage can in the corner.

"Toss them on in there," he said casually, "and we'll continue on to the next learning."

The can wasn't far away; most of the balls of paper went in. Margo, one of the last to toss, missed. She laughed, then felt she was trying too hard to show that it didn't matter.

"Twelve," said Ethan, sounding pleasantly surprised. "That's more than we usually get. This is a good group! Hmm … Tell you what. Let's try it a second time—crumple up a fresh piece of paper if you don't want to go rooting around in that old garbage can—and if *everybody*, I mean all fifteen of you, are able to sink it, we'll take an early lunch, and I'll buy coffees this afternoon. What do you say?"

This was fun; they were excited—but no one wanted to throw first. No one wanted to be the first to miss. Margo supposed this was all part of the lesson: *You can't win if you don't try.* And someone would miss, someone would have to be the *first* to miss. It might as well be her; it would take the pressure off everyone else. So she stepped up to the line and, with a humorous grimace, carelessly threw away her paper ball.

It went in. Everyone cheered. She curtsied.

Sonja, the shy single mom, threw next. It fell short. There were hums of sarcastically exaggerated disappointment and good-natured sighs to show Sonja that it was just a game, that no one really cared.

"That's okay," said Ethan, "but you know what? Let's keep going. If the *rest* of you, all thirteen of you, get them in, the offer stands."

In the end, he persuaded everyone to throw again. Altogether, only five went in.

"Sorry, gang," said Ethan, smiling and shrugging his shoulders impishly to show that this was exactly what he'd expected to happen—that this was, in fact, all part of the lesson. "Well, I think there just might be time for one more learning before luncheroo."

There were, on cue, a few mock-groans.

"So let's all sit back down and open our material to page thirty-seven …"

Most of the time, it's not that we're *not trying hard enough*. Most of the time it's *trying too hard* that defeats us. Desperation poisons all our efforts:

- We've all met that person, at the office or at a party, who wants desperately to be liked. But what's more unlikable than desperation?
- One person, desperate for a promotion, goes into their evaluation with sweat dripping from their brow. Another person, who doesn't care whether they get the promotion or not, goes into the evaluation with easy confidence, casual indifference. Who gets the promotion?
- An athlete wants desperately to win, so they clench every muscle in their body and tie themselves in knots with needless tension.
- Your golf game (or squash game or basketball game) is going very well, you're playing much better than usual—until you *notice* that you're playing well, and think desperately: "If I can just keep this up, it'll be my best game ever!" That's when, of course, you "choke."
- You can't sleep at night. You've got an important appointment tomorrow and you really really need to get some shut-eye. The later it gets, the more desperate you feel: "If I fall asleep *now* I'll still get five hours." "If I fall asleep *right now* I'll get almost four hours." "Oh God, I *need* at least *three* hours!" But the harder you *try* to sleep, the more desperate you get, and the more awake you feel.

Desperation—that is, wanting something really badly—is like a fear of dogs. Dogs only attack you when they smell fear. So being afraid of them is the worst possible thing you can do! And wanting something badly is possibly the worst way to get it.

An old adage says, "Whether you think you can or think you can't—you're right." In other words, the confident are successful *because they're confident*, and the unconfident aren't *because they're unconfident*. Confidence is always justified—and self-doubt is always justified, too.

Well, you could also say, "Whether you're afraid of dogs or not, you're right." But instead of "dogs," think "failure." Wanting badly to win is a kind of wanting desperately *not to lose*, and is the quickest way to failure.

Let's face it: You can't program yourself to be confident. (What could you possibly say to yourself? "Be confident, you loser"?) Confidence and success only come out of your *true self* in pursuit of its *real dreams*. To want something really badly and to try desperately to get it is a kind of bad faith, a self-betrayal, a backhanded admission that you're not completely sure you can get it, or deserve to. But when your true self is chasing after your true dream, the effort is effortless, and there's never any doubt.

Write down ten examples of things you've failed to get or goals you've failed to achieve because you wanted them too badly or tried too hard. (Use the back of this page if you need extra space.)

Margo did not believe she had ever wanted too badly or tried too hard; in fact, she did not believe such a thing was possible. All Ethan's and Jim Bird's assertions that nothing could be achieved through direct effort only strengthened her conviction that *anything* could be achieved through direct effort. Because they kept assuring her that she was powerless, she became quite certain that she was omnipotent.

(In the same way, of course, Jim Bird, after reading so many self-help manuals that assured him he was omnipotent—"Using the power of decision gives you the capacity to get past *any* excuse to change *any and every* part of your life *in an instant!*"—became only more certain that he was powerless. This is often what we do when confronted with an idea that conflicts with one of our beliefs: we exaggerate the idea, and exaggerate our own opposing belief; we make the familiar idea white, and the foreign black. This makes the new idea both easier and more enjoyable to combat. As Nietzsche said, even bad music and bad reasons sound fine when one marches off to fight an enemy.)

Margo ignored the instructions. She no longer even bothered trying to find the self-empowerment lesson hidden behind the self-acceptance doctrine; she simply wrote down whatever was on her mind. At the moment she did not want to think about the past, or mistakes she'd made, or her regrets. She wanted to think about the future. Wasn't that what she was here for?

She drew a horizontal line, representing her past, that, at the point of the present, branched into several arrows representing the future. Beside the arrows she drew question marks. Then beside the question marks she wrote down what she saw as all the possibilities.

Travel. (Norway? Korea?)

Acting again. (She had never been happier than when acting. But would this really be a change—or a regression?)

Horseback riding. (She had never even been near a horse. Would she like it? Well, it would be something different.)

Real estate agent. (Her friend Nyla seemed happy.)

Write a novel. (Because none of her plays had been produced in a long time, she believed that theater was a dying art.)

Divorcée.

She stared at this list for a long time.

THURSDAY.

"Your conscious mind," said Ethan, "is like a dog on a leash. It sniffs this and that and goes running after it."

To illustrate his point, he sniffed demurely in several directions. There were titters. Margo and Brad exchanged a wide-eyed look.

"But our unconscious mind, the sum of all our deepest wishes and dreams and ... what else? Just shout it out."

"Hopes!"

"Our real self?"

"Life scripts!"

"Desires?"

"Okay, yes, definitely, but what I'm looking for is—"

"Limitations?"

"Fears!"

"That's it! Yes, the unconscious is the sum of all our hopes and desires definitely but also yes let's face it our *fears*, and our fears, let's recall yesterday's learning, aren't necessarily what?"

"Bad!"

"Uncomfortable?"

"Well yes, our fears aren't necessarily *bad*, though they *can* make us uncomfortable, but that's okay because our comfort zone is what? Everybody!"

"Comfortable!," Margo and Brad shouted along with everyone else, but with a sarcasm that was detectable (or so they believed) only to each other.

"That's why they call it a 'comfort zone,' folks," Ethan dead-panned. "It's *comfortable*. And our fears and our dislikes are signals of *dis*comfort, but *dis*comfort is useful, isn't it. It shows us the limits of our comfortable zone. Like we said on day one: The mind *can't* make a heaven out of hell or a hell out of heaven—sorry, Milton. What you like is what you like, what you hate is what you hate. If you hate broccoli, and who here hates broccoli, show of hands? Yeah well, welcome to the club, ha ha. If you hate broccoli you don't say to yourself: Gee, I sure wish I liked broccoli, then I could eat a lot of it!"

Brad murmured in his Ethan voice, "I sure wish I was gay, then I could have sex with all those beautiful men!"

"Okay," Ethan was saying, "so the unconscious mind, which is made up of your dreams and your fears both, your unconscious mind is the master holding the leash. That's why we never get far. Unless we let go and let our master lead the way, we're only going to succeed in choking ourselves on that leash."

He had them write down seven "definers," or critical moments in their lives, then analyze whether they had acted as the dog or as the master. Had they run off incontinently towards what they *thought* they wanted, or had they pursued their true desires? Had they done what their intellect said they *should*, or that which their heart said they *must*?

This distinction was incoherent to Margo. Why should the two necessarily be at odds? Why couldn't her conscious, rational decisions at least occasionally correspond to her unconscious wishes? In fact, wasn't the process of decision-making, of thinking a matter through from every angle before acting, wasn't this precisely the way the conscious part of the mind figured out *what* the unconscious mind, or the whole self, wanted? She put up her hand.

"Sorry Ethan, and everybody, but forgive me if I'm wrong here, but don't you sometimes do exactly what you want to?"

"Sure. That's what we mean by pursuing your true desire, Mar, acting with your true self."

"But what I mean is, don't you sometimes *want* to do just what you *should* do? Don't you sometimes want to do what is right? Doesn't your ... dog sometimes go the same way as your master?"

"Can I answer that Ethan? Well Mar, the way I see it is last year for example I set this goal for myself? That I would make two hundred and fifty thousand dollars?" There were perfunctory murmurs of recognition; Lottie mentioned this figure almost every time she spoke. "Well I didn't achieve it and I've been trying to figure out why. Now it occurs to me that one of my definers was this business deal I got involved in. I won't go into the details," she said, then went into the details. "Anyway the point is, and Ethan correct me if I'm wrong here, but wasn't that my conscious mind *choosing* to get into that deal because I wanted it too badly? Wasn't that my dog running off ahead of my master? Like, instead of *letting* two hundred and fifty thousand dollars happen, I was *making* it happen?"

"Excellent, Lottie."

For not the first time that week, Margo felt like she was drowning in some invisible fluid. "But what if the deal had worked out?"

Ethan and Lottie stared at her blankly. She turned to Brad for support. He gave her a steady, compassionate look, as if she were some crazy but lovable aunt who should be placidly tolerated. She hated him at that moment.

Later, at lunch, however, he agreed with her. "It's dumb, all right. Because if your unconscious desires are really unconscious, you can't ever know what they are. You can say anything is your 'true' self. I came to this thing because I have a problem with commitment. Every time I meet a new girl, I think *she's* the one I want to commit to. But which is the true me: the one that sleeps around, or the one that wants to settle down? Should I be trying harder to be happy with the girl I'm with, or should I be trying to find the person I'll be happy with naturally, easily? Does settling down mean *settling*? Should I force myself to stay with a girl even after I get bored? Is that what love is? But then what if I meet someone new, someone—hypothetically speaking—intelligent, attractive, mature. Someone I can *talk* to. Should I just ignore her, pass her by? What if this is the woman I'm *supposed* to be with? But maybe I'm just fooling myself. Maybe this is just my way of wriggling out of the old relationship. But is it even possible to *make* yourself be happy with someone?"

Margo was disturbed by the intensity with which he asked these questions. This was not just rhetoric. He seemed to expect some answer. She felt as though he were petitioning her for advice, and did not like the implications. The word "mature" had stuck in her mind, and to combat the flattering possibility that he was flirting with her, she decided to take offense: He thought she was wise, knowing, experienced! He thought she was old!

"Oh, what the hell do I know?" she said. "I've never been happy, not really. Not for any length of time. Anyway, who wants to be happy? Have you *met* a happy person lately?"

"I don't know. Ethan?"

"*Exactly*. Happy people are morons. *Morons* are happy. Anyway, forget all that hogwash about your true self. You don't ever know how anything's going to turn out. All you can do is think it over and then do what seems right. Do what you want."

"But how do you know what you want?"

She looked at him. What *did* she want? How could she know? What test could she perform? Introspection was a myth; her consciousness, like her eye, could never be its own object. Her self—that dim, immeasurable, unlocatable, forever forward-facing, outward-looking self—could never know of what it was made. She could only judge her desires retrospectively: whatever course she finally took, that must ultimately be the one she had most wanted to take. Thus her behavior was an infallible record of her desires. It was, then, in other words, impossible to act contrary to her own wishes. For even to try quite conscientiously to do so was to make acting-contrary-to-her-own-wishes itself her wish! At that thought, she almost heaved a sob for all the pleasures she had denied herself, all the paths she had not taken, throughout her life—because *had* she taken them, they would have, by that very fact, been that which she had most desired. But no, that made no sense. Because, by the same logic, she must have desired the denials more than the acceptances.

What did she really want? If the only way she could assess her own feelings was by reviewing her actions, then no one could know her less than she did, because she, unlike others, had to rely on memory, on photographs and mirrors, to get glimpses of herself. And why should she feel such loyalty to a stranger? It didn't matter at all. Life was a map without wrong turns. She could do whatever she wanted!

Agh, but what did she *want?* She couldn't use her past as a guide, for even if she could detect there some pattern to follow, she would only be condemning herself to doing as she had always done. This would only prove Jim Bird's tenet, that we cannot change ourselves.

"Whatever you do," she blurted at last, with a smile she did not have to measure out in advance, "whatever you *do,* that's what you want."

Brad laughed. "But what to *do?*"

That evening after class she went up to her hotel room and called Bertie.

He didn't answer. She realized with a start that he probably wasn't home from the shop yet. This prosaic explanation seemed disproportionate to the momentousness of her act. She had finally broken down and called him—and he wasn't even home. How was this possible?

Her voice was still on the answering machine. She did not leave a message.

FRIDAY.

The next night she was sitting at her assigned table in the banquet room, scrunching up her napkin and getting unobtrusively drunk, when John came over and asked her to dance.

She had been in a good mood most of the day. She felt, as she supposed she always felt at the end of a seminar, that her life was going to be different from now on. This feeling was not attributable to anything Ethan or Jim Bird speaking through Ethan had said. Rather, two thoughts from her conversation with Brad the day before kept returning to her. The first was that whatever she did was what she wanted to do. The second was that she had never been happy.

And if you've never been *happy,* said her mind gloatingly, *what makes you think you ever* will be *happy?*

Okay. She would never be happy. She was incapable of it. This thought, curiously enough, made her feel quite content.

A placebo works because we expect it to work; that is, having swallowed it, we can stop fighting, or fleeing, or shrinking from the pain. Blake once said that, "He who binds to himself a Joy / Doth the winged life destroy"; and we could perhaps add, "He who thrusts from himself a Pain / Doth invite the same again." Just as chasing after happiness is the surest way to lose it, running from unhappiness is the surest way to bring it on. Margo, by resigning herself to her unhappiness, no longer had to fight it.

And since she would never be happy, no matter what she did or who she was with, there was no reason not to go back to Bertie— with whom she was comfortable, and about whom the worst that could be said was that he loved her unconditionally, and would not object, would perhaps not even notice, if she gained twenty pounds eating strawberry ice cream and cuddling with him on the couch in front of the television.

She wallowed in the idea of herself as fat and lazy and hedonistic—and alternately in the idea of herself as fundamentally, inescapably miserable. That morning, she slept in, was late for class, slouched into the room with her hands in her pockets, mumbled an incoherent (and insincere) apology, did not raise her hand when she had questions or objections, took no care to smile with her teeth, and, in short, enjoyed hating herself thoroughly.

But then in the afternoon, as a feel-good valedictory activity, Ethan had them write compliments and stick them on one another's backs. Margo's equilibrium was disturbed first by the fact that she could find so many kind things to say. She had felt all week like an outsider, alone with her doubts and her criticisms and at odds with the group. She realized now that in many ways she felt only respect and admiration for her classmates. When she had first arrived on Sunday night she had, as if by default, been irritated by how sane and healthy, how effortlessly normal, everyone looked. By "normal" she did not mean happy, she realized, but something more like unconfused, coherent. Unlike herself, everyone here seemed to have figured out long ago the knack of being themselves. Like characters in a play, other people were incapable of acting *out* of character. They did not dither or second-guess themselves (or if they did, it was only *characteristic* of them). Now, however, five days later, she was more impressed by her classmates' imperfections and uncertainties. Some of them, she had learned, were grappling with real problems. Louise was being tormented by an estranged teenage son; Carla was fighting for custody of *her* five-year-old daughter; Sonja was trying to balance motherhood, work, and an incipient romance, all without guilt; Shelly couldn't get in an automobile again after an accident and had lost her job; John was trying to find a passion that could replace the career that he had been forcibly retired from. Margo felt that her own obscure, obsessive worries (what to do with her teeth!) were trivial next to theirs, and she found it easy to write heartfelt compliments for each of them.

She was even more disturbed by the comments that she received. Not because they were negative—they were all, if anything, embarrassingly positive—but because they were so consistent. The same adjectives and phrases kept reappearing. The composite image that they conjured up was, startlingly, of a woman not so very different from the one that Margo aspired to be: strong, outspoken, courageous, opinionated, independent ...

But somehow this did not please her. Once, she and Bill and the daughters had been playing Adverbs, and Bill had done an impersonation of her. He had acted "Margo-ly" or "Mommily" by rubbing his hands together a lot and concluding all his sentences with a fruity "… I *think*." It could not have been less vicious, but she was deeply offended by this caricature of her. She had not realized that she rubbed her hands together when she spoke or that she said "I think" more often than anyone else. These were mild, inoffensive mannerisms to be sure, and perhaps she should have embraced them; but once she was shown them they became *conscious* mannerisms— that is, affectations. Thereafter, whenever she caught herself rubbing her hands together, she felt that she was doing an impersonation of herself.

That afternoon, too, she felt ridiculous, as if she'd been praised for playing a part well—instead of just being herself.

She had already been asked by Brad to dance, and had said no. Feeling guilty, if also a little flattered, by his hangdog look, she had explained herself expansively.

"Dancing these days is all improv. You just get out there and do whatever you feel like, with or without a partner. But when I was young"—she pulled out this phrase with a defiant absence of irony—"we danced to a script. You had to learn the steps first, but at least you always knew what to do. And then you could perform. There's no *performance* in this kind of dancing," she said, gesturing with repugnance at the few people twitching and jerking solipsistically around the dance floor. "It's either meditation or … showing off."

So Brad had gone off and found someone else to dance with—a blonde girl from one of the other connect groups whom Margo had not noticed before. Watching them, she was flabbergasted by the extent of her bitterness. This was the archetypal story of her life; this was the hell she had created for herself: to be always looking in from the outside; to be always waiting in the wings of life, never to be onstage. She could of course change her mind, go and ask Brad for that dance. But she could not be the sort of person for whom that would be the natural choice. She could never be the sort of person who would have said yes in the first place. She saw her limits but now was no longer wallowing in them. She hated herself keenly, and hated all the world, which at that moment seemed to her to be made up entirely of dancers.

Now John was asking her to dance. It was a slow dance; she would not have to improvise. She was surprised at how strongly she wanted to say yes, just to spite Brad.

"I'm sorry, John," she began, then stopped herself. She crumpled up her napkin and threw it into the middle of the table. "Will you hold that thought?"

She strode across the room. The vast banquet hall was a glittering ice cavern, and she skated across it. Though she might fall, she couldn't hurt herself: she would only slide off whatever she collided with ... She was drunk.

Jim Bird was talking to one of his connect group leaders, but she spoke anyway.

"I'm sorry to interrupt here, but Jim ... well, shit—how would you like to dance?"

He looked up at her with confused eyes, a mouth unsure whether it should smile or not.

"I'm sorry," he said at last, "but I don't actually really dance."

"That's what I thought," she said with dour self-pity. But by the time she had recrossed the room she was remembering her tone differently. *That's what I thought*, she'd said—but joyously, almost triumphantly, as if she had scored a point against him.

I would, said Nietzsche, only believe in a God who knew how to dance.

She danced with John, then found Brad and danced with him. She drank some more and fussed with her napkin. She ate chocolate brownies. She shared a cigarette with Brad in a stairwell or a parking lot. She had a long conversation with Lottie. She discovered a new way to dance: she moved until she did something that felt silly, then repeated that movement methodically, rhythmically, and made it her own. In the bathroom she wiped off what remained of her lipstick and laughed at something someone said. She would die one day, she supposed. She still missed Bill. She loved her daughters; she had no regrets. She liked herself, and wanted to change. She was happy, and she made a list of resolutions on her napkin and stuck it in her purse. Her ears were ringing. Brad shouted in the elevator. His breath was warm. Life was a piano, but the keys were out of order. She was paddling an iceberg. Healthy self, heal thyself. She laughed at the boyish reverence with which he took off all her clothes.

But she was only pretending.

SATURDAY.

The physicist Schrödinger (unlike Jim Bird, I do not think Nietzsche is the only show in town) once put forward the idea that consciousness only accompanies novelty. To the extent that an organism already *knows how* to do something, or has developed a routine of reflexes or habits to deal with a known situation, to that extent it is unconscious—as when we walk or drive down a familiar street without even being aware of our surroundings. Only when some new element, some differential, pops up, demanding to be dealt with in a new way, are we fully awake. The world around us fades from consciousness as we learn how to deal with it.

But not knowing how to deal with the world is, to say the least, distressing. Consciousness, then, is distressing. According to Schrödinger, the most aware individuals of all times, those who have formed and transformed the work of art which we call humanity, have always been those who have suffered most the pangs of inner discord. "Let this be a consolation to him who also suffers from it. Without it nothing enduring has ever been made."

The basis of every ethical code, he goes on to say, is self-denial; there is always some "thou shalt" or "thou shalt not" placed in opposition to our primitive will. Why should this be so? Isn't it absurd that I am supposed to suppress my natural appetites, disown my true self, be different from what I really am?

But our "natural self"—what Jim Bird calls our "true self," "living self," or "underself"—is just the repertoire of instincts and habits we've inherited from our ancestors. And our conscious life is a continued fight against that unconscious self. As a species we are still developing; we march in the front line of generations. Thus every day of a person's life represents a small bit of the evolution of our species. Granted, a single day of one's life, or even any one life as a whole, is but a tiny blow of the chisel at the ever-unfinished statue. But the whole enormous evolution we have gone through in the past, it too has been brought about by a series of just such tiny chisel blows.

The same is true of the individual. At every step, on every day of our life, something of the shape that we possessed until then has to change, to be overcome, to be deleted and replaced by something new. The resistance of our primitive will—shouting, "Do what's easy! Do what you've always done!"—is the resistance of the existing shape to the transforming chisel. For we ourselves are chisel and statue, conquerors and conquered at the same time. Deciding what to be, becoming what we are, is a true continued self-conquering.

*

What the age-old debate over free will boils down to, it seems to me, is this: Can we sometimes do what is hard, or are we condemned to always do what is easy?

The materialistic determinists, men like the famous philosopher who kindly wrote that introduction to James R. Bird's book on Nietzsche, believe that we always do what's easy. We are physical systems, and physical systems always follow the established routes. Clocks do not run backwards, water cannot run uphill, and a neuron firing in our brains can by no effort of its own pull itself up by its bootstraps and act counter to its habit. It does what it's supposed to, what it has always done.

I do not know much about the brain. I know that neuroscientists like to eulogize it as the most complex three pounds of physical matter known to exist in the universe—but always with the implication that it's still just a lump of physical matter, that we are still just fancy machines. (As Nietzsche put it, "The living being is only a species of dead being.")

But it seems to me that the material determinists want to have it two ways. We *are* our brains, they tell us; and (therefore) we are in thrall to our brains.

But if we *are* our brains, then we are not in thrall to our brains. You cannot point to one piece of our brains, one neuron among billions, and, noting how regularly and unimaginatively that piece behaves, thereby disprove unpredictability or imagination on the larger scale. It would be like pointing at my arm, which moves *every time* a certain pattern of electrical impulses reach it from my brain, and saying, "Your arm is not free to move or not move; therefore *you* are not free"—when I was the one, each time, who freely decided to move my arm in the first place. It would be like pointing at a soldier who always follows orders and concluding that the general has no power, or that the movements of the army are fatalistically determined.

The patience of the bricklayer (as a poet once said) is assumed in the dream of the architect; the obedience of the soldier is assumed in the freedom of the army. We think with our whole brain, and we need our individual neurons to follow orders predictably and reliably so that we can call up ideas or memories or biases or vague feelings or pros and cons whenever we need them. But what the whole system is going to do with all of that material, what the universe in your skull is going to produce or conclude or *decide* after mixing all those things together for a while, is astronomically unpredictable. Our decisions, our free choices, are nothing if they are not the fruit of deliberate thought. The more that we need to think about something before we act, the more parts of ourselves brought into play in making a decision, the more chemicals that get put into the beaker—the less certain the result, and the *freer* our will becomes.

I am the most complex three pounds of physical substance known in the universe? Okay. That sounds about right. That, to me, satisfies my requirements for a robust notion of a freely willing self. To me, a vast tumultuous physical system in disequilibrium but churning itself towards some unforeseeable state of temporary or relative stasis is a very good model of free will.

Sometimes, it is true, one desire or drive or motive will be much stronger than the others; it will be no contest. But do we really want to say that I am (as the famous philosopher puts it) "doomed by determinacy" to leap into traffic and snatch up my child? Wouldn't it be truer to say that I am acting in this situation with my full self, my true self? Maybe some decisions aren't really decisions. Maybe a lot of the time we go around on autopilot. Often our choices are obvious. But often they are not. That is when, as Nietzsche says, our various semi-independent drives must fight it out for supremacy. Consciousness is a battleground. But what we must remember, if we are not willing to foredoom the outcome, is that in any large enough street brawl even the underdog can win.

How does this happen? How does that one small part of ourselves whispering "No, do what's difficult, do what's *right*" ever emerge victorious? I think it is not through strength, but through perseverance.

Not enough has been said about the width—or rather, I should say, the *thinness*—of free will. We only ever act in the moment. But most of the decisions we make in life—whether or not to have children, whether or not to change one's career, whether or not to leave one's spouse—are ongoing decisions, spanning weeks, months, or years. Even the deceptively simple decision to give up strawberry ice cream, for example, must be remade continually—basically, every day for the rest of your life. No matter how fiercely you ball up your fists, clench your teeth, and simply WILL, once and for all, with all your might, that so help you God you will never eat another spoonful of strawberry ice cream *ever*, it is not enough. It cannot be enough, because there is no once and for all. There is once, and then there are all the other onces.

Here's another way of saying it: There are no big chisel blows, only many, many tiny chisel blows. Carrying out a resolution is like memorizing a poem, or learning to play the piano. It cannot be done in one single burst of will.

Once, many years ago, Margo was acting in a play. She came out of a wardrobe change, stood in the wings, and began to shiver violently. She was wearing a slinky, insubstantial evening dress, and the theater was cavernous and cold. Or perhaps she was nervous. In any case, she had about five minutes to get ahold of herself before her cue. When rubbing her arms and visualizing tropical climates didn't work, she finally, in frustration, just willed herself to stop shaking. It was good that she had five minutes; she needed that much time.

Her will at first did not have the slightest noticeable effect. She was not surprised: surely she could not *decide* not to be cold; it was an unconscious reflex, beyond her control! But she didn't know what else to do, so she persisted. She tried to remember what her body felt like when it wasn't shaking. She tried to focus on her breathing. No effect. She closed her eyes and moved her thoughts down into her twitching muscles. *Stop that,* she told herself. *Be quiet. Calm down.* Nothing. Unless ... Maybe she felt something. Maybe her left arm had, for a moment, shaken a little less violently than the other? She concentrated on trying to reproduce the effect. That alone took a full minute; and a minute, if you have your eyes closed and are attending solely to what is going on inside your body, is a long time. It is also a very long time to be continually applying willpower. It is a lot more difficult to will gently but persistently for five minutes than it is to will in any number of isolated bursts, however ferocious.

But it is the only way to make yourself stop shaking.

Our momentary decisions are like one-night stands. They can lead to a lasting commitment—to a resolution— or they can be thrown out in the morning. One night, in other words, counts for almost nothing; it is what you do the next day, and the next day, and the next, that matters—and no one day matters more than any other.

Margo, returning to her own room Saturday morning, found in her purse the napkin on which she had so cavalierly scribbled all those resolutions, and was disgusted with herself.

Jim Bird likes to talk about the self as an iceberg. The small part floating above the water is your conscious, "striving" self; the large, invisible part below the waves is the unconscious, "living" self.

Deceived by the apparent smallness of our "selves," we mistakenly believe ourselves to be highly mobile. We think we can do anything, go anywhere. We have an idea, we dream of a goal, and all we have to do is put the plan into action! We paddle this way and that but, strangely, we never seem to reach our destinations, or even get much closer to them. This is because our lower, larger, invisible selves are always, unbeknownst to us, being pushed around by hidden currents. Only our underself really knows where we're headed, and it is sheer folly to fight it. At best, we will only wear ourselves out. At worst, we slow ourselves down, impede our own progress, or even deflect ourselves from our proper course.

In other words, we can't change ourselves and are foolish to try; but if we're not careful we might do just that: *We might deflect ourselves from our proper course.*

We *can* deflect ourselves from our course. It is not easy—we are paddling an iceberg!—but it can be done. And it requires, above all else, that we *believe* it can be done. Without that belief, we will never bother to pick up the paddle.

I want to end this story on a positive note. Most readers find blatantly uplifting stories embarrassing, just as most people I know are too cynical about happiness to let themselves be happy. But to hell with it. I want to do something different.

For what it's worth, this is what I think: I think Jim Bird is wrong. I think we *can* change ourselves. I think who we are is, to some small but not negligible extent, our choice. I think, or want to think, that when Nietzsche said, "You will become what you are," he did not mean that your character is predestined or already decided. I do not think he meant that you will always be the same. I think he meant that what you are tomorrow (what you *will become*) is dependent on what you do today (what you *are*). But what you do, what you choose, what you are today, that's up to you.

I'll admit, it's kind of a burden, this freedom. It means that you're responsible (to some not negligible extent) for making the life that you want. It means that you're the author of your own story—or, anyway, that you have at least a modicum of editorial input.

And writing stories is not exactly a lot of fun. It's tedious, laborious, and usually unrewarding. And the worst part of it is that you're all alone. I mean, you have to decide everything for yourself! You have to decide what to write and how to write it. You have to decide what *not* to write. You have to decide what is good and what is bad. You have to create your own scale of values. You have to figure out what kind of story you want to hear and then you have to tell it. Nobody else is going to do it for you. You're your own boss and your only employee. You're the architect and the bricklayer. It's all up to you.

I'll be honest: it's not easy. In fact, I hate it.

But then, as Emerson said, "Everything good is on the highway."

In other words: Do what's hard. Do something different.

PART IV

SIGNAL TO NOISE

Presently a nurse came downstairs and delivered him a message.

"Miss Warren asks to be excused, Doctor. She wants to lie down. She wants to have dinner upstairs tonight."

The nurse hung on his response, half expecting him to imply that Miss Warren's attitude was pathological.

F. Scott Fitzgerald

HE WAS SEDUCING ONE of his competitors' wives when the deputy prodded him through the bars with a lawn dart. Instantly J. Jerome Singleton was on his feet, denying by his posture that he had ever been asleep. "Good," he grumbled, "now maybe we can get some goddamn thing straightened out around here." He smoothed the creases from his yellow sport coat, straightened his red tie, and dragged a comb back through his hair. He was appalled to discover that a fuzzy ruff had formed at the back of his head, as happened when he had been a few weeks without a haircut. His joints popped audibly; flashes of pain startled him, scurrying through his body like vermin through underbrush. I must be ill, he thought; I'm too young to feel this old. In fact, he was seventy.

From some obscure principle of pride or self-preservation, he avoided looking around him or at the two men who escorted him down a hall and outside to a parking lot where a white van was idling in the blue glow of dawn. He did not remember where he was; and though his eyeglasses were in his breast pocket (his right arm was numb from lying on his side in an unnatural position to protect them), he did not, for some reason, put them on.

The men jangled as they walked. Janitors or caretakers, he surmised: only the lowliest of employees carried keys or tools. Powerful men travelled light. He remembered a day in New York when he had lost his wallet, and how it hadn't mattered: doors were still held open for him, bills were still signed. Of course they were. A man's power comes not from any piece of paper, but flows forth from his status, his reputation, his very identity. The president of the railroad needs no ticket to ride.

He patted his pockets now for his wallet, his glasses, his comb—tickets he probably would not need, but was nevertheless glad to have.

Something about a train ride threatened to remind him of something—something unpleasant. Something about New York; something about Katy … Like a boy who swings his bat once, misses, and declares that baseball is for sissies, Singleton rummaged for the memory for exactly one second, then gave up.

The janitors put him up front and sat on either side of him, handling him with ironic deference, like an expensive package that they resented having to deliver. Apparently they were intimidated by him, without knowing exactly who he was. They did not work for him, then. They must be the competition's janitors. So he had been sent for.

"Let's get something goddamn straight," said Singleton. "I've got no gripe with you two. You're just doing your job. A man's got to follow orders. Man who doesn't follow orders—hell, I'm the first to see he gets thrown out on his ass, and forget the pension." He did not like being between them like this; he liked to face the man he was talking to, liked to look him in the eye. "You boys doing your job, doing a good job. All right. I'll tell your head honcho that myself. But," he said, grasping about for something to criticize, something that would explain his irritation and unease. Just then the van hit a pothole in the road, giving him the impetus he needed; he went on, shaking his finger at each of them in turn, "It's this goddamn approach that's all goddamn wrong. Ain't no way to do business. Waking a man in his—" He shied from that thought. "No class, no respect, no goddamn consideration," he concluded.

His escorts had been warned by the deputy that this little old man could be violent and was surprisingly tough. They therefore decided (with perhaps dubious psychology) that the best way to avoid provoking him was to avoid talking to him altogether. So, as they piloted him through the gauzy morning to their headquarters, they chatted instead about baseball stats.

Luckily, Singleton was too puzzled to become properly offended. Like any good American, he followed the game religiously; indeed, he had once come very close to successfully buying a major league franchise. But he recognized none of the players' names they mentioned. They must have been following the goddamn farm teams.

Years later, the story as Douglas Singleton told it to himself was that his father had left them no choice; that, in the words of the commitment papers, he had become a danger to himself and to others; that he needed help.

At the time, however, the story seemed to be less about his father than about the factory. The year-ends had come back and things were worse than they'd predicted. Brockmighton was threatening to pull out, and Douglas thought him capable of dumping his shares at a loss out of spite. If that happened, the bottom would fall out—that would be the end. Meanwhile, secretary number three had handed in her resignation for no good reason; that runt Patterson was inciting the union again for no good reason; and the sesame seed people had decided to jack up their prices, for absolutely no good reason—just because the old contract had expired; just because they could.

And now, on top of everything, his father thought it was a good time to go mad. After fifteen years of yawning through board meetings and drooling harmlessly onto his blotter, J. Jerome had suddenly decided that he was the only man who could turn things around. He began coming to the factory on Fridays, hanging around the assembly lines, and placing mysterious long-distance phone calls from behind closed doors—through which his rapid, haranguing bellow could nevertheless be heard. He was working on a plan, one of his big ideas. All Douglas had been able to discover was that it involved the purchase of one hundred and fifty thousand barrels of sheep dip.

"Sheep dip?" asked Bennett, the factory's lawyer. "What the hell's he going to do with a hundred and fifty thousand barrels of sheep dip?"

Because Singleton senior, who had founded Singular Soda Crackers forty years ago, had never technically resigned as president, Bennett knew that any deal he entered into with the sheep-dip people would probably be upheld in court. The lawyer had great respect for the law; and if the law was on Jerome Singleton's side in this matter, he secretly felt that right and reason must be on his side too.

"Who the hell knows what he's going to do with it!," Douglas screamed. "He's out of his fucking mind!"

Bennett said thoughtfully, "Of course, if that were really true, things might look a little different ..." And he went on to describe, in the neutral tone of a professional offering a footnote of only professional interest, the view the law took of the mentally deranged.

So it happened that Douglas visited a psychiatrist.

"The thing you must, I think, keep in mind," he began, "is that my father has always been a difficult man to get along with ..."

In that time and in that part of the world, it was possible to commit a person to a psychiatric institution without their permission—indeed, without their knowledge—if two family members and a psychiatrist could agree that commitment was desirable. Conveniently, the law did not stipulate that the psychiatrist must observe the allegedly deranged individual in person; and while a few guns-for-hire may have made a comfortable career of signing

every commitment request sent their way by lawyer friends acting on
behalf of rich clients, most psychiatrists, in that time and in that part
of the world, were more scrupulous.

Dr. Preston was a man of scruples. It was his own policy, entirely
self-imposed, to only sign commitment papers after a half-hour
interview with the lunatic—or, when this could not be arranged, a
one-hour interview with a member of their family. Because Douglas
Singleton was well-dressed, well-spoken, and had an honest face, Dr.
Preston agreed to waive the direct interview with the father, who in
any case could not just then be located.

Fortunately, the facts, gently and deftly extracted in under sixty
minutes from the son, spoke for themselves. "Difficult to get along
with." "Eccentric," "arrogant," "sure of himself." A "risk-taker,"
a "fast talker," a "bully." "Bossy," "unrealistic," "suspicious."
"Irrational," "naive," "restless," "sloppy," "irritable." It was from
such crude ore as this that the clinician refined his hard, gleaming,
diagnostic labels: J. Jerome Singleton, he concluded, was *impulsive,
overtalkative, overactive, antisocial, hostile, mendacious, agitated,* and
paranoid; he suffered from *inflated self-regard, monomania, flights of
fancy, loose associations*, and *emotional lability*. As for the one hundred and fifty thousand barrels of sheep dip that the old man was
at that moment trying to buy in New York City with his grandchildren's inheritance—well! Dr. Preston doubted that he would ever
encounter a more perfect illustration of *delusions of grandeur*. Sixty-
three minutes after Douglas Singleton had entered his office, the
doctor inscribed his diagnosis on the commitment forms—"mania
with intermittent depressive features"—and signed his name with
a solemn, sympathetic, and (because of those three extra minutes)
more than usually confident flourish.

Douglas was stunned. He had heard the term "manic depression" before, but, like "syphilis" or "elephantiasis" or "homicidal

psychopathy," he had never applied it to any living person of his acquaintance. And this, what his father had, was apparently even worse. Not knowing that the doctor's roundabout diction had been cultivated to avoid needless professional squabbles over terminology, Douglas saw in the wordy diagnosis the embarrassed periphrasis of the doomsayer: A man might survive a heart attack, but never a "cardiac infarct." That word "mania," too, shocked him as "manic" never could have, for it revealed more clearly the horrible truth: A manic person, one suffering from mania, was a *maniac*.

Douglas was stunned—and moved. All his guilt evaporated. His father needed help.

To Germaine Singleton, "finding help" for Jerome meant finding for him a "retirement" or "care" home—in other words, a place for him to die. She was relieved that Doug had seen what she had seen— that Jerome was cracking up—but even more relieved to realize that Doug did not expect *her* to nurse Jerome through his dying.

Some part of her still believed that marriage entailed such obligations, even when the marriage had not been a happy one. Her grandmother had nursed *her* husband through eight years of consumption, and Jerome's mother had nursed *her* husband through what had probably been but which no one would call prostate cancer.

Five years ago, Germaine had nursed her own mother through an even more catastrophic deterioration. Celine's mind had crumbled like a stale cake months before her body started to fail. In her senility she became flamboyant and maudlin, as if she were patterning her dissolution after that of a drunk from a radio play. She wept, raged, smashed things, then became lugubrious and childishly stubborn, refusing to do anything but sit on the floor and sulk. At a later stage she became bizarrely and violently anti-religious: she berated the poor Anglican minister in the street, smashed two of the Catholic church's stained glass windows, and tore the arms off crucifixes and planted them in the garden like tomato stakes. One time Germaine tracked her down in the cemetery, barefoot and bareheaded in the rain, babbling to herself and weaving wreaths of dead flowers. Another time—one of the worst—she discovered her in the cellar, completely naked, filling jars with her own feces. (Weeks later, when Celine was in one of her communicative periods, she revealed that she had been trying to disprove the existence of the soul: if her output, she reasoned, equaled her input, then none of what she consumed could be going to the nourishment of her spirit.)

Germaine could not go through that again. As far as she was concerned, she had done her duty once, and once was enough.

She should by rights have been the first to die. It was only fair. After all the times Jerome had left her, it should have been her turn to leave him; after all the times she had taken care of him, it should have been his turn to care for her.

But of course it could never have happened that way. He would never feed her, dress her, clean her. Had she been the one to fall ill, he would not have stuck around. He would have run off again, and the responsibility would have fallen to Katy or one of the boys. Yes, J. Jerome Singleton was a great one for running away. He was doing it again, now. He was leaving her again, one last time.

It had been amusing at first, watching him grasp at ad hoc excuses for his little confusions. When she caught him removing his socks in the middle of the day, it was because his feet were hot. When she found him sitting in the car in the garage, it was because he needed tobacco from the store. (It was ten years since he'd given up chewing, fifteen years since he'd driven a vehicle, and more than that since he'd visited a shop.) When he lost his bearings or failed to understand what was going on around him, he blamed his eyes or the poor light. When he handed her the telephone in dismay, it was not because he had forgotten to whom he was talking, or why, but because the goddamn receiver wasn't working, or because the idiot caller refused to speak up. To abet these excuses, he stopped wearing his hearing aid and his eyeglasses—claiming, of course, that they were uncomfortable, ineffective, broken, wrong.

All this had been more or less entertaining. But one day she had come upon him in Doug's room, standing at the window, eyes unseeing, hands trembling with anxiety or frustration—reminding her exactly of the stray cat she'd once found cowering and hissing in the pantry: having wandered in somehow from the street, it had not known how to get back out.

She had spoken his name, twice. He had looked at her like she was a porter or a maid: impatiently, and without recognition.

He was leaving her, a bit at a time. That was just like him, too. He could never make a clean break. He would leave this life the way he'd left his marriage: trying not to burn any bridges, so that he could return if he didn't like what he found out there in the world.

Well, he had never left a note or made a speech any other time he had run off; so why should she be given the satisfaction of a proper goodbye this time?

Actually, that wasn't quite true. The time he was in the hospital, seven or eight years ago, for a polyp on his lung, he had thought he was dying. She got her deathbed farewell then. Breathing laboriously, looking small and pale and very sorry for himself, he confessed to her that he had never really loved any woman, that he was simply not capable of it. He said he was sorry.

That was it. That was his idea of making amends, of tying up loose ends: telling her he'd never loved her. What a burden that secret must have been to him all these years; how happy he must have been to finally get it off his chest! Shriven, he collapsed back onto the bed and ... fell asleep.

She called that dying badly. A good death was one that gave others as little trouble and sadness as possible. Reassuring lies whispered through teeth clenched in agony—that was her idea of dying well. Jerome Singleton had died a bad, selfish, inconsiderate death. But again, why should it have been otherwise? He had lived a bad, selfish, inconsiderate life.

He had loved no one; he had cared for no one. He never would care for, or take care of, anyone but himself.

And if he wouldn't have done it for her, why should she do it now for him? Why should anyone have to care for someone who would not care for them?

She would do it for her children, of course. If the obligations of a wife were sometimes conditional, those of a mother were not. And if there was one key theme to her self-story, it was that she was a good mother. It was a mother's job to care for her children—not vice versa. She had been a good mother; she would not let death undo that. She would not be babied by her babies. If it had to happen, if she was doomed to fall apart like her mother and her grandfather before her, let it happen among strangers. If she could not die with dignity, at least, please God, let her die quietly and anonymously, somewhere out of sight, out of mind. Let someone else take care of her.

Now, hopefully, a precedent was being set. If Douglas agreed that none of them, none of the family, should have to take care of Jerome, then perhaps he would, when the time came, do the same for her: "find help" for her; find a place for her to die.

"What day is it?" asked the man behind the desk, as if he knew, but couldn't, just at the moment, remember.

Singleton, circling the chair he had been offered, said (because he did not know), "Never mind what goddamn day it is. It's tomorrow in Japan and we're twiddling our thumbs in Memphis and cooling our heels in Atlantic City like a bunch of goddamn greenhorns."

The man behind the desk squeezed his nose thoughtfully. "And what month are we in now?"

"Look," said Singleton, alighting briefly on the edge of the chair and looking the man first in one eye, then the other, "I don't want to get in your way here, but then you've got to not get in mine, neither. Man can't scratch his own back. Those goddamn cornpones brought me to the wrong office, you hear what I'm saying?" He indicated that the room they were in was too small to belong to anyone important by shaking his arms at the walls, like an epileptic on the verge of a fit warning bystanders to stay back. "I'm here to see the big cheese, the man in charge, *your boss*. Understand?"

The nose of the man behind the desk was soft and porous. When he squeezed it, it took some time for it to return to its normal shape and size. "Could it be ... May, for instance?"

"Talk to me about time," sneered Singleton, resuming his pacing, "when time's wasting. Ten thousand dollars a day!" he roared. "That's a thousand dollars every one hundred forty-four minutes you're costing me," he said, making calculations on his fingers, "that's five hundred every seventy-two, nearly a hundred dollars every fif-goddamn-teen minutes and we're standing around here like a couple of monkeys at a movie show."

The man behind the desk squeezed his nose and listened to the crackling it produced in his ear as it reinflated. On the sheet of paper in front of him he wrote, *Sensorium impaired.* When the old man ran out of breath, he asked casually, "Have you ever had syphilis?"

Singleton stopped mid-stride. His hands gripped and shook fistfuls of empty air like a pair of ravens grappling with garbage. A cloud of rage engulfed him.

Two minutes later, the man behind the desk, who was the resident in charge of morning admissions that day, wiped Singleton's spittle from the back of his hand and wrote on the form, in the blank provided for syphilis, *Undetermined*. A few more strokes of the pen were enough to bring the interview to a conclusion. One stroke ratified the referring doctor's diagnosis (the resident thought of the manic-depressives that came in as "the loud ones," and Singleton certainly fit that description); other strokes prescribed what Singleton would eat, where he would sleep, what drugs he would swallow or be injected with, and to a large extent how he would be treated for the next several weeks or months of his life. After the new intake had been led away, still uttering imprecations, the resident went to the toilet and washed his hands vigorously—in defiance of the doomed and self-pitying part of him that said it was futile, it was too late, he'd already caught another cold. The colds that you caught in the nuthouse were not like normal colds. They were worse. They were more like flus than ordinary colds. He didn't know why, but crazy people just got sicker than regular people.

Singleton's belief, that he had been brought here by a competitor to make some business deal, had never had much more substance than a dream recalled a few minutes after waking. The strange gift-giving ceremony of the fat man in the shower cap could not be reconciled with that belief—and so the dream faded. No alternative hypothesis came to mind, however, for this scene was quite unlike any other in his experience.

"This is the only towel you get," said the clothes-room attendant, shaking a swatch of cloth the length of his forearm in Singleton's face like a penalty flag. Singleton tried to snatch it from him, but the man had more to say. "So don't *lose* it," he concluded. Then he relinquished the prize with a huff of resignation, as if he knew for a fact that his warning had fallen on deaf ears, that Singleton was going to burn or tear or bury the towel as soon as he was out of sight. "Well, let's see what you have in your pockets."

This struck Singleton as a good idea. By showing his tickets, he could perhaps figure out what train he was on.

The clothes-room attendant took his job seriously. Because it was his duty to confiscate all potentially dangerous items, he felt that the safety of the hospital depended on him. Because the safety of the hospital depended on him, he felt entitled to more than the starvation wage the hospital paid its attendants. To bring his salary more in line with his responsibility, he confiscated each week a few items that would, perhaps, have made dubious weapons (although, to be sure, a watch chain can, in a pinch, be used as a garrote; some cigarette cases have rather sharp corners; and even a cufflink would not feel so nice stabbed into your eye). Because he stole from the patients, he felt tenderly and paternal towards them. Because he felt a little guilty, he did his job well.

So he applied himself to the matter of Singleton's eyeglasses and hearing aid with the same fastidious deliberation he brought to more dangerous or profitable items. It was his general policy to let anyone who came in the front door wearing glasses keep them— reasoning that, if they had managed to get around in the world without losing or breaking them, they could probably be trusted to preserve them in the more circumscribed world of the hospital. Singleton, however, kept putting his glasses on and taking them off, so the clothes-room attendant did not know if the general policy pertained. Finally, recalling that three of his intakes had smashed their glasses already that month, he decided, somewhat vindictively, to commandeer these. To avoid a dispute, he reassured Singleton that he would not miss them because nothing visibly interesting ever happened here anyway. He kept the hearing aid too, because it was fragile and presumably expensive (though not, he thought, pawnable), and because he could not imagine where the old man would get replacement batteries for it. Yes, it would be better to save the hearing aid for special occasions, such as visits, or Christmas. In any case, Singleton apparently had one good ear, and that was more than some people could say. He also took Singleton's sport coat, tie, shoes, and suspenders. He let him keep the comb.

Singleton was too bemused to protest. He had found in his left front trousers pocket not his wallet, but a wad of newspaper folded to look like a wallet.

When her brother called, Katherine was either having a midlife crisis or an affair.

The man she was in love with (if she was in love with him) was nearly young enough to be half her age. He also was obnoxious and emotionally fragile, already had a girlfriend, and happened to be one of her husband's graduate students.

But it had been such a long time since any man had given her the unambiguous compliment of his desire; and the reminder that she was still a sexual being, a bundle of nerves still capable of becoming excited and exciting other bundles of nerves, had been as poignant as a glimpse of a forgotten self in an old high school photo.

Her heart had only started thudding after Elroy left the bathroom that night of the party, but it had not stopped thudding since. She was a wreck; anything was possible. She was going to smash everything, throw everything away, for a fuck. Was she?

Yesterday she had finally called him. He hadn't even given her a chance to offer the pathetic, flimsy cover story she had prepared (shopping, errands, lunch?). He had cut her off, affably enough, saying that he was "with people" and would see her soon. (The affability was somehow worse than curtness, which would at least have acknowledged the impropriety of her call, and what it signified.) To the interpretation of those two minutes of words she brought all the flailing, anguished creativity she had brought to her reading of Restoration poetry, twenty years earlier, when she'd needed to churn out another essay. For twenty-four hours she churned out brilliant hypotheses, each of which, in the moment she considered it, was absolutely convincing. He wanted her—yes. He loathed her—correct. He had been drunk that night, didn't remember groping her in the bathroom—unquestionably. Everything was possible.

She was still producing hypotheses when Doug called to tell her about Jerome.

The incongruity struck her like an affront. She felt as if, on page 500 of an 800-page novel that she was engrossed in, the author had suddenly embarked on a completely new story or introduced a completely new character without even so much as a paragraph break to announce the divagation.

She agreed (too readily) that their father was crazy, but scoffed at Doug's claim that she was his favorite, and denied that she could do anything to help. She wanted nothing to do with any scheme to clap anyone in a nuthouse—not even J. Jerome.

(Years later, long after Elroy had vanished from her self-story, this was the version of events she clung to: she told herself that she had told her brother that she washed her hands of the whole matter.)

But that night she was ruffled. Three hours later, when the phone rang again, she did not even pick up. She was thinking about her father.

The words "manic-depressive" sank into her like a stain setting into a tablecloth. Disparate parts of herself came together; old beliefs and memories reorganized themselves around this magical phrase like iron filings around a magnet. Before now, she had had to rely, when telling the story of her father, on homely psychologisms like "abrasive," "unreliable," "arrogant," "obnoxious," "inconsiderate," "sexist," "self-absorbed," "hard to get along with." Now she saw how all these traits could be—in fact, *had been* all along—subsumed under the one precise, unemotional, clinical term. The reason no one had ever been able to get along with goddamn J. Jerome Singleton was that he was crazy—really, honestly crazy.

Take for instance that preposterous family myth that she had been his favorite. All her brothers remembered were the times he had shown an interest in her, the times he called her from the road, the times he inveigled her into coming to Chicago, Boston, New York on the train to visit him. What they forgot, or had never seen, was how quickly Jerome's fatherly moods passed, how often she would find herself alone on some empty station platform or cooling her heels in some extravagant hotel room, a thirteen-year-old girl left to her own devices in a huge alien city. If he never invited Doug or Aaron or Tom, he also never abandoned them.

She had never understood these sudden inexplicable changes of heart of his. So many years she had wasted trying to figure out if her father loved her, hated her, or was simply indifferent. Now at last she saw that all of these had been true—in succession. "Manic depression" suggested to her exactly this changeability, this oscillation between extremes. It made sense. Her father was a manic-depressive. She heard herself saying it, wryly or matter-of-factly, but always without self-pity: *My father was a manic-depressive. He hugged me and pushed me away. He called me to him, then ran off. He gave me a piano but left the lessons to me; and he never came to the recitals. (He bought Tom a car, but only after he'd enrolled Tom in a mechanic's course!) When I wanted to build a kite, he ordered the kit, lent me his tools and his workshop (which the boys weren't allowed to use—too dangerous!); then, on the day we were supposed to launch it, he disappeared. That is how I see him: encouraging me, even running alongside me;*

then, suddenly, gone. And I am alone, left holding the string. I was his
favorite, and he didn't give a damn about me. He was fickle. He was
flighty. He was manic-depressive.

The ringing phone brought her out of her reverie, but she did not
pick up. Instead she went for a walk. On West 68th she saw an old
man in a bright green sport coat coming towards her, rubbing his
hands and grimacing with self-importance, his tongue between his
teeth—and she was thrown back thirty years to the day she'd crossed
the street to avoid him.

She was on her way to school; she didn't know he was back in
town; he hadn't been home in months. For some reason, she pretended she didn't see him. She crossed the street. She was twelve and
she had snubbed her own father.

At least, she'd always assumed she had. Now she saw another
possibility: she had been scared of him. And she had been right to be
scared. For he was crazy. He had always been crazy.

But the man on West 68th Street was not her father. In fact, he
was not even holding his tongue between his teeth; he just had large
lips.

When she got home she took the phone off the hook. Elroy
seemed as trivial as a nightmare on waking. Subsumed by her past,
she could not remember how any part of him connected to any part
of her.

But the next morning, with two days before Carl was due to
return, she put the receiver back on the cradle, telling herself that she
was not committing herself to anything.

Singleton did not know where he was or who these people were, but
he could see that they were only doing their jobs. He understood
that he had been gripped by the cogs of some vast machine, that he
was passing through the works of some immense bureaucracy; and

his admiration for large, inexorable organizations (which reminded him of his factories), coupled with his dread of having his memory lapses detected, persuaded him to keep quiet for the time being. For about twenty-four hours he let himself be carried along like a cracker on a conveyer belt. Then character reasserted itself.

Identity is memory; and if we believe the latest theories of the psychologists, memory is stored in the connections between brain cells. Thus, for a memory to become established, to become part of ourselves, it must find connections to other parts of ourselves. New thoughts, new experiences, new ideas must find echoes already in us, if they are to be entertained, felt, or believed. This takes time. New memories establish themselves slowly, like spreading stains—or like strangers settling in to a new town.

This is why, as we age and our minds deteriorate, new experience loses its capacity to impress itself on us, and why our distant youth begins to seem more vivid than what we did yesterday, last week, or last year. Old memories are like tomato plants: they have many roots.

Sometimes this trend is more pronounced; sometimes it is quite catastrophic. Sometimes the last year, or the last five or ten or twenty years of our lives, evaporate altogether, while the rain of new experience, of present day-to-day existence, dwindles to a faint drizzle, which scarcely dimples the face of the water; and, with so little downward force to oppose them, the deepest currents rise to the surface. Then the past grips us, while the present becomes shadowy and unreal. When today's events do manage to pierce the bubbling upsurge of ages past, they reach us faintly, as if from a great distance, and often in isolation, untethered to other memories—just the way, in fact, that memories of our distant childhood reach most of us in midlife. This curious inversion sometimes leads to the mistaken belief that the recent past is ancient history, and vice versa.

This explains, for example, why Singleton wrongly placed the memory of his missing wallet in the distant past, when in fact it had occurred only a few days earlier. But it also explains why, fifteen years after Singleton had returned home to his family, fifteen years after he had retired from the active life of a manufacturing magnate, he began suddenly to revert to his former self. As he forgot where he was and what he was supposed to be doing, he could only remind himself *who* he was. That information was stored deep.

J. Jerome Singleton was a great man, a rich man, a powerful man, a captain of industry. He was a force to be reckoned with. His name was known. He was somebody, goddamn it. Events depended on him. People were waiting for him. He was needed elsewhere. He did not belong here.

Alvin had caught sunstroke on the beach and wandered into a well-to-do neighborhood where his odd behavior was interpreted as ravening drunkenness probably compounded by insanity. He had fully recovered within twenty-four hours, but within twenty-four hours he was in the asylum. Now he had to wait the minimum ninety days to get out, like everyone else.

Scott's wife had caught him masturbating. Without a word, she'd left the house for a week; when she came back, she suggested, in her clear unabashed schoolteacher's voice, that it was her opinion and the opinion of her closest friends that he was mortally oversexed, and that what was obviously called for was a long rest far away from everyone who knew him, and her. He had been too embarrassed to argue; secretly he agreed; his mother had caught him masturbating once, too, and had whipped him, and wept.

Syed drank too much. He didn't even like drinking, really. When he drank he was outgoing but stupid. When he was sober he was clever but shy. He was lonely, so he drank. Every few months he was clapped in here when the little glowing cellophane creatures made their reappearance. He knew, when he was sober, that they were hallucinations brought on by D.T.; but at the moment they appeared, they were more real, more obviously independent of his perception of them, than any other thing he had ever seen. More than their grotesque appearance or the insulting things they said, it was the awful intensity of their existence that terrified him.

Cliff felt an exhausted tightness in his belly one day which he could not explain. It felt as if he had just done two hundred sit-ups, or vomited all night. It felt, he decided, like guilt. He wracked his brain for possible causes, scouring his past for every error, mistake, and sin he had ever committed. Each transgression, in the moment that he considered it, seemed more than adequate. The pain in his guts got worse, and with it the conviction of his loathsomeness. Now all he could do was hold himself and sob broken apologies as he recalled each evil afresh.

Baltazar, who was thirteen, suffered from night terrors, which did not cause him much worry (because he did not remember them) but troubled his parents enough to send him away to be cured. In the asylum, however, his screams troubled his roommates —strange grown men with angry faces who were too embroiled in their own nightmares to feel sympathy. Instead of bringing him glasses of chilled apple juice like his parents did, they shouted at him to shut up, or else. The problem worsened. Baltazar grew to hate himself for what he could not control; and rather than wait for the thrashing he deserved and which was constantly being threatened, he actively pursued his punishment, insulting and irritating the men relentlessly until they struck him.

Digby treated strangers like they were old friends.

Claude had lost his wife in a car accident.

Immanuel felt ashamed. Most of the time he was able to hide his shame from others behind a façade of aloof derision. But recently he had begun to have a recurring nightmare which kept him from sleep. He lost his welding job, and a finger, before checking himself in to the asylum for the paraldehyde that clouded his waking mind and took some of the bite out of his dreams. Years later, he remembered nothing of the hospital, could recall none of the staff or his fellow patients. For him, those three months were simply the time of the bad dream. In the dream he was very ill, but could not stay home. He had to go out; something had to be done; someone was waiting for him. Then it happened. Always, inevitably, in some crowded public place—in the street, at school, on the train, at his mother's shop—the worst possible thing happened: he was sick; he vomited. A hundred people turned to look with disgust at the mess he had made. He was so horrified, so ashamed, that the only thing he could do, each and every time, was get down on his knees and try desperately to lick it back up, scoop it into his mouth and swallow it again.

But everyone has a story. Life as we know it is less like a cohesive novel than an anthology of unrelated short stories whose protagonists, caught up in the development of their own individual plots, take no notice of one another. Novels, unlike collections of stories, promote the illusion that humans are not completely, or not always, incarcerated in their own concerns—that it is sometimes possible for our storylines to intersect, or even merge. Perhaps that is why people prefer novels to short stories: escapism.

All Singleton knew was that he was in the wrong place. All he saw around him were broken, inferior animals: a man placing chess pieces on the keys of the piano while working the pedals with his feet; a man lying under a table, shaking his legs in the air like they were full of bedbugs; a man sitting in a trash can chatting amiably to God, chuckling appreciatively at His replies, saying "Thank You, thank You, I'm glad You feel that way"; one man howling with frustration when another told him, with obvious malice, that it was Tuesday; one man stroking another's head till he fell asleep; a man kicking a boy of thirteen, who laughed a brittle, bitter laugh and chased after the man for more; a man wrapping himself from head to toe in countless colorful scarves; a tall, wilted man spinning slowly in a circle; a bird-like, fidgety young man whose wet brown eyes were like two separate living entities in the dead mask of his face; a man whose huge, grinning face looked like something carved out of wood to scare a child; a man bawling like a child, and gasping, again and again, "I'm sorry, I didn't mean to"; another who moved his hands over his body in an elaborate sequence repeated precisely and endlessly, and who could say nothing but "Cars need to eat too," over and over.

Perhaps most appallingly, there were at least a dozen men who behaved perfectly normally, playing cards, reading, smoking, or writing letters—and implying by their normalcy that there was nothing abnormal, nothing even unusual, about the behavior going on around them.

When the orderly at the end of the hall, whose name was Brian, saw Singleton coming, his heart sank. He did not like getting into tussles with the patients, whom he believed were too mixed-up to know what they were doing. He felt sorry for them—almost as sorry for them living here as he felt sorry for himself working here. Clearly the last thing any of them needed was an ass-whooping; but sometimes they left him no choice. They always picked on him—him, the biggest guy in the place! That's how mixed-up they were.

"You best get your ass back in the dayroom now, Signalton," Brian suggested.

"Forgot something, can't find my keys," Singleton said, making impatient shooing gestures, "so if you'll excuse me for a moment while I—well, man, are you deaf or just stupid? Get out of my way."

"I think probably you best just go on back now, Signalton."

"My name is Singleton goddamn it, J. Jerome Singleton Singleton *Sing-gull-ton*, and you're costing me ten thousand dollars a day!"

"It says Signalton on your forms," Brian said (truthfully), hoping to deflect the old man with trivia.

"Don't you think I know my own name! If you don't let me out that door right this very minute, so help me God I will rip your tonsils out and mail them to your widow. I will—I will eat your *boss*."

"I sure would if I could," Brian said softly, "but you've been here long enough now I guess to know it ain't up to me. Only ones that got a grounds pass are allowed out in the afternoon. So come on now, Signalton, why don't you just ..."

Singleton heard not a word of this. Because he was a loud man himself, calm or soft speech always struck him like a sanctimonious reprimand. This man was *defying him*. Anger flooded through his body like a toxin; it became an audible buzz in his ears. He squeezed his fists till his arms shook. Then he lowered his head and rammed the man in the belly.

For a moment, as the world tilted, he saw the door at the end of the hall swing open, and he saw himself emerge once again, through the sheer force of his will, triumphant.

The paraldehyde they poured down his throat unmoored him; he drifted through scenes half dream, half memory.

"You want to know my secret?" he asked the fawning elevator operator. "Always double down on aces. Put the money you make back into the business right away—that's the only way it'll grow. It takes backbone, a little fire in the belly, but you can't be afraid to let your balls dangle. Take it from me." He gave the boy a five-spot.

He looked at it coldly. "What am I supposed to do with this?"

"Don't ask me—never saw it before in my life. Guess you found it on the sidewalk or in one of your pockets or something."

The inspections agent continued to stare at the envelope, as if it might move.

"These goddamn peas now," Singleton sighed. "These goddamn stalks and stems—let me tell you, I fired the sonofabitch let those through. You want to know my opinion, it was Hardy sent that sonofabitch my way. Goddamn agricultural sabotage is what it is—if we're calling a spade a spade. I grow A-grade peas—ask anyone in the county. Come back to the farm, take another look at those peas—that's all I ask. There's a man. Say, you reading this?"

FINGERS FOUND IN PICKLE FACTORY.

The reporter whistled dubiously. "Who saw the finger?"

Singleton slid the piece of paper with the Pole woman's name and address across the table. "You treat her gently now. She don't speak English too good and they threw her out of her job and she doesn't want her name in your goddamn scandal-rag. But she wants to do her duty, wants people to know what's going on in those factories, wants the truth out. And I'm sure she wouldn't say no to a little vig on publication neither."

"What's the matter, can't find a place for her at your—"

Singleton shook an index finger in the reporter's smug face. "You keep me and my factory well out of it, you understand? I know Dallas Cullins and I know who your father is and I know my way around a goddamn libel suit, let me tell you."

The retraction was printed a week later and seven pages deeper. Too little, too late: he'd already won the government contract.

"A good story doesn't die," he told the trashy torch singer. "Once it's told, you can't untell it. Mrs. O'Leary's cow didn't start the Great Chicago Fire!"

"I heard that one before," she said, drunkenly determined to not be impressed.

"But a thing takes on a life of its own. The truth never stood in the way of a good story. Course, that's the *problem* with the world. You can't *change* nothing, all you can do is print goddamn retractions and corrections and addendums and— You come into the world like an immigrant after an election: the government's already in place, all you can do ... all you can do is respond to its stupidities. *They* decide the agenda, *they* the ones choose the game, all you can do is bicker over the rules ..."

"Shucks now, angel, what's the matter?"

He slapped her hand away. "Goddamn it, don't *fuss*. One thing I hate is being fussed over by a woman."

That stupid comment about immigrants! He had to be drunk. When she touched his hair again, he threw his glass at the wall, missing the piano player's head by inches. They threw him out.

He cackled and whooped in the night air. He didn't need them. He didn't need anyone. He was his own man. He'd made himself out of nothing, less than nothing. Goddamn them all. Goddamn *her*. Those twisted teeth, those idiotic peasant's costumes spattered with flour ... Always fussing over him in that ignorant immigrant's accent ... Too stupid to know the difference between a boy's name and a girl's name ... He'd overcome all that. He was as American as goddamn baseball. "I almost owned a Major League Baseball franchise!" he roared. "But they wouldn't take my goddamn bid 'cause I don't belong to a *club*, I never been to a *university*, I don't wear a little *ring*. *I* made a fortune without any of their advantages! Aw goddamn it, sweetie-pie, you're getting mustard all over my good slacks."

"Gimme some more napkins, pa, huh?"

Her hands, coated in orange soda, shimmered in the sun like lizard skin. She was the most beautiful perfect little creature that had ever existed. His heart was suffocating him; he jumped to his feet and opened his mouth like a bird bursting into song: "Goddamn you to hell you lousy sonofabitch Ruth, scratch your ass if you're going to scratch your ass but step up to the plate and *swing* if you're going to *goddamn swing goddamn it!*"

Germaine turned to the man seated opposite. "What business are you in, Mr. Hencks?"

Singleton simpered apologetically: *Women!*

"I am a musician," the man said stiffly.

Singleton upgraded their tickets. When Germaine quailed at the cost, he bellowed, "The world takes you at your own estimation and I will not fraternize with artsy-fartsy goddamn riff-raff!"

In the dining car they were seated next to the owner of a Milwaukee steel mill. He told the man (because the world takes you at your own estimation) that he was in manufacturing. He patted Germaine's distended belly and said, "My wife too." He laughed in her scowling face. "As you can see, she manufactures her own unhappiness."

The steel mill owner chuckled. His wife—or daughter—smiled.

"Not everything," Singleton told her. "Not quite everything—only *just about*. Sure there are things I can't do. For instance, I ain't cut out for television—there's a fact. A man must accept his limitations or this world of limitations won't accept him. My genius is basically for deal-making. I'm an idea man, a conceptualizer. I invented price ranges, did you know that? Same exact product, different packaging, three prices. Because there's those who always buy the cheapest product—they think they're being thrifty; then there's those who always buy the most expensive product—they think they're getting quality; and then there's everybody else—they don't want to be ripped off, but they don't want to eat shit, either. Tell me, your husband ever talk to you like this?"

"What makes you think I was ever married?"

"You're a hoot and a holler, doll. I like you. Who was your father?"

"Perhaps," she said, "we should discuss terms."

"To be honest with you," he said, circling the chair he had been offered, "I don't like mixing business with women."

"Neither do I."

"I *like* women, you see. But business—business is brutal. I like my business competitors to be men. I like my chicken to have bones in it."

"Not everyone you make a deal with is your competitor, Mr. Singleton. There is such a thing as a mutually beneficial—"

"Men pay lip service to that idea too, but let me tell you something, sweet pea: it's just the polite ceremony around the duel. The aim in business is always to shoot the other guy before he shoots you."

"Your people don't want me to sell to you," she said. "Neither do my people."

"But you—you don't like being told what to do, do you? Sure—I know your type. I can read a woman like a billboard. Bill-*broads*, I call 'em. Heh—you like that?"

She stood by the open door and said, "I'll call you when I've made up my mind."

"I get it. You want to talk it over with your accountant, your manager, your brain trust—the *boys*. I understand."

"What hotel can I reach you at, Mr. Singleton?"

He could not remember. "Never mind," he said. "Never you mind. Maybe *I'll* call *you*, angel. Yeah, maybe I will. Maybe I will and maybe I won't. Never mind."

He wasn't licked yet, goddamn it; he still had a few tricks up his sleeve; they weren't going to farm him out to the minor leagues yet, goddamn it.

She had been weak. He would be strong.

The chairs in this house had cushions on the seats and the cushions had dust on them. In this house, everyone whispered.

The boy he was playing with kicked him in the leg. "Ha ha, you're hurt!"

"No I'm not," he spluttered in rage and incomprehension. "*You* are!"—and he kicked the boy as hard as he could. The boy's mother yelled at his mother, but it didn't matter: he'd made the boy cry. Jan was happy. Jan was strong.

"What do you want a hundred and fifty thousand barrels of sheep dip *for*, anyway?"

"You think I'm going to tell *you*?" he screamed.

The train was moving so slow, he half expected water to come pouring in when he opened the window.

"Would you mind terribly closing that, please? The smoke ..."

"Goddamn it, a little coal dust never killed no one." He stuck his head out the window and gulped wind. The little old couple excused themselves to the dining car.

"They call me eccentric," Singleton said, "but goddamn it, it ain't me—it's the times that're *un*eccentric. We used to ride cable cars hanging upside down from the straps—nothing to it. We used to sing 'Oh, Lady Be Good' in the street—and no one blinked. We drank gin neat from iced melons and made egg-nog in June—big deal! We rode from New York to Milwaukee in the dead of winter with the windows all open wide—just to make the gin taste warmer, goddamn it."

Each of these moments came to his mind as clearly as the faces of his grandchildren.

The manager informed him that the matter of his bill had been satisfactorily resolved—and that there was a telephone call waiting for him.

"Of course it has," Singleton said irritably, mistaking the man for a bumptious bellboy. "I told you it would be."

"The call, I gather, is of an urgent nature."

Singleton rubbed his hands together. But it was not the baroness; it was little Dougie.

"You've got to come home, Dad. It's Kate."

What was she doing back there? Why wasn't she in New York? She'd escaped all that, like he never could—so why had she let them drag her back? Something must be terribly wrong.

Doug and Germaine were waiting for him at the station. He was shocked by how old they looked. They walked him to the car, their faces as solemn and flaccid as those of board members.

"What for the love of God is going on here? Why are you behaving like two goddamn robots? Where is she?"

"She's at home," was all they would say.

But she was not. Instead, waiting for him, in the house that he had helped design and paid cash money to be built, were the deputy and the sheriff.

"It's best if you don't make a fuss here, Jerome, but just come along with us now."

Their moist eyes and embarrassed posture gave them away: Katy was dead.

"What the fuck is going on out here?" said a voice pained with bewilderment. It belonged to a man with a neck as thick as his head, which protruded from his beige uniform like a big pink pencil eraser. The face had a disrespectful expression on it.

Singleton said, "You watch who the hell you think you're talking to, goddamn it."

The orderly, who was known in the hospital as Bullneck, opened his mouth. His scalp began to tingle. With a heroic, indeed angelic effort, he closed his mouth. This man was a new intake.

"Get back to bed," he stuttered at last. "And don't let me catch you out here making that bloody racket again."

Singleton began to vibrate. "How *dare* you—"

It was Bullneck's belief that, since the patients of the asylum had something wrong with their heads, the best way to correct their behavior was to hit them in the head, the way you might slap a fuzzy television.

Singleton had never been sucker-punched in his life. Instinctively he reared back and kicked the man in the shin as hard as he could.

Bullneck's screams soon brought assistance, as well as onlookers. When the orderlies had pinned Singleton's writhing body to the floor, Bullneck asked, "Now are you going to shut up or do I have to really hurt you?"

Singleton choked on his hatred. "Goddamn you to hell you goddamn sonofabitches!"

Bullneck slapped Singleton's face as hard as he had ever allowed himself to slap any patient's face. "I *said*, are you going to shut up or—"

"By all the gods in heaven you'll pay for this you goddamn dirty whoring sonofa—"

Bullneck clapped his hand over Singleton's mouth and squeezed.

(Years later, he would remember none of this. He would recall the poor wages, the snooty doctors, the terrible working conditions, and the patients who spat on him; and he would admit that there were times when he had lost his temper. But he would not recall wanting to kill this old man who would not shut up; he would not recall how earnestly he had tried to crush his face in his fist. It was a moment that did not fit into his self-story—for he was not, he believed, a cruel or violent man.)

"There's only one God in heaven," he said, and squeezed.

Singleton bit his hand.

He'd thought he knew what dying was: dying of malaria in that sti-
fling thatch hut in Peru; freezing to death that night in a Minnesota
cornfield; awaiting the imminent explosion of Hardy's bullet
cutting into his chest; drowning in the anonymous Atlantic after
falling overboard like a goddamn fool; dying of an old, broken lung
in a barren hospital room. But he'd been wrong. None of those
were dying. Dying was this flailing panicked fight, this all-out
war against death. He could not breathe—he was a sucking lung
submerged in the ocean. Every nerve in every tissue of his body
screamed like a firecracker—every cell within him burned with life,
fought against death—he had within him a dying animal, a wild
thrashing shrieking rodent—he kicked, punched, clawed at their
faces, whipped his head from side to side, gnashed his teeth—an
arm as strong as the bole of a tree snapped the cartilage in his neck
like a dry wishbone—hatred, indistinguishable from the will to live,
seared his veins—they were killing him—*the goddamn sonofabitches
were killing him*—

He bought her an ice cream cone. "Thanks, pop," she said sarcastically. He tousled her hair sarcastically. They went into their funny-
walk routine. The passersby gaped. They were the show; everyone
else was just onlookers, just passersby.

"And that of course," he said, "is the famous Waldorf Astoria
where maybe you'll stay someday, huh."

"I won't need to," she said, slipping comfortably into their future-
making patter, "I'll own an apartment across the street, right there."

"What," he said, aghast, "you won't own the whole building?"

"I *do* live here, Dad," she said. She was old now. "Remember?"

He didn't want to remember.

"Dad, it wasn't me. It was you." She huffed a sigh—she was thirteen now, fourteen. "*You're* the one dying."

He threw back his head and his shoulders and quickened his pace. She had to jog to catch up.

"Then why does your age keep flimflamming around like that?" he demanded.

She explained it to him. He was reviewing his life one last time before leaving it. His life, as they said, was flashing before his eyes.

His bruised, burning, straitjacketed body told him that she was telling the truth. He let out three quick sobs—thinking of his patents, his factories, his grandchildren. "I'm not leaving nothing," he said.

She wouldn't meet his gaze.

"You might not have to leave *everything* behind," she said at last. She explained it to him.

Everyone was against Dr. Ngi. They didn't like him because he was new, because he was short, and because he was foreign.

They had liked Dr. Kenneally, his predecessor, well enough. His approach to administration had been, for forty-two years, that of a man about to retire: he didn't attend rounds, didn't like reading incident reports, didn't insist on proper stock-taking of the medicine room, and commandeered all the meat for his staff. Of course they liked him.

Dr. Ngi, on the other hand, was young, and subject to the belief that bad situations can sometimes be ameliorated. He was trying to make the asylum into a hospital—a place where the ill might actually, once in awhile, recuperate. This made him unpopular.

The latest controversy was his no-television policy. The nurses and orderlies hardly cared what the patients did—what horrors they

observed, what trash they took into their brains—so long as they
kept quiet. The television kept them quiet. According to the nurses,
and even now some of the doctors, the dayrooms had become much
noisier and more violent since the TV ban. But Dr. Ngi simply could
not believe that murder mysteries and garish news reports of fires,
plane crashes, and natural disasters were conducive to the mental
health of his inmates. Perhaps a person had to get worse before they
would get better. But he could hardly argue this to his beleaguered,
volatile staff. Instead, to placate them, and not always because he
thought it was in the best interest of the patient, he authorized each
day more of the requests that came his way for paraldehyde, veronal,
insulin, and isolation.

On top of all his other worries, Dr. Ngi made a point of seeing
patients personally. He did not have the time, but it was one more area
in which he was determined to outshine the repugnant, beloved Dr. K.

He sent the sobbing man away with a grounds pass, and called
in the next.

"I guess you're the one I've been waiting for," said the old man
as soon as the door was opened to him, nodding with approval at
Dr. Ngi's open report book. "Katy told me there'd be someone
to take down the things I've been holding on to. Well, I've been
thinking it all over for I don't know how many days, and let me tell
you it hasn't been easy, a lifetime is a long time and I don't know
how much longer I could have remembered some of this, but if
you're going to get it all down there in your book now then I guess
maybe I can start letting some of it go. I hope there'll be enough
time."

Dr. Ngi, whose English was functional but largely devoid of
idioms, did not fare well with fast talkers. He nodded seriously,
matching the patient's expression, gestured to the chair, and consulted the man's file.

"My mother was not a bad woman but she was weak," said Singleton, circling the chair he had been offered. "I've left behind many things about her but I don't want to forget it all. She was always kind to me, it must be said. Those *sarmale* she used to make— No, goddamn it. Let me start with the important things. The companies I started and the money I made, all that was well and good but the best thing I ever made, because I made her make herself, was Katy. She never understood that. She always got me all wrong. Well, all right, maybe that was the price I paid, but let me get it straight for the record. She thought I told her she could do what she liked—that I didn't give a damn. But what I tried to tell her was, Do what you *want*. Make the world be the world you want to have around you. Goddamn it, I had to show the boys what to do each step of the way because they didn't have the mettle, I had to give Doug the cracker factory because he couldn't have done anything else, but I always tried to get Katy to surprise us, because she had it in her. I wanted her to be *like* me by *not* being like me—by not being like *her* old man, either. When she was twelve—and get this down, because this is what I want to save, more than anything else. When she was twelve, I came home on the train ..."

But Dr. Ngi had stopped listening. He wrote in his careful hand, visualizing the correct spelling of each word before putting it down, and avoiding all those troublesome pronouns: *Greatly agitated. Flights of fancy. Loose associations. Logorrhea.*

Two weeks earlier, in the weekly team meeting which Dr. Ngi himself had initiated, Dr. Alban and Dr. Niederwaldt had criticized him, in front of everyone, for mistaking an "obvious case" of manic depression for schizophrenia. Well, they would find no fault with his diagnosis this time; here was a textbook case. With defiant pride he wrote out the words: *Schizophrenia, with paranoiac features.* Then, while the patient talked on, he filled out a chit for thirty days of insulin shock therapy, to be repeated in forty-five days if necessary.

The sheep-dip baroness allowed herself to be talked into selling to Singular Soda Crackers a token ten thousand barrels of sheep dip— which Douglas Singleton, who did not know what to do with them, did not insist be delivered.

Germaine Singleton, on visiting day several weeks later, was delighted to see how calm and quiet Jerome had become. Though she was somewhat discomfited by the bars on the windows and con- fused by the youth of some of the guests, she liked that the doctors here were mostly foreigners and that the nurses were mostly fat, ugly, ill-bred, and discourteous. The thought of dying badly in a place like this gave her an anticipatory thrill of spite.

Years later, when her father finally passed away, Katherine Osbret, née Singleton, surprised herself by weeping at the funeral.

Everyone was surprised by the will—by just how much he had left behind.

PART V

THE INNER LIFE

Very few of us go through life, or even through one day, on an even emotional keel. No one of artistic temperament ever does; and the closer the individual of artistic temperament approximates genius, the surer he is to display waves of exaltation and depression which can scarcely be distinguished from manic depressive insanity.

Joseph Collins, M.D.

A HUNDRED YEARS AGO, in May, 1884, Freud received his first shipment of cocaine from the Danish pharmaceutical company Merck. He was then twenty-eight, and hoping to make a name for himself—or at least enough money to permit him to marry his fiancée. *The Interpretation of Dreams* was still fifteen years away. The coke was frightfully expensive.

He started by taking a twentieth of a gram, presumably by mouth. It made him feel good—or rather, it made him feel normal:

The psychic effect of *cocainum muriaticum* in doses of 0.05 - 0.10g consists of exhilaration and lasting euphoria, which does not differ in any way from the normal euphoria of a healthy person. One feels more vigorous and more capable of work; on the other hand, if one works, one misses that heightening of the mental powers which alcohol, tea, or coffee induce. One is simply normal, and soon finds it difficult to believe that one is under the influence of any drug at all. This gives the impression that the mood induced by coca is due not so much to direct stimulation as to the disappearance of elements which cause depression. One may perhaps assume that the euphoria resulting from good health is also nothing more than the normal condition of a well-nourished cerebral cortex which is "not conscious" of the organs of the body to which it belongs.

Freud had high hopes for cocaine. It relieved hunger, so he thought it might work as an anti-nauseant. His sister, in fact, had found it useful in dispelling seasickness. One researcher had found it effective in forestalling asthma attacks. It might have some application in the treatment of diabetes. In America there were numerous reported cases of using it to ease the withdrawal pains of morphine addiction. And, of course, it made people feel good. As Freud pointed out, there was no shortage of tranquilizers capable of calming frazzled nerves, but as yet nothing one could prescribe to "increase the reduced functioning of the nerve centers." Perhaps here was a potential cure for melancholia—that is, for depression.

But Freud's hopes were never quite fulfilled. The fame that should have been his was snatched away by a colleague, Carl Köller, who discovered the potential of using cocaine as a local anesthetic in eye operations. This application, in fact, soon came to be recognized as nearly the only legitimate use of an unpredictable and often dangerous drug. Within a year, reports of addiction and toxic side effects had begun to appear in the medical literature. Freud, whose name was associated with the drug thanks to his popularizing articles, was denounced for having unleashed "the third scourge of humanity," after alcohol and morphine. (In fact, one of his own good friends, Ernst Fleischl, who had, in the course of treating a phantom pain in his amputated thumb, become addicted to morphine, subsequently became, in the course of being treated for morphine addiction by Freud, addicted to cocaine.)

Freud defended himself, somewhat belatedly, in 1887 by saying that no one without an innate weakness was susceptible to "cocainism"; that is, no normal, healthy person could possibly succumb to addiction. He also blamed the needle: by mouth cocaine was harmless, under the skin sometimes dangerous.

This last argument, however, was a bald contradiction of what he'd written in an earlier paper. In 1885 he'd gone out of his way to reassure those harboring "unjustified fears" that "even subcutaneous injections—such as I have used with success in cases of long-standing sciatica—are quite harmless. I have no hesitation in recommending the administration of cocaine for withdrawal cures in subcutaneous injections of 0.03 - 0.05g per dose, without any fear of increasing the dose." But two years later, he considered it "advisable to abandon so far as possible subcutaneous injection of cocaine in the treatment of internal and nervous disorders." He further covered his tracks by removing from his list of published works the incriminating 1885 article. And even *fifteen* years later, in *The Interpretation of Dreams*, he was still absolving himself: "These injections in the dream reminded me once more of my unfortunate friend who had poisoned himself with cocaine. I had advised him to use the drug internally only, while morphia was being withdrawn; but he had at once given himself cocaine *injections*." Apparently Freud's conscience wasn't quite clear; no wonder he was having troubling dreams.

But in 1887, three years after he had first experimented with cocaine, three years after he had written his first "song of praise to this magical substance," maybe Freud hoped no one would catch the change of heart; maybe he wasn't aware of it himself. His enthusiasm, in any case, had suffered a blow; his interest began to flag. With this last, limp attempt at saving face, Freud put the whole mess behind him. "The Cocaine Episode," as his biographer Ernest Jones disparagingly called it, was at an end.

The problem with this story, thought Devon, as he stood up and rubbed his hands together in the cold garage, was that Freud was again—or still—using cocaine as late as 1895. He admitted as much quite guilelessly in *The Interpretation of Dreams*, where he submitted one of his own dreams to analysis:

What I saw in her throat: a white patch and turbinal bones with scabs on them. The scabs on the turbinal bones recalled a worry about my own state of health. I was making frequent use of cocaine at that time to reduce some troublesome nasal swellings, and I had heard a few days earlier that one of my women patients who had followed my example had developed an extensive necrosis of the nasal mucous membrane. I had been the first to recommend the use of cocaine, in 1885, [*sic*] and this recommendation had brought serious reproaches down on me. The misuse of that drug had hastened the death of a dear friend of mine. This had been before 1895, i.e., the date of the dream.

Or was this guileless? To what exactly was Freud admitting? The "at that time" seemed to imply that the "frequent use" was, at the time of writing, a thing of the past; in other words, sometime between 1895 and 1898 or 1899, when he wrote the book and analyzed the old dream, he had given up the habit. And the phrase "to reduce some troublesome nasal swellings" suggested that his use of the drug had had, at least in his opinion, a clinical justification. But did this particular method of application preclude all others? Was he, through this limited confession, implicitly denying that he had used it in any other way, or for any other reason?

And he was worried about his state of health. It could not have been the nasal swellings themselves that worried him so much as the possible side effects of their *treatment*. He must have been afraid that he, too, like the patient who had "followed his example," was going to end up with an "extensive necrosis of the nasal mucous membrane"—in other words, a dead, blown-out nose.

But this didn't prove much more than that in 1895 he had begun to worry that putting the stuff up his nose might not be good for him in the long run. This bad dream might only have persuaded him to go back to taking the drug by mouth. Or it might not have changed anything at all. The only word that Devon had on the matter was, of course, Freud's. And Freud did not always tell the strict truth—as he'd first demonstrated in 1887, then again in another passage from *The Interpretation of Dreams*:

> *Injections of that sort ought not to be made so thoughtlessly.* This sentence in the dream reminded me once more of my dead friend who had so hastily resorted to cocaine injections. As I have said, I had never contemplated the drug being given by injection.

Devon went into the house, moving almost on tiptoe. He looked at his digital watch: it was 10:56. For a moment he could not make these numbers mean anything; he wasn't even sure if it was morning or night. Then, gradually, the bricks of his life fell back into place around him. Barb was on the phones tonight, and Devon was home alone with Clyde. He crept on stiff legs past Clyde's open bedroom door but did not look into the darkened room, the only dark room allowed in the house. He closed the bathroom door softly behind him. He held his breath, thinking he had heard Clyde's voice. When no sound came, he went to the medicine cabinet and looked in the mirror.

Which was it: *still* or *again*? Did Freud use cocaine regularly for ten years, or did he at some point quit, then resume the habit? But even this by no means exhausted the possibilities. What was really meant by "regularly," after all, or "habit," or, for that matter, "quit"? How often had Freud taken cocaine? Once a week? Once a month? Three times a day? How much did his use vary over the years? How many times did he "quit"? Once? Once a week?

His mind was off again, racing pleasurably.

There was, unfortunately, very little concrete evidence to go on. During his engagement, which lasted four years, Freud wrote to his fiancée, Martha, almost daily. Aside from the published articles, these letters seemed to be the main source of information about Freud's cocaine use—indeed, about much of his private or inner life at all; but even today, a hundred years after they had been written, most of them remained unpublished. Jones, in researching his sycophantic *The Life and Work of Sigmund Freud,* had been given complete access to the letters; a few years later Freud's own son had edited a sparse, one-volume selection of them, which, not surprisingly (they spanned something like fifty years, and Freud had been a prolific letter-writer) featured some sizeable gaps: like the maddening *three-year* gap between letters 107 and 108, dated July 13, 1891 and June 7, 1894. Between what Jones had chosen to reveal and what Ernst Freud had permitted to see the light of day, Devon could glean very little that was definite. It was like connecting the dots, but the spaces between the dots were astronomical.

The first mention of cocaine appeared in a letter to Martha dated April 21, 1884, when Freud was still awaiting his first shipment:

I am toying now with a project and a hope which I will tell you about; perhaps nothing will come of this, either. It is a therapeutic experiment. I have been reading about cocaine, the effective ingredient of coca leaves, which some Indian tribes chew in order to make themselves resistant to privation and fatigue. A German has tested this stuff on soldiers and reported that it has really rendered them strong and capable of endurance. I have now ordered some of it and for obvious reasons am going to try it out on cases of heart disease, then on nervous exhaustion, particularly in the awful condition following withdrawal of morphine (as in the case of Dr. Fleischl). There may be any number of other people experimenting on it already; perhaps it won't work. But

I am certainly going to try it and, as you know, if one tries something often enough and goes on wanting it, one day it may succeed. We need no more than one stroke of luck of this kind to consider setting up house.

Unfortunately, the very next letter in the *Letters of Sigmund Freud* was dated more than a month later—May 29—and contained no mention of his cocaine studies. The entire month of May, when he had actually begun to experiment with the drug, was missing.

The next reference to cocaine appeared only in June, when Freud assured Martha, whom he was about to visit, that he wouldn't be tired, "because I shall be travelling under the influence of coca, in order to curb my terrible impatience."

Then there was nothing, nothing at all for nearly a year. On May 17, 1885, he wrote:

When the letter came I was suffering from migraine, the third attack this week, by the way, although I am otherwise in excellent health. I took some cocaine, watched the migraine vanish at once, went on writing my paper as well as a letter to Prof. Mendel, but I was so wound up that I had to go on working and writing and couldn't get to sleep before four in the morning.

Then in January of 1886 he wrote from Paris:

Charcot invited me (as well as Richetti) to come to his house tomorrow evening after dinner. You can probably imagine my apprehension mixed with curiosity and satisfaction. White tie and white gloves, even a fresh shirt, a careful brushing of my last remaining hair, and so on. A little cocaine, to untie my tongue.

The next day he reported:

> We drove there in a carriage the expenses of which we shared. R. was terribly nervous, I quite calm with the help of a small dose of cocaine, although his success was assured and I had reasons to fear making a blunder.

Devon noted that Freud had written "11 P.M." above the date of this first Paris letter, and in it he apologized for having so exhausted himself working and writing that he could barely hold the pen. The same thing had also happened the night before: "Last night," he wrote, "I went on writing the outline of my anatomical paper till I just couldn't keep my eyes open." Did this mean he was no longer taking cocaine in the evenings, that he had learned to avoid getting "wound up" too late in the day? He was evidently using the drug in Paris as a social lubricant—to combat shyness, to calm himself in company, to loosen his tongue—but not, perhaps, as an aid in his academic work.

Two weeks later, still in Paris, Freud wrote to Martha:

> It is now 6 P.M. and at 9:30 I am going to Charcot's, not without the fear of having a most unamusing evening. Needless to say, I have fewer preparations to make than for the first time, but I have felt so out of sorts all day that I haven't done any work.

Later in the same letter he suddenly admitted:

> The bit of cocaine I have just taken is making me talkative, my little woman. I will go on writing and comment on your criticism of my wretched self ...

And two pages later:

> Oh, how I run on! I really wanted to say something quite different.
> Here I am, making silly confessions to you, my sweet darling, and really
> without any reason whatever unless it is the cocaine that makes me talk
> so much.

The letter included a postscript, time-stamped, as it were, 12:30 A.M.:

> Thank God it's over and I can tell you at once how right I was. It was so
> boring I nearly burst; only the bit of cocaine prevented me from doing
> so.

But in his first article on the subject Freud had written:

> The effect of a moderate dose of coca fades away so gradually that, in
> normal circumstances, it is difficult to define its duration. If one works
> intensively while under the influence of coca, after from three to five
> hours there is a decline in the feeling of well-being, and a further dose
> of coca is necessary in order to ward off fatigue.

So, if he had taken that first bit of coke at 6:00, when he was writing
the letter, it would have more or less worn off by the time he reached
Charcot's at 9:30, three and a half hours later; in any case, it certainly
couldn't have staved off boredom for the entire evening. Unless he
was now taking *immoderate* doses, one had to assume he had taken
a further dose before going to Charcot's. And when he returned to
his room after midnight, he sat down to write a letter to Martha. He
must have realized he was going to be awake all night.

Devon again had to pass Clyde's bedroom on his way back to the
garage. This time he looked in, a solicitous but unworried smile on

his face. Usually Clyde lay on his back with his head propped up by two or three pillows, staring dolefully out the door, waiting for sleep as though for a visitor (or, Devon sometimes thought, for death). But the room was dark and Devon could see nothing. He lingered there in the doorway for a moment, his smile frozen, waiting for his eyes to adjust. Clyde had not been sleeping well since his return from the hospital, and Barb had asked Devon to keep an eye on him.

A grunt emerged at last from the darkness. "What is it?," Clyde muttered.

"How you feeling?"

"Fine," said Clyde.

"Good," said Devon, sincerely. It *was* good that Clyde was feeling fine. It was no holiday being shut up in the hospital, even if you had someone like Barb there to look out for you, to bring you books and illicit snacks. Devon would never forget the one and a half days he'd spent "under observation" in that hospital, eight months ago now, after what Barb and others gently referred to as his "breakdown" but which he preferred to call his crack-up. But that had been different.

"Good," he said again.

Clyde said nothing.

"Well, good night."

"Yeah, all right."

In the kitchen Devon gulped two glasses of cool, delicious water. He felt that he was on the verge of a major discovery. It was almost a physical sensation, this feeling that the world's doors were unlocking themselves and waiting for him to step forward and open them.

He did not need Barb's sly, condescending look of approval to remind him that he had not felt this good in months. Only now that he was feeling good again, *right* again, could he admit to himself that he had gone through something like a period of depression. At the time, he'd sworn that there was nothing wrong with *him*; it was not *him* but *life itself* that was fucked up. But of course that was the tricky thing about depression: it so thoroughly blackened your view that everything you looked at, anything you turned your thoughts to, appeared black enough to be the cause of your unhappiness. It was all too easy when you were depressed to look at the world and say: No wonder I'm depressed—how fucking depressing it all is!

Devon supposed one also had to guard against the opposite fallacy. Perhaps happiness bathed everything in a golden light, made anything you looked at seem the probable cause of your happiness. But no, his newfound optimism was not delusive or manic; it was simply normal. *This* was what it felt like to be alive and healthy. This was the way a well-fed cerebral cortex was supposed to feel. His depression had made him forget this feeling, made him forget that time could be relied on to unfold its promises. Depression was a sort of temporal cage: inside it, you simply could not imagine that anything would ever change or improve; you were chained to the wheel of this one endless moment of misery. But when you were not depressed, the future lay spread out before you like a landscape of possibilities. When you knew with an overpowering, bodily certainty that the present moment was *not* an isolated prison cell but a vestibule opening onto a vast field where there was fresh air and room to run, you felt almost omnipotent.

"Hey!," Clyde called from his room.

"Sorry!"

Devon turned the light in the kitchen back on. Clyde needed the lights in all adjacent rooms and hallways to be on at all times, even while he slept. He also could not abide closed doors anywhere in the house (the bathroom door was his only grudging exception). He had, since his return from the hospital, become even more obstinate in these demands. As far as Devon could tell, Clyde did not fear anything imaginary, like monsters or ghosts, but rather feared broken communication. That was also why he refused to be left alone, why he needed to have someone in the house with him at all times: he needed to know that if he ever called for help, someone would hear him.

"Sorry," Devon said again, then returned to the garage and to Freud.

There were very few direct references to cocaine in Freud's published works. At least, the index volume of Winston's battered old *Standard Edition* listed only a handful of page numbers under that word. There were the confessional dream analyses in *The Interpretation of Dreams*. There was a potted summary of "the cocaine episode" in his *Autobiographical Study*. Then, tucked away in the *Fragment of an Analysis of a Case of Hysteria*, there was this:

> I had begun to suspect masturbation when she had told me of her cousin's gastric pains, and had then identified herself with her by complaining for days together of similar painful sensations. It is well known that gastric pains occur especially often in those who masturbate. *According to a personal communication made to me by Wilhelm Fliess, it is precisely gastralgias of this character which can be interrupted by an application of cocaine to the 'gastric spot' discovered by him in the nose, and which can be cured by the cauterization of the same spot.* In confirmation of my suspicion, Dora gave me two facts from her conscious knowledge: she herself had frequently suffered from gastric pains, and she had good reasons for believing that her cousin was a masturbator.

The middle sentence was not actually italicized by Freud, but seemed nevertheless to Devon to be typeset in a special font. He read it through several times but it did not acquire a firmer foothold in the paragraph. It did not belong there. It should have been relegated, at best, to a footnote. (And Freud, Devon had soon discovered, had no antipathy to footnotes.) It was bizarre enough that Freud believed that masturbation had something to do with stomach pains. It was equally bizarre that this Wilhelm Fliess believed that the nose had something to do with stomach pains. But what relation did the two beliefs have to each other? What did the nose have to do with masturbation? Who was Wilhelm Fliess?

Among the books that Devon had brought home from the McSeutor Library was, he was sure, the complete letters of Freud to Wilhelm Fliess. It took him a minute to find it; the garage was a mess, and he had not improved matters much by rescuing several boxes of Winston's library from storage. Tomorrow he would go out and buy shelves, and a little table, and a space heater. Tomorrow, after all, was not a hypothetical proposition, but a real place where things got done.

It gave him a thrill—a cool fluttering in his chest, as if from the wings of some giant moth—to see that the letters to Fliess spanned the critical years 1887 to 1904. He began to leaf through the book at random, allowing his attention to be drawn to paragraphs and sentences that a previous reader had bracketed in pencil and annotated in the margin with a question mark, exclamation point, or both.

Wilhelm Fliess was an ear, nose, and throat specialist from Berlin who had some strange ideas. According to Fliess, there was "in the nose, as in the cerebral cortex, a specific localization for the individual distant symptoms in other organs." Swellings of the nasal mucosa and pathology of the turbinate bones and the sinuses were, in his view, responsible for such diverse symptoms as pain in most parts of the body, migraine and other types of headaches, heart problems, respiratory difficulty, gastrointestinal upsets, and, finally, all manner of disturbances in the functioning of the female genitals, causing dysmenorrhea (painful menstruation), miscarriage, and more. In clinical proof of all this, Fliess cited the visible swelling of the turbinate bone during menstruation, the occurrence of vicarious nosebleeding during menstruation and pregnancy, and the fact (Devon had to read this twice) that cocaine applications to the nose were capable of inducing accidental abortions.

"The number of symptoms adduced is great," wrote Fliess,

> and yet they owe their existence to one and the same locality—the nose. For their homogeneity is demonstrated, not only by their simultaneous appearance, but by their simultaneous disappearance. The characteristic of this whole constellation of complaints is that one can bring them temporarily to an end by anaesthetizing with cocaine the responsible area in the nose.

In other words, thought Devon, the "nasal reflex neurosis" was a catch-all diagnosis for any malady whatsoever that seemed to clear up rather nicely when you put cocaine up the patient's nose.

This preoccupation with the same drug that Freud had more or less single-handedly brought to the attention of the European medical community must have been what brought the two men together. Even Jones (while airing the obligatory diagnosis of transference and latent homosexuality) had touched on the truth:

> Both Freud and Fliess suffered from migraines, and the two men conjured up various theories, none of them very fruitful, to account for this distressing disorder. Then, as was fitting in his relation to a rhinologist, Freud suffered badly from nasal infection in those years. In fact, they both did, and an inordinate amount of interest was taken on both sides

in the state of each other's nose. Fliess twice operated on Freud, probably cauterization of the turbinate bones; the second time was in the
summer of 1895. Cocaine, in which Fliess was a great believer, was also
constantly prescribed.

It was prescribed, apparently, not only by Fliess to Freud, but by
both men to their patients. In May, 1893, Freud wrote to Fliess: "I
am now making this diagnosis very often and agree with you that the
nasal reflex is one of the most frequent disturbances. Unfortunately,
I am never quite sure what to do then." So he sent his patients to
Fliess for operations, who returned the favor by sending his own
patients to Freud for psychoanalysis; and in the meantime both prescribed cocaine for a host of problems.

Devon dropped the book on the concrete floor, stirring up a little
cloud of sawdust. Absentmindedly cracking his knuckles in precisely
the way he had trained himself not to do in court, he stood and
began pacing.

How much cocaine had Freud himself really been using? It was
impossible to tell. There were few direct references to his personal
use, and the gaps between these few were wide enough to accommodate any theory. At any rate, an absence of proof was not proof
of abstinence.

All Devon, or anyone, knew for sure was that in May of 1893
Freud was writing to say that he had interrupted a migraine by
applying cocaine to both nostrils. In January of 1895 he was
"keeping the nose under cocaine," that is, repeatedly painting his
nostrils to prevent renewed swelling. In April of the same year he
was pulling himself out of some kind of "miserable attack" with an
application. In June he was admitting quite bluntly, "I need a lot
of cocaine." Then, abruptly, in October of 1896—the day of his
father's funeral—he was claiming to be done with it: "Incidentally,"

he wrote, "the cocaine brush has been completely put aside." And that was all he wrote.

Devon twisted a kink out of his neck with a loud crack and padded into the kitchen. What he needed, he decided, was a timeline. Yes! He could already see it: a luminous ruler into which he would drive the key dates like posts, after which the gaps would become as clear and well-defined as missing puzzle pieces. The procedure was so straightforward that it would be less like noting up a case than solving an engineering problem, less like connecting dots than fitting tongues into grooves. In his imagination he could hear the oiled ball bearings rolling against one another as another piece of the mechanism fell into place.

About three and a half hours later, he realized that a timeline was not, after all, a useful idea. The chronology was not what mattered. It was not the objective but the subjective, not the outward appearance but the secret inner life that he was after. He did not care *when* Freud had needed a lot of cocaine or when he had put the cocaine brush aside; he wanted to know *why* Freud had needed a lot of cocaine, and *how* he had put the cocaine brush aside. He wanted to know what it had been like for Freud, being Freud, at that time of his life.

And this, Devon realized, was what he could never know. It was not just that all his source material was translated from a language he did not understand, or that so many letters and other documents were inaccessible to him, or that the pertinent letters he did have were written to Freud's fiancée or closest friend and therefore drew on a private stock of idioms and anecdotes. It was not just Freud's secretiveness (he had set the tone in 1885 when he had burned all his papers and boasted to Martha, "let the biographers worry, we have no desire to make it too easy for them!") or the frequent inscrutability of his prose that made Devon despair. He would have been in no better a position if Freud had been here in the garage with him and feeling talkative.

Because there was, around every mind, every inner life, an impenetrable wall. Most people never invited you in, and even those who did did not have keys to half the doors in their own houses. A year ago Devon had spent fifty hours interviewing Rodland Miller—the most willing and forthcoming affiant imaginable—and still he hadn't been able to foresee what would happen when they put him on the witness stand. There came a point in every interrogation and in every line of research, no matter how deep you went or how meticulous you were, when the information simply dried up. The more closely you looked at anyone, alive or dead, the more distantly they looked back.

The only way to get into another's life was to project yourself there, imagine yourself into them. He remembered now why he had given up reading the biographies of great and famous men. It was because every life was, viewed from the outside, more empty space than dots, and every biographer had therefore no choice but to connect the dots in his or her own individual, imaginative way. Most historians and biographers were too timid, however, to speculate much. But speculation was the only road to truth. A line, however it was arrived at, said more than any number of dots. Fiction, because detailed, would always be truer than fact, which could only ever be partial.

A short story or film about Freud as a young man experimenting with cocaine or grappling with addiction would be more telling than the most assiduously researched biography, because the facts could never puncture the wall, could never push through to the inner life. Devon, however, had always disliked so-called literature, with its unabashed irrelevances, its cloistered melodramas, its idiosyncratic ways of slicing up and presenting the universe. Stories and novels seemed to him both obscenely private and obscenely trivial, like the dreams a stranger insists on sharing with you. For this reason, as he moved down the bright hallway towards the bathroom, the floorboards creaking explosively beneath his feet, as he crept past Clyde's black room and the sure sense of eyes upon him, as he closed the door delicately behind him and stood before the mirror, Devon imagined he was watching a movie: *The Story of Freud and Cocaine*.

Freud, deep in thought, walking through the streets of Vienna, the four fingers of each hand slotted primly into his waistcoat pockets.

Freud in his office, persuading one of his fidgety patients that she was hypnotized. He retreated behind the desk to write a letter while the woman pretended to be asleep.

Freud seated before the fireplace, reading aloud, with sonorous pride, his son Martin's latest poem.

Freud in his study, carefully, but with an air of nonchalance, tapping his last remaining crumb of cocaine onto a piece of brown paper. He hesitated, thinking perhaps of Martha's silent disapproval—or of his dead friend Fleischl.

Freud in his study, putting a pinch of the white substance on his tongue, thinking with self-satisfaction that when the supply of one's vice was limited, using it was a kind of virtue, for one was also thereby using it *up*, getting rid of it.

Devon corrected his picture of Freud, remembering to cast him not as a sour, shrewd, bespectacled old man clutching a cigar who unaccountably spoke English with a lisping Austrian accent, but as a pudgy thirty-five-year-old in a shabby suit who spoke gruff but eloquent German (and French and Italian and English) and who suffered from migraines and a propensity to bleed from the nose into his thick, lustrously oiled moustache.

He saw this Freud seated on a train, red-faced and sweating, eyelids lowered like shutters against a coming storm, afraid that his screaming heart would explode or seize up in his chest.

Freud at Charcot's, gauche, unsure of himself, hungry to make a good impression. He wondered if anyone was laughing at his French. He wondered if anyone could tell that he had taken a bit of cocaine before stepping into the carriage with Richetti. He glanced in a mirror and decided that no one could. The light from this lamp was peculiar, that was all. He looked the same as ever.

Freud, at 2:00 A.M., creeping through his apartment, moving almost on tiptoe, afraid to disturb Martha or the children.

Freud, seated behind a patient, struggling not to fall asleep.

Freud going through a period of depression—not that he called it that. There were simply good days, when work was a joy and an adventure of perpetual discovery, when the words flowed effortlessly from his pen and he marveled at his own perspicacity; and there were bad days: "Fathomless and bottomless laziness, intellectual stagnation, vegetative dreariness. I have never before even imagined anything like this period of intellectual paralysis. In times like these my reluctance to write is downright pathological. Every line is torture." On bad days he sat at the window, fingering his bust of Aristotle like a lecturing phrenologist, despising himself for ever having thought himself worth something, capable of something great. Sometimes, on his bad days, if there was work to do, he took a little cocaine, and felt almost normal again. There was, of course, no evading altogether the bad day; it could only be postponed. Indeed, the next day he would probably feel even worse. But it was a universal truth, he felt, that humans would always elect to pay for a present pleasure with a future pain. It soothed him to think that he was only acting in accordance with intransigent human nature, as everyone must do.

Now here was Wilhelm Fliess: short, barrel-chested, wide-eyed, bursting with health and confidence, yet holding something back, like a tightly coiled spring. Fliess came bounding up to Freud, pumped his hand up and down, cracking his arm like a horsewhip, and congratulated him effusively on an excellent lecture.

Freud, reading a letter from Fliess, frowned.

Freud, writing a letter to Fliess, smiled.

Freud on his way to meet Fliess for their annual "Congress." This time, it was not just the train causing his anxiety: Fliess had threatened to "take another look at that *Shnoitsl*"—which meant another operation. Freud did not like going under the knife at any time, but there was, he felt, something uniquely terrifying about having the soft, sensitive tissues of the nose pierced and peeled apart by cold surgical instruments. (Years later he would write to his friend, "I find it very expedient that surgeons never take the pain they cause into account; if they did, they obviously would not find the courage for many a thing. I still shudder—an echo—at your heroism in the early period of our friendship. I could tolerate nothing at all.") It was, he told himself, the nature of the operation itself that caused his grief and trepidation, not the surgeon or his methods. Indeed, he felt sure that he could never have put himself under the hands of anyone but his good friend Wilhelm.

(In fact, though Freud would hardly admit it, he had good cause for anxiety. One of his own patients, Emma Eckstein, had nearly died following one of Fliess's operations. The good surgeon had, it turned out, left half a meter of gauze behind in her nasal cavity; when, two weeks later, Freud's colleague Dr. Rosanes found and removed it, the poor girl had a near-fatal hemorrhage. The "flood of blood" made Freud woozy; he had to leave the room. But then again, as he'd swiftly reassured his friend Wilhelm, and as he now reassured himself, that ordeal had not been Fliess's fault, but Rosanes's, for pulling out the gauze so recklessly. Freud also could not entirely discount the possibility that the poor girl was bleeding hysterically in order to monopolize his, Freud's, fatherly attention. The mind, after all, was a mysterious place.)

Freud settling himself, with heroic nonchalance, into a suitable *fauteuil* in Fliess's crisp, lavender-wallpapered hotel room, while Fliess chewed on a crust of bread and went about the room without haste, patting his pockets and laying out his gleaming instruments on a nearby armoire.

Fliess took his friend Sigmund's head firmly between his rough, dry hands and tilted it backwards. He bent over from the waist, his back as straight as a well pump handle, and peered, unblinking, down into Freud's nose. He made a satisfied gurgle in his throat and murmured, "Just so." Then, without another word, he reached for the cocaine bottle, withdrew the brush, and generously spackled the inflamed, bright red interior of both nostrils. Within a minute the blood vessels had begun to constrict and the swollen tissue visibly to subside. Within five minutes, as the drug, unbeknownst to either man, passed through the Schneiderian membranes, into the bloodstream, then percolated through the blood–brain barrier and into the brain, Freud began to feel much better indeed: it was as if all the doors and windows in his head had sprung open at once and all the dark corridors in his mind had been flooded with sunshine, and he could see that they went on forever, corridors upon corridors, rooms adjoining rooms, and he realized that he could move as far as he needed to in any direction, at his own pace, in his own time. It was not too late. Someday he would do something great. He did not even notice when Fliess made the first incision—though some time later he did notice that Fliess was spending a lot of time fussing about in the wrong nostril. But he would have been a fool to worry: his friend Wilhelm was a great man, a genius, the best of all doctors.

*

Devon remained in bed, or rather on the bed, for several minutes after he heard Barb arrive home. Then he got up, changed his clothes, and went down the hall to the kitchen, turning off lights as he went. At night, having every room lit made the house feel open and institutional, like a museum or an office. In the morning, however, as the first blue glow began to ooze in through the windows and render the lights superfluous, the house felt exposed and sterile, like a waiting room or a morgue.

Clyde was a bluish swath of fuzz protruding from a chink in his cocoon of blankets.

Barb was at the stove, hunched over a frying pan, with her usual undecided look of attending to everything at once. Devon sat down at the table with an involuntary groan, for he knew the sausages were for him. He resented the assumption that he would be awake, let alone hungry.

"Good morning, sunshine."

He looked around for cigarettes; that is, without moving his head, he moved his gaze across the portion of tabletop directly in front of him. The thought of chewing and swallowing anything seemed as pointless and alien as the wartime atrocities of savage tribes, but he could imagine a case being made for sucking a cloud of chemicals into his lungs.

He felt as though he had been tricked. The way he felt now was the most forceful and concise refutation imaginable of his earlier optimism. He was being chastised for his meaningless enthusiasm with this meaningless despair.

He had been wrong. He had been wrong about Freud. He had been wrong to be excited. There was nothing exciting about Freud's cocaine use. Until last night he had somehow taken it for granted that Freud was a great man, someone to be admired. He must have formed this opinion twenty years earlier during his undergrad, when, in preparation for a psychology course, he had read a few of Freud's "classic" works. *Totem and Taboo* and *Civilization and its Discontents* had proved spectacularly useless as background to an introduction to the physiology of the retina and the localization of brain function, but he had nevertheless come away with an impression of Freud as a brilliant and fearlessly independent philosopher of the soul—an impression that had probably only been inflated retroactively by the extent of his disappointment with the psychology course, and its circumvention of philosophy and of the soul.

His erratic reading of the past three nights had at first corroborated this impression. Freud was certainly brilliant (he seemed to have memorized a lot of Goethe and Shakespeare, anyway), and he was undeniably a good writer (his prose, at least, proceeded with a stately grace and polite, almost wheedling formality that obscured the occasional incoherence of his ideas or the faults in his logic), and Devon had been positively delighted to discover passages like this, which seemed to reveal the torment of a genius at loggerheads with the unimaginative fools around him:

> I am pretty much alone here in the elucidation of the neuroses. They look upon me as a monomaniac, while I have the distinct feeling that I have touched upon one of the great secrets of nature. I cannot talk about it to anyone, nor can I force myself to work, deliberately and voluntarily as other workers do. I must wait until something stirs in me and I become aware of it. And so I often dream whole days away. Everything in me is very quiet, terribly lonely.

But then there were also passages that Devon simply could not digest, theories of Freud's that were not any less bizarre than those of his friend, Wilhelm Fliess, to whom he wrote things like this:

Now, a child who regularly wets his bed until his seventh year (without being epileptic or the like) must have experienced sexual excitation in his earlier childhood. Spontaneous or by seduction?

Devon could not decide if this was just plain silly nonsense, or evil, irresponsible nonsense.

He had only wasted a few nights on Freud, granted. But he had also wasted a few nights on James Joyce, a few nights on William James, a week of nights on De Quincey. His thesis—that there were great men who had achieved greatness not *despite* the drugs they used but *because* of them—was slipping away from him. What was slipping away, in fact, was the indefensible contention that there had ever been, that there ever could be, such things as "great men."

He had no thesis. There was no project. There would be no book. It had been a stupid idea anyway. Had he really thought that a polemic against the current drug laws would win back for him the status and respect that he'd lost? Had he really believed that a writing career would make up for the one that had been taken from him? He felt chastened for his delusions, like an ignorant, misbehaving child.

He had been wrong. Depression was not the feeling of being imprisoned. Happiness was not the feeling of freedom. It was exactly the other way around. Happiness was being tucked snugly into a single moment. Happiness was a winding hike through dense woods to who-knows-where. Happiness was blind.

Depression was having all the future spread out before you. Why take a step down any path at all if you could already see where it led? Misery was walking down a long straight hall, driving down a long straight highway. He could see exactly where he was headed; there would be no surprises, and no exits.

Barb put her chin on her shoulder and looked at him.

"Rough night?"

"No," he said.

She was not discouraged; his first response to most questions in the morning was "No."

She transferred the spatula from one hand to the other. In her left she held it like a surgical instrument; in her right, like a club.

"Up late working again?"

"No," he said, this time in the tone that meant "don't ask."

"Couldn't sleep?"

"No," he said, and she could tell that he had stopped listening to her.

She looked at him closely, her forehead wrinkled with concern. He was still depressed. She did not know what to do about it. On the phones it was easy: you made sure they were safe, that they were not going to hurt themselves, and then you listened. They wanted to talk—that's why they called. She did not know what to do with someone who did not want to talk.

He had been getting better, too; that was what was so frustrating, so disappointing, about these funks of his in the morning. In the last couple of weeks he had begun to smile again, even to laugh. She didn't claim to understand what he was up to in the garage with his books so late every night, but it was clear anyway that he had an *interest* again. This made her so happy that she was tempted at times to embrace him, or to cry.

She turned back to the stove and herded the sausages to one side of the pan to make room for the eggs. There was one thing at least she could do for Devon, and that was make sure he ate. A body could do nothing if it was not well-nourished.

"What about those bookshelves?" she asked.

He scowled up at her, as though she had used one of his own arguments against him. "What about them?"

"Should we get them this morning? The Do-It will be open by eight. I'm sure Clyde would come along."

"No," he said, his tone close to "don't ask."

"The early bird gets the worm …?"

"They'll still be open later," he said, though he didn't sound as if he believed it.

PART VI

THE BLOOD-BRAIN BARRIER

McNarry couldn't understand how any psychiatrist could bring himself to testify for the prosecution: The entire aim of psychiatry was to unravel the causes of behavior. And if all behavior had a cause, where was guilt?

Meyer Levin

The psychologist must himself be psychologized.

L.S. Hearnshaw

ON JULY 9TH, 1980, Mike Burger was having dinner with his wife, Roz, and four friends at a restaurant in West Hollywood.

Q. Now, can you tell us, Doctor, what the defendant was thinking and experiencing at the time of, and leading up to the time of the instant offense?

Their friends were waving their wineglasses around and talking loudly, as if to make up for Mike and Roz's silence.

A. I can tell you that, following the perceived insult in the foyer, that his thought processes are disordered. His mental state is predominantly one of confusion and disorientation. The sights and sounds, and smells of the restaurant are reaching him as if from afar. He is experiencing a profound depersonalization—

Roz's gaze briefly met Mike's as she left the table. Mike was breathing heavily.

Q. Can you define that last word for us, Doctor? I'm sorry to interrupt.

"This shit has got to fucking stop," Mike said. The others looked at him. Mike stood and strode across the room.

*

A. A sense of not being himself. A sort of feeling of detachment from reality, you might say. A sort of feeling of being on autopilot, or being in a dream.

He pulled a man out of his chair and threw him to the floor and began kicking him in the face, muttering the word "motherfucker" repeatedly.

Q. Was he angry? Was he … "enraged," as the newspapers put it?

Someone screamed. Two men tried to pull Mike away. He thrashed free, elbowing one of them in the face, breaking his nose with a crunch, and the other backed away.

Mike kicked the man on the floor in the stomach. "Get up, motherfucker." A thick sob emerged from the man's bloody, shattered mouth; he did not get up. "Have it your own way." Mike began stomping on the man's back, neck, and head.

A. He was not angry. On the contrary. He was dissociated from his feelings. It was like he was in someone else's body, watching someone else do these things. Like watching a movie.

Abruptly he stopped. The room had half emptied out, and those who remained stood staring at him, aghast. He spat on the man's crushed skull and returned to his table.

He picked up his fork, put a piece of broccoli in his mouth, then made a face. He threw down his fork; everyone in the room jumped. "Well?" he shouted. Aside from some stifled whimpering and the dripping of spilled wine, the restaurant was silent.

He sighed and slumped in his chair. "Where's Roz?" he asked.

*

Eight months later, Joseph Massick, counsel for the defense, took his hands out of his trouser pockets and folded them behind his back.

Q. Doctor, I would like to thank you for your time and for your testimony. This has been a difficult, a most thorny case, and I would like to thank you for lending us your expert assistance in disentangling the truth from the many falsehoods that surround this matter. And now, I would like to ask you one final question if I may, and that is this. Doctor, did you, as a result of reading about this case, reviewing the reports of eyewitnesses and police officials, and most importantly interviewing the defendant for many hours on several occasions over the course of the last two months, did you arrive at a conclusion as to whether Mr. Burger was, at the time of this lamentable incident, able to appreciate the criminality of his conduct, or to conform his conduct to the requirements of the law?

Daniel Strickland leaned into the microphone.

A. Yes, I did.

Q. And what was the conclusion you arrived at, Doctor?

Strickland glanced at his notebook, but only for a moment.

A. I concluded that the defendant at the time of the crime was suffering from a psychological disorder which made him unable to conform his conduct to the requirements of the law.

He paused, as if waiting to be asked more. But Massick, who had been moving his lips almost imperceptibly as the psychologist gave this answer, sat down.

Q. Thank you, Doctor.

THE COURT: Doctor, would this be a good time for a recess?

Strickland looked at Mike Burger, who was looking out the window.

A. Thank you, Your Honor, but I'm all right to continue. I don't mind.

THE COURT: All right. Ms. Lattimann, you may begin your cross-examination.

Q. Good afternoon, sir.

A. Good afternoon, Ms. Lattimann.

Q. Can you tell us again, Professor—I'm sorry, I can't help but think of you, in looking at you and listening to you, as a professor. Do you have any objection to me calling you Professor?

A. It's very unusual. Not even my students call me Professor. But I will try to get used to it.

Q. All right, sir. Thank you, sir. It's your image you present and your background that makes me—I mean it very respectfully.

A. Thank you.

Q. Can you tell us, Professor, when you first met with the defendant.

A. Certainly. It was January first.

Daniel Strickland sat watching television in a dark, cavernous room with a woman who wore too much make-up.

"Three," she said, counting down with the crowd on the television. "Two. One!" She clicked a photo of the screen, then one of Strickland. "Happy New Year!"

"Happy New Year to you, Beryl."

Later, she wept.

"Nineteen fifty-nine," she said. "Shirley MacLaine, Deborah Kerr, Robert Stack. George Scott. *Anatomy of a Murder*—now that was when they made movies. Oh God. Everything turns to shit."

Strickland frowned and nodded.

Beryl gave him a fierce look. "Well? Aren't you going to say I'm catastrophizing?"

Later, she slept.

*

Someone who did not know the words was singing Auld Lang Syne. Someone was watering down the whiskey. Someone was patiently picking infinitesimal grains of cocaine out of the carpet. Someone was on their hands and knees, making kissing noises at the cat, which cowered beneath an end table.

"Five billion dollars for how many, fifty people? That's—ten million dollars a person! I don't care if they *are* Americans."

"Here puss. Here puss puss."

"Just another histrionic personality disorder in other words."

"It's a hundred million and you teach statistics."

"Here puss, got some nice ... what are these?" She tasted one and made a face. "Macadamias?"

"Guatemalans. They're good in salads."

"Say what you will about histrionic but at least they'll never bomb us. Rest of the world, U.S.A. *is* Hollywood and not even the Iranians would let their crazy government bomb bloody I don't know, Paul Newman."

"My dear drunken dear, Guatemalans are people."

Strickland came in holding a large bottle of champagne by the neck, like a club. He leaned over a woman who was sprawled with dignity across an armchair.

"Happy New Year, dollface." He tried to kiss her but she sat up.

Martie said, "Honey please don't interrupt. Nigel was saying something very interesting about the economic crisis."

"The solution is simple. Let them keep the hostages; we'll keep the money heh heh."

"I think that's wonderfully appalling," said someone.

"What's wrong with your cat!"

Electronic sockets projected from the creature's bare skull.

"Evan brought him home from the lab. I forget why."

"Because he's used up," said Evan. "Be careful, he's blind, too."

Someone clapped Strickland on the back and screamed, "Dan's here! We can finally pick."

The men lined up and drew keychains from a hollow African idol. After each turn the hostess put the statuette's head back on and shook it like a cocktail mixer.

Strickland pulled out a turquoise rabbit's foot to which a flashlight, flip-top lighter, garage door opener, and some keys were attached.

"Lucky Jim," said a plump woman, taking him roughly by the arm. "Goodnight, my husband," she called, waggling her fingers. "I'm leaving with this other, strong, manly good-looking man who is not you." Failing to get a reaction, she led Strickland away. He resisted, trying to catch his wife's eye.

Someone drew the hostess's keys and she put down the idol with a squeal.

"Who's left?" shouted Nigel, pushing his glasses up his nose.

"Just me I guess," said Martie.

"Then I guess it's you and me tonight heh heh."

"Looks like it."

Strickland was yanked brutally from the room.

Strickland drove, but she was the one who kept her eyes on the road while he cast little inquisitive glances her way. Nothing was said for a long time.

"He used to be different," she said at last. "People always say, After that operation she was a changed woman, he was a changed man." She laughed. "I always thought that meant changed for the better."

"And he's ..."

"Oh he was always a bit of a swinger, I didn't mind, both of us were I guess. He just never used to take it so seriously. All this theory crap. Erotogenic zones, modern civilization, polymorphous sexuality and the decline of genital supremacy. It's a bit of a drag."

"… I know how you feel."

"But then I'm not a psychologist. I was probably the only one."

"Some of us are psychiatrists," Strickland joked. "Not me," he hastened to add.

"No? What're you?"

"A psychologist. I'm Dan."

"I know who you are. It was you we were all waiting for."

"My reputation precedes me."

"Trace," she said. They shook hands lightly, ironically. "I'm Ted's wife."

"Ah yes," said Strickland. "I don't know Ted very well. He's an experimental man, isn't he?"

"You mind if I smoke?"

"It's your car. I don't mind."

"Did you see what they did to that cat?"

"Lookie what we have here," she said.

Strickland crouched beside his five-year-old son. "Sergeant Bonzo," he said, "what are you still doing awake?"

"Melanie was mean to me. Who's that?"

"I'm sorry to hear that. Did you walk away, or were you mean back?"

"Walk."

"Good man. This is a friend of mine. Her name is Trace."

Trace leered at the boy over his father's shoulder. The boy ducked his head, exaggerating a pout to hide a grin.

"Let's go find your sister," said Strickland. "Sorry about this."

Trace whispered, "Is there someplace I could go for a little pee-pee?"

"End of the hall. And the, ah ..."

"I'll find it!"

When she was gone, he asked the boy, "Do you know if Melanie paid the sitter?"

"I did it."

"Good man," said Strickland. "Uh, how much did you give her?"

Melanie sat in front of the television, which showed one man bludgeoning another to death. Strickland gestured his son out of the room. The boy marched off with dignity.

"Everything cool?"

Melanie swiped at her eyes with a hand but said nothing.

"Home a bit earlier than we expected. Lousy party?"

She shook her head. After a pause, she said, "And where's Martie?"

"Staying with a friend tonight."

She snorted.

"Want a drink?" he asked.

"No."

"Think I'll have one."

"Good for you."

She came into the kitchen while he was pouring. She did not acknowledge him, but sat down at the table briskly, as if meeting someone who was already late. Strickland took his drink to the window while she sat cracking her fingers.

"Catch the fireworks at all?"

She slumped forward and buried her face in her arms. He sat down beside her. He nodded, frowning. He reached out to touch her, then hesitated.

"Your mother ..."

She walked out of the room.

*

Strickland watched his son get into bed and pull the sheets up to
his chin.

"Light on or off?"

"Off. On! On."

"Definitely on?"

"Definitely."

"Goodnight, Bonzo."

"I'm sleepy."

"Good. Then you'll enjoy your sleep very much."

"Wait! Dad?"

"What is it?"

"How much does it cost to buy a whale?"

"A blue whale?"

"No, a big one."

"A big one. Probably somewhere between seventy-five and eighty
thousand dollars."

While the boy pondered this figure, Strickland turned off the
light and slipped away.

The woman, Trace, was sound asleep on top of his bed.

She wore nothing but a sheer negligee. He reached for a blanket,
then changed his mind.

Q. January first. And when did Mike Burger beat to death Antonio
DiRosa in The White Grape?

A. The date of the instant offense as I believe it is called was July
ninth.

Q. Nearly six months later.

A. I beg your pardon?

Q. It is true that you only finally interviewed Mike Burger for the
first time nearly six months after the killing?

A. I will take your word for it on the math. It was several months later, yes. Undoubtedly. As I understand it this sort of delay is not ...

Q. Do people not sometimes change substantially in six months? Or even one month? Professor?

He turned off the television and lay down on the couch.

A. They can. Certainly. Sometimes.

The next afternoon, Mike Burger pulled his car into Strickland's driveway. He scowled up at the house for a moment, whistling a tune, before going to the front door. He had a loose, springy gait, one that seemed to bring into play every muscle in his body.

Strickland's son looked up from the card game he was playing on the floor beside the couch where his father lay.

The barrage of knocks brought Strickland to his feet, kicking cards across the floor as he stumbled around in search of his glasses. "Where is everyone?"

Mike was peering in through a window when at last the door opened.

"You Strickland?" he said, bounding back up the steps.

Strickland took an involuntary step backward. "Yes."

"You the shrink?"

"Psychologist. Clinical—yes, I'm Daniel Strickland."

"This your house?"

"Yes. It is. My house."

Mike grimaced and fingered his upper teeth as if adjusting a denture. "Guess I was expecting some kind of office or something with waiting rooms and magazines and shit."

"Ah," said Strickland. "Of course. You're Mr. Burger."

"Lawyer sent me."

Strickland offered his hand and Mike shook it.

"I keep an interview room in the house," Strickland explained. "I have an office at the university but I don't often use that for my clinical appointments. I prefer to see people on their own turf—or let them see me on mine. Ah yes. This is my son," he said, sounding slightly perplexed. "Ben, this is Mr. Burger."

"Mike," said Mike. "None of that mister shit for me."

"Are you my mom's friend?"

"Don't think so." Mike considered. "Don't know. Who's your ma?"

"No no," said Strickland, "this—Mr.—Mike is my friend, Ben. He's one of *my friends*."

"My mom is staying with a friend, I thought maybe you were him."

"She ain't at my house, swear to God, Your Honor." Mike had begun investigating the room, picking up pictures from the mantel and replacing them indifferently. "This her?"

Strickland said, "Is Melanie around somewhere?"

The boy shrugged, watching the visitor.

"Benjamin."

The boy detected the undertone of urgency in his father's voice, but so did Mike. They both looked at him.

Strickland hesitated only a moment. "Will you kindly keep Mike here company for a few minutes while I get dressed?"

The boy looked at Mike and shrugged. Mike shrugged back.

"I guess I could teach you about aquatic mammals."

"Sure, and that's great actually, 'cause actually I don't know shit about aquatic mammals."

When Strickland had left the room, Mike said, "He looks dressed to me."

Strickland took a quick shower, shaved quickly, and quickly got dressed. While buttoning his shirt he suddenly stopped and looked around the room. He went to the window. Only Mike's car was in the driveway.

There was a note on the night table.

THANKS FOR A <u>WONDERFUL</u> NIGHT
I WILL NOT SOON FORGET
P.S. DOWN WITH GENITAL SUPREMACY ANYWAY
XXX OOO TRACE (TED'S WIFE)

Ben had opened a book on Mike's knees and was standing beside him, turning the pages fussily.

"Some of them aren't even mammals."

"What about that one?"

The boy shook his head. "That's an orca. Sometimes people call it killer whale but they're not supposed to."

"Well, they breathe air, don't they?"

The boy scowled, uncertain, and his mother decided to save him.

"They call them killers because they like to eat meat. They're excellent hunters."

The book fell to the floor as Mike stood. "Shit. Here. Thanks, kid, for the lesson." He added, "I liked the expensive whales best."

"Oh good," said Strickland. "You're here."

"You must be the Missus," said Mike.

"You just missed a very sweet moment," Martie told her husband.

"Yes, well. Mike and I will be in the interview room for a little while. You know what that means, Ben."

"You're not home."

"Good man. Mike?"

Mike shrugged and followed him from the room. Martie stared at her son for a moment, then went the opposite direction. The boy looked at his book and card game.

"All right if I smoke in here?"

"I don't mind."

"I'm smoking all I can while I'm still in the world. To be honest I don't even like the shit that much."

Strickland had settled himself into one of two comfortable armchairs that faced each other at a slight angle. He had in his lap a few books and a notepad. Now he picked up a pen and asked, "Still in the world? You can sit down."

"If it's all the same to you I'd rather just …" Mike paced demonstratively before the window. "I've never been much good at sitting."

"What did you mean by while you're still in the world?"

"Not in hoosegow. Not in the clink. Not in fucking jail, man."

"I understand." Strickland wrote a string of random numbers at the top of a page. "I thought today we could start out with a few simple cognitive tasks."

"Like tests? Like mental sanity tests?"

"More like memory tests."

"Well shit. It's what I'm here for. Fire at William."

Strickland said, "Seven. Five, three, two, eight, seven …"

"This somebody's phone—"

Strickland held up a hand and finished, "Five, nine, zero, four. Now, how many of those can you remember?"

"Seven, five. The last one was four. I wasn't paying attention."

"That's fine. Let's try another." He wrote and circled a 2, then started a new row of numerals, reading them aloud as he went.

"Four, two, eight, seven, nine, six, six, one, two, five. Now give them back to me."

"Shit, man. Four two eight, uh seven, six maybe. That's all I know. And two sixes and a five at the end there."

Strickland wrote and circled a 4. "This time let's try it backwards. Ready?"

Mike sat down.

Strickland showed Mike a cartoon from one of the textbooks. In the foreground a disgruntled-looking man wore only one shoe, and in the background a car sped away, leaving behind a cloud of dust or exhaust.

"What happened in this picture?"

"Man, what *didn't* happen."

"Guess."

"Could be anything."

"Then just make up a story."

"Shit, I don't know. Could be this guy just got his ass kicked out of this fucking car for some reason."

"… Why? Who's in the car?"

"Probably his wife," Mike laughed. "She caught his dumb ass in bed with some skanky bitch and dumped him on the side of the road somewheres. Middle of fucking nowhere somewheres. Didn't even have time to put on both shoes, sorry-ass motherfucker." Mike looked at Strickland. "Something like that, could be."

"That's fine."

"Yeah?"

"If I said to you, a table and a chair, what are they, what do they have in common, I think the answer would be furniture. Agreed?"

"Yeah, okay."

"What about a pair of pants and a shirt?"

"Clothes."

"How about a bicycle and an airplane?"

"Shit you get around in. I mean vehicles. Or not vehicles, but like—transportation. Right?"

"That's fine. How about a fly and a tree?"

"A fly and a tree? Things that got leaves—no. I don't know. I don't know that one."

"That's fine. If I say don't cry over spilled milk, what does that mean?" On the notepad, he wrote *fly + tree = leaves?*

"It means the past's in the past and there's no use getting all het up over it."

"How about: People in glass houses shouldn't throw stones."

"It's when people who are involved in bad shit, they shouldn't go round accusing others of—whatever. It's like—hypocritical, right?"

"That's fine," said Strickland, writing *vocabulary!?* "How about: If wishes were wings, pigs would fly."

"No. Never heard that before."

"That's why I gave it to you."

"Ha!" Mike gave a sly grin. "Okay, well, I guess it's like if—a person can get what he wants if he wants it bad enough."

"Not bad," said Strickland, capping the pen and putting the notepad aside.

"That okay? I got it right?"

"It doesn't have one single interpretation. Very few people get that one. But your answer is not bad, not bad at all."

Mike settled back in his chair with a slight smile and looked around for his cigarette.

Strickland walked Mike to his car.

"What about a fly and a tree?," Mike asked.

"Life."

"Life? Motherfucker."

"See it now?"

"Yeah, I see it."

"All right."

"Just ... weird comparison, right?"

"How so?"

"Well, not weird. But I mean they're pretty fucking vastly different."

"Well yes, but so are a bicycle and a plane. Vastly different."

Mike shook his head. "That's for sure."

They reached the car. Mike stood looking down the street.

"So that means I'm okay in the head?"

Strickland pursed his lips. "That's not a very clinical way of putting it. But yes. I think you're probably okay in the head."

"That's what you'll tell them, then?"

"Who?"

"Whoever. The jury. The lawyers. Whoever."

"When's your trial?"

"Fuck knows. February something if they don't change it again."

"Then let's not put the cart ahead of the horse. You know that one?"

Mike grinned and fingered his upper teeth. "Yeah, I know that one."

"Let's meet again in four days." Strickland glanced up at his house. "On your turf, this time."

"My turf?"

"Your place. We still have a lot to talk about."

Q. You are not a forensic psychologist, are you, Professor.

A. No. I admitted as much under Mr. Massick's examination.

Q. In fact this is your first time, as an expert witness.

A. That's correct. I believe I said as much.

Q. Well, you're doing just fine, Professor. You're a natural. Let me be the first to say.

A. Thank you, Ms. Lattimann.

Melanie said, "And this is the guy you leave Ben alone with?"

"Melanie," said Martie.

"What."

"You know what. Don't interrupt."

"I gave him the abbreviated cognitive battery," Strickland resumed. "Everything was within parameters—pretty normal," he added for Melanie's benefit. "His digit span—that's his memory—was maybe a bit low for his IQ. Careful, this is hot."

"I don't like yams," said Ben.

"Could indicate intrusion of emotional factors," Martie said.

"I thought of that. But the strange thing is, he didn't strike me as overcontrolled. That is, he had no problem expressing his feelings. For the most part he was polite and obliging, eager to make a good impression of course, but he also sighed and grumbled at times, openly expressed his resentment about the court system, showed some bitterness on the TAT …"

"Why is that a problem?," Melanie asked. "That he has feelings."

"Normally, a case like this, where a guy blows up, goes berserk, with little or no provocation—well, you expect to see a history of bottling things up."

"So he just killed this guy for no reason? Great! So he's crazy."

Martie said, "We don't use that word, dear. And it's a little more complicated than that."

"According to his statement to the police," Strickland said, "the other guy's group got seated first."

"So your client," said Martie, "expressed his resentment."

Melanie guffawed. "By beating the guy to death!"

"I don't like yams," said Ben.

"These aren't yams," said Melanie, "they're sweet potatoes. You like sweet potatoes. Ow! Fuck!"

"We told you it was hot," said Martie.

Ben perked up. "That kind of language …"

"Yes, Ben," said Strickland. "It's all right at home."

"But not at school!"

"Yes, Ben," said Melanie, "we know, Ben."

"Run it under cold water, Mel?," Strickland suggested.

"Forget it. It doesn't hurt."

"Could be an undercontrolled hostility pattern," Martie mused, gazing through her daughter.

"I thought of that too. The problem is the delay. First there's some sort of argument, apparently, in the foyer, while they're waiting for a table. But it's broken up, his friends break it up, everybody seems to calm down, nobody needs to be kicked out. Then twenty minutes later he gets up from his dinner and … attacks the guy."

"Beats him to a bloody pulp, you mean."

"Melanie."

"What."

"You know what."

"Anyway," said Strickland, "if he had *no* impulse control, he should have flown off the handle right away, there in the foyer."

"What about his attachment pattern?"

"What's a tachment pattern?," Ben asked.

"Don't interrupt," Melanie told him.

"Melanie."

"Now what!"

"You know what. We agreed you're not to mother him."

"All I did was tell him not to interrupt."

"I think it's for the individuals talking to decide whether or not an interruption has taken place."

"Well, I·was talking too, wasn't I? Or don't I count?"

Martie put down her fork. "Daniel," she said, "may I bring you in as mediator at this point?"

"That's fine. Let's all just take a little breather."

Melanie said, "Forget it."

"Ben," said Martie, "an attachment pattern is the way you relate to people as a grown up, because of the way you were related to when you were a child, especially by your mother. Now, you need some orange on your plate to go with the green and brown."

Melanie made a choking noise. "I wonder what kind of attachment pattern *I* have."

Martie put down her fork. "Melanie, if you are looking for a reaction, you won't get one here. You had a perfectly healthy and loving upbringing, as you well know, and if you are finding it difficult to relate to people with respect and on a footing of equality then the reason must lie somewhere in the five years you lived under your father's roof."

"It was only a joke!"

"Fuck fuck fuck," said Ben.

"Daniel," said Martie, "did I raise my voice just then?"

"Well, I don't know …"

"Never mind. I think I know when it is time to calm down and consider alternatives. In fact, I will excuse myself, I have a late appointment with a client, thank you for a lovely meal. And look into this man's attachment pattern is my advice to you. Goodnight, Ben. Goodnight, Melanie."

After a long silence, Ben asked, "Where is Mom going?"

"You heard her," said Melanie.

"You don't know what he heard," said Strickland, then told his son, "She has a late appointment with a client." After a pause, he added, "She has to go to work."

"If you believe that," Melanie muttered.

"Will you two wash up?," Strickland asked. "At least run them under the tap. Then it's easier later."

Q. What exactly is your specialty, Professor? You do have a specialty?

A. I am a clinical psychologist.

Q. So you run a clinic?

A. I use the word 'clinical' to distinguish it broadly from so-called experimental psychology, which is the sort generally done in a university setting, usually on undergraduate students, and usually with some form of pencil-and-paper multiple-choice questionnaire, to determine for instance whether men or women have better will-power and burning questions like that.

MR. MASSICK: Now Your Honor, I think I must object. Ms. Lattimann has already agreed to accept Doctor Strickland's credentials as an expert witness.

MS. LATTIMANN: These questions, Your Honor, are not about the doctor's credentials but his method. I am trying to get a clearer picture of what his general method is when assessing someone.

THE COURT: Which I do not doubt you will use to shed light on the particular method of this particular case, Ms. Lattimann. Objection overruled.

Q. Now, I don't think you answered my question, Professor.

A. I'm sorry, I've quite forgotten your question.

THE COURT: I think the doctor can be forgiven for that. Let the record reflect that there was laughter in the courtroom, Miss Reporter. Not a lot, but some. And would you kindly read out Ms. Lattimann's last question.

REPORTER: You run a clinic.

A. Thank you. No, I do not run a clinic per se. I see patients in various settings, and these meetings are all clinical in the sense that I provide a form of cognitive and behavioral therapy, or counseling, but I do not have a clinic, no. To answer your question.

Q. People who are insane or who have mental disorders come to you and you cure them.

A. Ah. That is a mouthful. I would perhaps object to the term "insane" and to the concept of "cure." But otherwise, in general, you could say that yes, people with mental disorders or psychological disturbances come to me for help and I try to help them.

Q. You help people.

A. I do my best.

A frail, perspiring young man with thinning hair sat slouched over a tidy kitchen table and said rapidly, "I even explained it to her, I said very clearly—I know I can have a tendency to mumble but I said it quite clearly—I said Hi, my name's Robin but most people call me Coby, she said All right I'll call you Coby, I said Actually I prefer Robin, she said Okay I'll call you Robin, but now already she's calling me Coby like everyone else."

Strickland frowned and nodded.

"That doesn't matter I realize, but it gets under my skin. I try not to let it get under my skin but I can't help thinking about what I could have said differently. It's the same as at the grocery store last week. I have to park out at the edge of the parking lot—I told you about this—where there aren't any cars around or I feel hemmed in, but then on the news the other day I heard there was this warning to women about some guy who was going around supposedly selling perfume and when you smell it it's actually chloroform, I couldn't get it out of my head even though it was broad daylight and I'm not a woman." He gave Strickland a quick defiant look. "Actually to tell you the truth I think I get all worked up because I'm actually afraid women will think *I'm* the guy, one of these guys going around trying to abduct them with a bottle of fake perfume. But what can I do? I need groceries," he finished miserably.

After a long pause, Strickland said, "I think that's probably an urban myth. Chloroform, to the best of my knowledge, does not operate so quickly."

"That doesn't matter. That's not the point. It sounds true."

Q. As a doctor of psychology—I'm sorry, as a clinical psychologist, you do your best to help people.

A. That is correct.

Q. And is that what you've done in this case?

A. I beg your pardon?

Q. Shall I have the reporter read back the question?

A. I heard the question correctly, but I do not understand the question.

Q. What you have said to Mr. Massick's questions, what you have told the jury and the honorable judge and everyone else in this courtroom—it will help Mr. Burger, won't it?

Massick stood up.

A. I don't know what will help Mr. Burger, Ms. Lattimann. I am a doctor, not a lawyer.

Massick sat down.

Strickland sat at his desk, thinking.

Mike, as a child, holding his mother's hand, waiting with his mother and her friends for a table in a posh restaurant.

The maitre-d' saying, I'm sorry, but we have a table for only eight at the moment.

His mother dropping Mike's hand and laughing, That's okay, we'll take it, the boy can wait, I'm starving!

Mike, as a child, being left behind.

"Ridiculous," Strickland muttered, rubbing his neck.

A crash came from the living room.

Martie told her daughter, "Well, that wasn't a very intelligent thing to do."

Melanie stomped out of the room.

"What was that about?," Strickland asked. Glass shards were scattered across the floor.

"That girl has a serious punishment complex. She needs to be told that she's doing everything wrong. You know, her father was always correcting her posture …"

"But what's it all about?"

"Oh, evidently I was insufficiently appalled to learn that my daughter is a bisexual. Or thinks she is. Or wants to think she is. Or wants me to think she is."

Strickland tapped on Melanie's door, then opened it. The room was empty.

He tapped on the closet door, then opened it.

She was standing there, almost hidden by clothes.

"Hey," he said.

She groaned.

"Look," he said. "Your mother …"

"Aw, *fuck* my mother!" she said, and slammed the door in his face.

Strickland wandered the halls of the courthouse.

"Excuse me," he asked a sharply dressed woman pulling a trolley stacked with boxes of files, "is there a list somewhere of the cases, the court cases, currently in session?"

They stood before a list posted to the wall.

"What are you in the mood for?"

In a small courtroom with mahogany paneling, a police officer in uniform sat in the witness box, his face pressed against the microphone, and read tonelessly from a report he held in his lap.

"At which juncture Officer Daniels and myself—it says Officer Miller here, but that is myself—Officer Daniels and Officer Miller proceeded to question the suspect, period. New paragraph. The questioning began at seventeen fifty-four—that is written as one seven, uh colon, five four—and continued until one eight four five, that is one eight colon four five, open parenthesis five one minutes, close parenthesis period. The suspect gave the officers—and here is a typo, it says notal, N O T A L, but it should say—well, I'll just read what it says. The suspect gave the officers notal cooperation in answering the questions put to him by officers Daniels and Miller, comma ..."

Strickland stood and, with little gestures of apology and gratitude, shuffled out past the other spectators.

The corridors were suddenly bustling. He heard his name called. But there was no one here he knew.

Someone shouted "Dan!" again, right in his ear, and grabbed his arm.

"You!" he said.

Trace smirked at him. "'You,'" she mimicked, then sighed. "You, he said. He remembered where she worked, but not her name."

"Actually," he grinned guilelessly, "it's exactly the opposite."

*

"I never told you I was a court reporter?" She bit her lower lip. "Then it's just a coincidence."

She sat on folded legs, leaning over the table. With the base of her cup she made little overlapping circles of coffee on the tabletop.

Strickland sat stiffly upright, one leg draped neatly over the other, knee atop knee. "Is that so bad?" he said.

As if changing the subject, she said, "I thought you were going to call me. After all …"

"But I don't have your number," he protested.

"I left you that note."

"But no number!"

"You were supposed to track me down. That was supposed to be the whole fun of it. Really, with your big brain …!"

"I'm actually not very smart sometimes."

She withdrew a pen from her purse and scribbled on a napkin. "There," she said, sliding it across the table like a poker bet. "Now you don't have to be smart anymore."

"Come on," she said.

"Should we be in here?" he asked, entering the courtroom cautiously.

"It's a public building. Anyway, I work here. Right here, as a matter of fact."

She showed him the equipment she used.

"And you can get down everything everybody says?" he asked.

"We use a kind of shorthand. And you always got to compare it with the tapes before filing anything officially. But yeah, mostly everything."

"Show me."

Her fingers hovered above the typewriter. "Say something."

"Uh … The world is too much with us. Uh, late and soon, getting and spending, we uh, lay waste our powers. Little we see in … nature that is ours."

She rolled her eyes. "Say something *quick*."

With an effort, Strickland babbled, "Once upon a time there was a boy who got his foot stuck in a radiator and some cats then came along and jousted one another with the footballs in the heart-attack revelation of the final days of September and all the mothers were whimsical so whimsical in their summer dresses. How's that?"

Trace read it back to him. He clapped his hands and she curtsied.

There was a moment of silence. They looked away.

"You know, it's funny," he said.

"What?"

"It's only now that I feel like … Although technically …"

"Yeah?"

"Never mind."

"Well, hell's bells. I gotta go." At the door she turned back and said, "When you call …"

"Yes?"

"*If* you call … let it ring once, hang up, then call again. That way I'll know it's you."

"All right. When I call."

He sat in the witness box. Furrowing his brow, he leaned forward and said, "That is correct." The loudness of his voice in the empty room startled him. He smirked, allowed the smile to grow cold, then said sarcastically, "Yes, I suppose you *could* say that."

In the cafeteria, Strickland said, "And potatoes and the steamed vegetables."

"It's only zucchini today, that all right?"

"That's fine. I don't mind."

Strickland stood at the front of a small classroom, listening to a debate among his students.

"Yes, but self-reflectiveness can be conceptualized as a self-organized subject-object relation where both the subject and the object of attention are the self."

"We all know what introspection is, there's no need to define it."

"What I would like defined is this suicidal ideation. Why not just say thoughts of suicide?"

"So … he killed his family because he was depressed and wanted to die?"

They looked at Strickland, who said, "It's not a true story. You tell me."

After a pause, a girl in a black turtleneck said, "Quite probably his ego boundary had expanded to include his family, so naturally suicide would include them as well."

Strickland raised his eyebrows and pursed his lips.

She said, "He just never got around to himself."

Strickland sat in his office, watching a video. On the screen, Orson Welles said, "Well thank you, Doctor. Now uh, can you tell us how far this tendency to what you call schizophrenia had progressed with Artie Strauss?"

The distinguished, goateed man on the witness stand crossed his legs and said forcefully, "Not with any degree of exactitude. We do know that the habit of lying, indulging in fantasies, and telling stories which the boy developed in infancy had progressed to the stage where he himself was having difficulty distinguishing between what was true and what was not true …"

The girl in the turtleneck appeared in the doorway.

"Oh, hi!" Strickland jumped up and fumbled for the remote control just as the phone rang. They both laughed. "Sorry, Marianne, I'll just—hello?"

"Come now," cried the television, "you are an expert and under oath, is your diagnosis insanity or not!"

He gestured for her to wait but she shook her head, mouthed an apology or a promise, and was gone.

"Under oath I cannot answer that, sir. Insanity is a legal term, not a medical one. I am a doctor, not a lawyer."

"Yes, sorry, hello?"

"Daniel Strickland?"

He trotted up the wide steps of the school. "I must have gotten my days mixed up. Howdy, Sarge."

"Hi."

The boy's teacher, a young woman in a yellow floral-print dress, wrung her hands in satisfaction at this successful reunion. "He was no trouble, Mr. Strickland."

"What'd you learn today, Benderson?"

"Buts."

"I often stay a bit late on Tuesdays over my correcting."

"Butts?"

"Conjunctions," she explained. "Ands and buts and what else?"

"Ors," said Ben.

"Very good. One little matter," she said, dropping her voice. "Since you're here."

Ben went on ahead to the car, alternately clomping and scuffing his feet like a zombie.

The teacher wrung her hands. She had a smattering of freckles across one clavicle.

"Ben," she said, "likes to eat … dirt."

"Yes. We know."

"Oh!"

"It's called pica."

"I thought that was only pregnant women."

"Apparently not." After a moment he elaborated: "We think perhaps it came about as a result of little tidbits left in some of the houseplants by his half-sister. She believes in composting."

"Tidbits?"

"Teabags and carrot tops and egg shells and things."

She looked with dismay at the boy buckling himself into the back seat of the car.

"Egg shells too?"

"My wife assures me it's a phase."

"Yes, but is it … healthy?"

"Oh," Strickland sighed, "a lot of them at that age toy with the idea of saving the world. Especially the ones from so-called broken homes. Form of compensation, presumably … But she'll grow out of it. We all do."

"Melanie? Martie?"

Ben said, "Nobody home."

Strickland said into the phone, "Is Stephanie there? Daniel Strickland. Yes, Ben's … No, it'd be for now. Yes. No. Thanks anyway."

He looked at his son.

He stopped the car but did not get out.

"It won't be more than a couple of hours," he said.

"Okay," the boy said.

"Just be … nice to her, all right?"

"I'm nice to everyone."

"All right. Good man. And stay away from the pool."

Beryl cooed, "What a lovely surprise. Come in, young man, come in."

Strickland said, "It won't be more than a couple of hours."

"That's fine, of course it is, we'll be just fine won't we young man."

"Well, see you later, Sergeant."

"Okay," the boy said. "Thanks."

When Strickland was gone, Ben said, "This is a big house."

"It was my husband's. He was a faaamous movie director. Do you like movies?"

"I like documentaries."

"Good! I'll show you some photographs."

"Do you have a …" He gazed out the tall windows, then pulled himself away. "Anything to eat?"

Strickland walked along the narrow sidewalk, looking at addresses.

He noticed a young man proceeding methodically from car to car, trying the door handles. Strickland opened his mouth, closed it, then stepped out into the street.

"Excuse me," he called. "Can I help you?"

The man looked over, his face blank.

"Are you … Are any of these cars yours?"

"… Yeah."

"Well … which one?"

"I don't know, man."

Strickland came closer so he would not have to shout. "I'm afraid I don't understand. You don't know which is yours?"

"I forget where I parked," the man said.

"But ... This will sound stupid of me, but ... that doesn't make any sense."

"I locked my keys inside."

"But ... is one of these cars yours or not?"

The man cast a thoughtful glance over his shoulder. "I might've parked on a different street, I guess."

"Wait a second."

"I'll keep looking. Peace, man."

He disappeared around a corner, and Strickland stood there, frowning at the parked cars.

As he came up the walkway, a child ran out the front door and across the street, calling out in a loud whisper to a group of others, "He's coming!"

The building was even more rundown inside. The corridors were dim, the walls peeling. The sound of an argument filtered down the stairwell.

Mike's wife, Roz, threw open the door, holding it for a moment at arm's length as if ready to slam it shut again. "Oh good," she said.

Strickland hesitated. "I'm ..."

Mike's bellow came from inside the apartment: "It him?"

"Well, come on in. He's in the den."

Mike came bounding across the cluttered room to shake his hand. "Well," he said. "Sure enough."

"Hello again, Mike."

Mike kicked a toy truck across the room. "Fucking kids' fucking shit," he apologized.

They sat down.

"So here you are. My turf." He whistled some. "Doing all the whistling I can while I'm still in the world," he explained. "Don't let you whistle in the clink."

"That seems harsh."

"Naw," said Mike. "It ain't respectful. Some of those guys there for life. Man, get the fuck out of here!"

Strickland turned his head. One of the children he had seen in the street ducked out of sight.

"Man, I told them motherfuckers two hours. What's it been, five fucking minutes?"

Roz said, "Your pop is gonna whoop your asses something good." To Strickland she said, "We don't uh, have no uh, any coffee. Mike can't drink it, on account of his kidney."

"Kidney, shit. I got stomach problems."

"You want some tea instead?"

"That's just fine. I don't mind."

"That bitch thinks she knows everything because her sister is a big-shot fucking nurse, but she don't know shit."

"You had these stomach problems long?," Strickland asked.

"*That* is *it!*" Mike leapt to his feet, stomping noisily in place. From the hallway came screams and the clatter of fleeing footsteps. Mike sat back down. "Fucking monsters got minds of their own."

"You may as well tell them to come in," suggested Strickland.

Mike said, "Huh?"

Strickland sat with Mike, Roz, and five of their children in the den. A sixth appeared in the doorway.

Roz said, "Well, come on over, dopey."

Without taking her eyes off Strickland, the little girl crouched at her father's feet and pressed her face against his leg.

"Clamantha," Roz told Strickland.

"Well, that's all of them," said Mike. "The whole goddamn brood."

The children fidgeted. Their parents stared at the floor.

Strickland sipped his tea. "What would you all be doing right now if I wasn't here?"

"What *wouldn't* we be doing," Mike muttered.

"Getting our ass whooped," said Joan, the oldest girl.

"Got that right," Roz said.

"Playing basketball," said Clarence, the oldest boy.

Strickland put down his cup. "Oh?"

The children ran around the blacktop. Clarence got ahold of the ball, bounced it off Clamantha's head, and executed a perfect layup.

Mike shouted, "Now you know better than that! You gotta get behind the line before you throw again."

The girl looked over at her mother, who stood with her arms crossed at the edge of the court. "Don't look at me," Roz said. "Get him back."

"That's travelling," Mike called. He was agitated, hopping in place. "And that's holding, Clem, goddamn it. Okay, give me the ball, give, me, the ball. There's no point in playing unless you're gonna play proper."

"I'm captain!"

"I'm captain," Mike corrected him. "Me … and Dan."

"Oh no," Strickland laughed.

The children stared at Strickland, then clamored: "I'm on Pop's team!"

"I pick first," Mike said, "and I got Clarence." The boy hooted and yanked the ball out of his father's hands.

Strickland looked at Roz, who shrugged and rolled her eyes.

He nodded at Clamantha. "Do you want to be on my team?"

The others laughed. "He picked *Clammie!*"

Mike picked the next biggest boy.

"You playing?," Strickland asked Roz.

"Everybody plays," said Mike.

"He picked *Ma!*"

Mike crouched in front of Joan and grimaced. "You feeling it?"

"I'm feeling it."

"You bringing it?"

"I'm bringing it."

"Then let's do it." They slapped palms and knuckles together solemnly, then let out a wild war cry. "That's my team," he told Strickland, "you can have the other two."

The two youngest children looked at each other, crestfallen.

"Team meeting," Strickland said. "Emergency team huddle. All right. Now. Listen up. As your uh, team captain, I have only one thing to say. I order you … to go out there … and have fun."

Roz said, "You heard the man. Now let's see some hands." She put hers out, and the children slapped theirs down onto it. Strickland laid his on top.

"C'mon, you lazy slop-buckets!," Mike screamed. "We're starting without you!"

They played basketball. Strickland and Roz and the kids tripped over one another and fell laughing to the ground. Mike's team danced around them, scoring point after point.

"We're the best!"

"The best at *sucking!*"

"The best at sucking at being *losers!*"

Strickland lifted Clamantha into the air, but before she could shoot, Mike, gibbering with glee, slapped the ball out of her hands. Soon the youngest children grew discouraged and drifted to the sidelines, and without opponents the older kids grew bored, till only Mike, radiant in triumph, and Strickland, ruddy with exhaustion, stood alone on the court with the sun going down behind the apartment blocks.

"Forty-one to one," Mike said. "Not bad."

"I wasn't keeping score."

"Losers never do."

"I'm parked down here," Strickland said.

Mike shook his hand. "Good game, man. You don't give up."

"Neither do you."

"I like to win."

"See you next week."

Strickland stood in the street, staring at a gap in the row of parked cars.

Mike opened the door. "Forget something?"

"This will sound funny."

Strickland stood on the sidewalk with his hands in his pockets while Mike paced back and forth in the street, muttering, "Motherfucker. This is my neighborhood, man."

A car honked at him. He slammed his fist down on the hood but stepped aside.

He joined Strickland on the sidewalk. "This burns my fucking ass, man."

Strickland smiled, but then his face went blank. "Oh no."

Beryl told Ben, "Just pretend that no one is watching you. That's all acting is: pretending you're all alone. Now try it again."

Ben put down the teddy bear and looked at it. "I wish they didn't kill you," he announced.

"Yes," Beryl cried, "but without words! We don't talk when we're alone, do we? Only crazy people talk to themselves."

The doorbell rang.

"Speak through your actions," she said on her way to the door. "Your body is your instrument."

Ben laid his head on the bear's breast.

In the car, Ben said, "And her husband is a famous movie director and if we had a VCR we could watch his movies when we got home like we did at her house."

In the driver's seat, Mike said, "Listen, I been thinking. Cops ain't gonna do shit. Bunch of goldbricking dogfuckers." He glanced at the rear-view mirror. "Pardon my Portuguese. What I'm saying is, give me a couple days to check it out."

"Check it out?"

"Make some calls. See what turns up. I know some people work in this shop. Sometimes these shitheads try to move hot cars through them. What is it, a '77?"

Strickland said, "I'm bad with cars."

Martie watched Ben get into bed.

"Brush your teeth?"

He showed her the inside of his mouth.

"Good man."

"Mom? The brown man is going to help Dad find the car."

"So I heard. And we don't say brown man."

"How come?"

"We say black."

"But he's not black."

"That's just the way it is." She sighed and sat on the edge of the bed. With some difficulty she explained, "It has to do with equality. Now, your skin isn't exactly white either, is it? But we say white people and black people because white and black are the most common, the most basic colors."

"So Penny is black too?"

"No, Penny is oriental. It's a little complicated at first, but you'll pick it up."

"Mom? What's a goldbricking dogfucker?"

After a pause, she said, "Well, it must be some kind of idiom. Tomorrow maybe we'll look it up."

"Mom? I want to be an actor."

"You can be anything you want, dear."

"I want to be an actor."

After a pause, she said, "Then that's what you should be."

Strickland was at his desk.

"I just had the funniest conversation with Benderson," Martie said.

Strickland sighed. "I didn't know what else to do," he said. "You weren't here, I didn't exactly want to take him along to the home of a— And Stephanie wasn't home, it was supposed to be your day to pick him up I thought, and I'm not leaving him with that Barbara girl anymore I've decided, she doesn't even talk to him, she just listens to that Walkman the whole time, it'll stunt his socio-intellectual development and I didn't think that was what we wanted."

Martie looked at him sadly.

"I'm sorry," he stated. "Did I raise my voice?"

"No. You never do."

"Maybe I need a time out." He rubbed his neck. "It's been a long day." After a minute, he chuckled. "Believe it or not, I played ..."

But when he looked up she was gone.

*

Q. Now, Professor, in your testimony to Mr. Massick you mentioned, I believe it was, let me get this right, intermittent explosive disorder. Is this correct?

A. That was my diagnostic impression, yes.

Q. When you say diagnostic impression, do you mean diagnosis?

A. Yes. That is what I mean, yes.

Q. Because when you say an impression, it sounds like, I don't know, something less than a diagnosis.

A. Thank you for bringing that to my attention. I should have said diagnosis.

Q. By what date precisely had you arrived at this diagnosis?

A. I don't think I could pinpoint the date with any degree of exactitude.

Q. Well, was it January first? Was it yesterday?

A. It took some time. These things take time. It is not the same as with medical diagnosis, where you can simply tally up the presenting symptoms and arrive at a conclusion.

Q. So symptoms and conclusions play no part in psychiatric diagnosis?

A. I don't believe I said that. Of course they do. But psychiatric— psychological symptomatology, etiology, these things lie beneath the surface, you must get at them, it is a gradual process and often there is resistance.

Q. You mean, your patients lie to you?

A. Not exactly. Not consciously. They—there are things they don't like to talk about.

Q. Such as the murders they committed?

Strickland said, "Huh?"

"I said," said the cabbie, "twenty-five eighty."

"Jesus."

*

Massick said, "Come in, Doctor. Have a seat if you like. You'll forgive me for standing, I've been in court all morning. Well. Now.
You'll forgive me for cutting straight to the chase scene: What can
you tell me about our mutual friend, Mr. Burger?"

"Well ..."

"Quite a guy, isn't he. Quite a character. Family man too, which
is always a bonus in my line of work. Beautiful wife. Bunch of rug
rats, I understand. In the army too. Good citizen. Likable guy. Full
of beans. Can't keep a man like that down, no, not for long. Says
what he means and means what he says. No damn good at all on the
witness stand. Though don't think I wasn't tempted. He'd win over
eleven of them and get stuck in the craw of one bitter old little old
lady. But that's the jury system for you: any twelve meatheads picked
out of a hat know the law better than one intelligent man who's
dedicated his life to it. Imagine if they tried that in any other line of
work. If you had to get twelve people off the street to fix your car,
or take out your appendix—or do what you do, Doctor! But what
can I do? Every man wants to go before a jury of his peers. Every
man wants to be found not guilty. In this case, not guilty by reason
of insanity is the best we can do. So be it. All right. So give it to me
straight. Mike Burger. In your professional opinion."

Strickland opened his briefcase. "Well, I've prepared a prelimi-
nary report, and I thought—"

"No no no, just give it to me in your own words."

Strickland looked at the thick sheaf of paper in his hand. "These
are my own words."

"Summarize it for me, doctor. I'll be reading reports and motions
and counter-motions and responses and counter-responses and affi-
davits till the Los Angeles River wets its bed and one thing I can
tell you is they're not worth the paper they're printed on. When
you're paid by the page, why say in ten words what you can say in a

hundred? No, I'll take it from a man's mouth every time, thank you, and when the courts start reading cases instead of hearing them, *well*, that's when I'll know it's time to shuffle off this jurisprudent coil and retire back home to Alabama. In the meantime here we are, mano a mano, so give it to me in your own words."

Strickland put the report down on the desk. "I haven't come to any firm conclusions, of course, but judging from what I have seen so far, I think the most likely diagnosis is going to be something in the nature of an impulse-control disorder."

Massick, who had been pacing, sat down abruptly.

"In other words," said Strickland, "for the most part he is absolutely adequately adjusted—lively, likable, all those things you said. But evidently he has … outbursts. Now, we all have those. But his are way outside the normal, the acceptable range. Which strongly suggests pathology."

Massick sat silent.

"That's it in a nutshell," Strickland said. "If you read through my report you'll no doubt be able to get a better idea of the legal, uh, ramifications …"

Massick stood again. "Tell me something, Doctor." He perched on the front edge of the wide desk and crossed his arms thoughtfully. "What you just said … It's all a lot of pigwash, isn't it?"

"Pardon?"

"A load of crap. Hooey. Horseshit. Nonsense, Doctor. Isn't that so?"

"I'm obviously sorry you feel that way, Mr. Massick, but I …"

"With all due respect, sir, you psychiatrists are all alike, aren't you? A bunch of goddamn charlatans?"

"I can't help but feel that perhaps I haven't expressed myself as clearly as I could have. And that if you had looked at my report, perhaps … But in any case, if you feel that way I don't suppose I can be of much use to you, or to Mr. Burger. I'm sorry to have wasted your time."

Massick leapt up and made placating gestures. "You'll have to forgive me, Doctor, but that's the quickest and surest way I've found of testing a witness's mettle."

Strickland stared.

Massick grinned down at him like a proud parent. "You're a cool customer. You'll do just fine on the cross."

"On the cross?"

"Cross-examination."

"You want to put me on the stand?" asked Strickland. He could not completely hide his pleasure.

"Now, you put an emotional man like myself or Mike Burger up there and start hammering at him and he'll either go to pieces, or he'll fight back. It makes good theater, and the jury may even love you for it—but they won't trust you anymore. The one thing an expert must be, is dispassionate."

Strickland pursed his lips modestly.

"Where to, my friend?"

Strickland looked in his wallet. "The police station."

The bored cop said, "Anything of value in the vehicle?"

Strickland looked puzzled and fatigued. "No. Nothing of value. Just the vehicle itself."

"Anything in the glove compartment?"

"I don't think so. No. Nothing valuable."

After jotting something down, the cop sat back in his chair, as if calling it a day. "And this man you saw in the street," he said finally. "Think you could identify him?"

"You mean … pick him out of a lineup?"

"Or recognize him from a photo."

Strickland sighed. "Are you familiar at all with the research of Elizabeth Loftus?"

The cop looked at him with serene blankness.

"There's a Russian proverb," said Strickland. "'He lies like an eyewitness.' Never mind. I don't trust myself. I wouldn't trust myself to get the right guy. I wasn't really paying attention."

Strickland entered a phone booth, dialed, let it ring once, and hung up.

Then he lifted the receiver again.

Trace pulled up to the curb in a station wagon, rolled down the window, and smirked.

Strickland scuffed his feet forlornly.

She laughed. "Need a ride, stranger?"

"I'm glad they stole your car," she said. "I bet I never would have heard from you otherwise. I should have thought of it myself."

"Did you steal my car?"

"I'll never tell."

Strickland fumbled with his chopsticks. Trace, with a huff of exasperation that stirred her frizzy bangs, slid around the table to give him a lesson.

"Grasp the first one like a pencil." She took his hand and showed him. "Then the top one is your pincher doodad. Like this."

"I think my method is unimprovable," said Strickland. "It's the mushrooms that are to blame. They're slippery buggers."

"Then why don't I have any problems? See?" She popped a mushroom in his mouth.

*

"Best part of the meal," she said, cracking open her fortune cookie. "Whoa, whoa. You've got to eat the cookie first or the fortune won't come true."

He chewed slowly and made a face. "Worst part of the meal."

"Oh, I've got two! Twice as much future as you. 'The first week of next month will be a good time to complete unfinished tasks.' I hate the ones that are just advice. 'You are creative but can also be diligent when it is called for.'" She considered this. "It's not a fortune, but it's true."

"True of everyone."

"No it isn't!"

"It's vague and it's vaguely flattering. Anyone would recognize themselves in that. It's like astrology."

"I don't believe in astrology. I believe in personality." She peered at him. "What are you?"

"What am I what."

"I'd peg you as either INFP or INFJ."

"Oh God. You mean this Myers-Briggs thing."

"I can't decide if you're introverted intuition with feeling or introverted feeling with intuition."

"Come on. There is absolutely no foundation to that system, absolutely no experimental data that would—actually, it's impossible even to imagine what experiments *could* be done to validate it. It's entirely unfalsifiable. Unfalsifiable and unverifiable."

She watched him contemplatively, her chin resting on one upturned fist.

"It's not science. It's not even psychology."

"Judgment, definitely," she decided. "INFJ."

He laughed.

"But that's okay," she said. "I'm a perfect ENFP myself, so we've got good overlap but also good ..." She fitted her fingers together and made a locking-into-place sound. "Meshing. Opposition. Complement-ariness. Now read your fortune."

"'A smiling face is half the meal.'"

She looked down at their plates. "Yuck."

They laughed.

Strickland asked, "Do you really think I'm an introvert?"

Q. About how common is this intermittent explosive disorder?

A. I do not have access to any precise figures at the moment, but I should say that it is not extremely common.

Q. In fact the DSM, the psychologists' manual, says that it is extremely rare, does it not?

A. No doubt you are correct. Thank you.

Q. How many times have you seen it? In a patient. How many times in your career have you made this diagnosis?

A. Well, Ms. Lattimann, I could not say.

Q. You don't know or you don't remember?

A. Diagnosis, in a clinical setting, diagnosis is of a secondary order of—it's not an issue of primary—it's tangential to the main thrust of treatment.

Q. Professor, for your sake and my sake and the sake of the jury, may I with all due respect please remind you to please answer the question directly.

A. Thank you, yes. I will try. Could you repeat the question?

THE COURT: Miss Reporter, will you kindly read back the last question for the doctor.

REPORTER: How many times in your career have you made this diagnosis?

A. With all due respect, Ms. Lattimann, diagnosis, putting a generic name to a cluster of individual and often unique problems or symptoms, well it does not play a large part in my clinical, therapeutic work.

Q. Your Honor, I would ask that the witness be directed to answer the question, please.

THE COURT: Answer the question if you can, Doctor.

A. I am trying, Your Honor. To the best of my knowledge, and in light of what I just said, I suppose the answer must be not very often.

Q. Professor, I will try to make this easy for you. Before Michael Burger, did you ever, have you ever made this diagnosis before? Please answer yes or no.

A. No. But as you pointed out it is very rare.

Q. How many patients do you see, Professor?

A. On an ongoing basis? It varies.

Q. How many patients do you see right now?

A. As I said, it varies.

Q. How many patients did you see in the last seven days?

A. Two. But perhaps I could be permitted to elaborate?

THE COURT: Just wait until you're asked a question, Doctor.

Q. What are your diagnoses of those two patients, Professor?

A. Well, one is suffering from a form of chronic depression, and the other, a sort of generalized anxiety.

Q. Are those diagnoses—chronic depression and generalized anxiety—are those in the DSM, Professor?

They stood beside the car on an embankment, looking down at the city.

Trace said, "Old people holding hands … Finding money in the pockets of clothes you haven't worn in a long time … Days that are sunny and rainy at the same time. What else … Oh!—when somebody out of the blue smiles at you like they know you, but they don't. I love that … What about you?"

Strickland smiled and shook his head.

*

In the car, she said, "Jealousy. A crime of passion."

"But the guy was a complete stranger."

"Maybe. Or maybe the wife is hiding something. Maybe your friend finally had enough and just pow!—snapped."

"I don't know."

"It's obvious. You just can't see it because you're above all that."

"I don't know."

"Do you want to come in?" he asked.

"Why?"

"I ... I thought maybe you'd like a cup of coffee."

"Oh. In that case."

"I don't know where everybody is ..."

She looked at the framed photographs on the mantel. "Nice."

"Do you have—kids?"

"Kids are amazing. No. Ted didn't want any." She let out a bark of laughter. "Neither did I. How old is he?"

"Five. Yes, five ... Hard to believe. Children are the most amazing clocks. Five years used to mean nothing to me. Now it's ... well. His lifespan." He shook himself out of his reverie. "How do you like your coffee?"

"No sugar. Lots of cream. Till it's like the color of my skin."

She showed him an arm.

He stood in the kitchen with his forehead against a cupboard.

He poured coffee, added cream, looked at it. Added more cream, looked at it. Added more cream. Looked at it.

"What's the matter?" she asked.

"Oh, nothing. Kink in my neck. I sleep funny."

She put down her cup. "How often?"

"Every other day or so."

She stood behind him and put her hands on his shoulders.

He stiffened. She waited. He relaxed.

She began feeling his neck, his shoulders, his upper back. His head fell forward.

"That's better," he murmured.

She laughed. "I haven't even done anything yet."

The front door opened and closed. He stiffened again.

"It's not a kink, it's repetitive strain. You hold yourself too tight. Hello."

"Oh," said Martie, "hello."

Strickland got to his feet, but his wife was already climbing the stairs.

"Should I leave?," Trace asked.

"No. I don't know. No. Finish your coffee …?"

"I'll take a rain check, how about."

At the door she said, "See you tomorrow night, smiling face."

Strickland leaned in the doorway, hands in pockets, and watched his wife brush her teeth. She raised her eyebrows at him in the mirror.

"Are you smoking again?" he blurted.

She spat in the sink. "What?"

"It's the middle of the day and you're brushing your teeth."

Without looking at him she said, "They felt furry. I had wine at lunch."

He stepped forward and put his arms around her.

"Oh-*kay* …" she said.

He let her go.

"I've got to pick up Ben in … five minutes ago," she explained.

He sat on the bed and watched her remove jewelry, change her shoes.

"I don't think we should keep secrets from each other," he said.

"I agree. Why, do you keep secrets?"

"I think we need to talk."

"You sound like a movie. Instead of announcing that you want to say something, why don't you just say the something that you want to say."

"Very well. All right. Are you …"

She sighed. "I've really got to go, hon."

"… Trace—she only gave me a lift home."

"That was nice of Trace."

"Well, you weren't going to ask."

"What you do … Listen, I don't have time for this."

"Then I'll come with you."

They rode in silence.

From the back seat Ben said, "Penny was running around when teacher was out of the room and she fell but nobody tripped her. She had to go to the nurse and also she cried."

Neither Strickland nor Martie replied, but glanced disapprovingly at each other for not replying.

Eventually Strickland said, "Listen … Do we have to go to this party thing tomorrow?"

After a long pause she said, "No. Not if you don't think it's important anymore."

"'Important'?"

"'The therapeutic value' *et cetera*—those aren't my words."

"You make it sound like I dragged you into it kicking and screaming."

"As I recall, you were the one who—No," she decided, "I'm not going to say what I was about to say."

"Please, by all means. Say it. I implore you."

"Mom," Ben asked, "are you and Dad having a disagreement?"

"I was going to say that I am not the one who was nearly reprimanded for certain no doubt wondrously cathartic liaisons with one of my students now I really do think we've made enough of a negative impact on a certain young person's emotional psycho-development for one day. *Yes*, Benjamin, your father and I were having a disagreement but now we're having a time out. How do you feel about that? All right?"

Ben said, "The black man's here again."

"Where'd you find it?"

"I know some people." Mike grinned and fingered his teeth. "I got some connections."

Strickland looked inside the car. The back seat had been slashed and cigarette burns covered the dashboard. The glove compartment held only a blackened soda can.

"Well," he said.

"They bagged the shit out of it a little but it still goes."

Strickland circled the vehicle. "Took the license plates," he noticed.

"Sure. Gotta do that if you're gonna sell it."

"Well. Thanks, Mike. I appreciate it."

"Come on."

"What?"

Mike tossed him the keys. "Take the motherfucker for a spin."

"That's easy to fix," Mike shouted over the rattling noises coming from the engine. "That's just timing, any asshole can fix that."

Glancing at the cars backing up behind them, he said, "Better get off the express. Take Wilshire—I know a place."

Mike slapped palms and knuckles with the bartender.

"How the fuck are you, Mike?"

"How the fuck *ain't* I, man."

"I thought your fucking ass was in clink."

"Naw. Not yet." He leaned against the bar and surveyed the room like a man expecting to be recognized.

Strickland lowered himself onto a stool and peered at the bottles behind the bar. "Guess I'll have a little chat with Mr. Daniel."

The bartender looked at him.

"Jack Daniel's," he said in his normal voice. "Ice, no water."

"Coming right up."

"His friends call him 'Mister,'" Strickland explained.

Winking over his shoulder at Strickland, the bartender said, "This guy your lawyer, Mike?"

Mike turned slowly around, as if afraid of forgetting something. "This guy," he said, "is my fucking headshrink, man."

"No shit."

"I'm his fucking headshrink," Strickland agreed.

"Gonna get this piece of shit off on an insanity plea?"

They all laughed.

"Before that," Mike said, "it was the fucking pulp mill. Nasty fucking place, the pulp mill. I still get dreams. Fucker I knew had his arm ripped off in the fucking winch."

"Jesus," Strickland said. "Did you see it?—happen?"

"Naw. Different shifts. Still, that kind of shit … Before that it was Houston. Man, I did everything in fucking Houston. Construction, windows, sweeping up in a bolt factory. Chopping meat, deliveries. Even selling socks with the fags in a fucking department store."

"A lot of jobs."

"And we were only in Texas six months that time!"

"Why so many?"

"Aw, shit. You ever known a boss that wasn't a fucker? Anyway, I like variety." He gulped at his drink and said, "No, that's one thing I can't ever stand is super—you know, superior fuckers telling me what to do. I never was able to stand that shit. Not even in high school. Our football coach—now there was a disrespecting super-superior motherfucker if you ever saw one. I showed him." He grinned at the memory. "I was good, too. No shit. Halfback. Fucking solid, you know." He jumped into a pillar-like stance above his chair. "But fuck it, man. Can't push a guy around. Can't tell a guy what to do."

"What about the army?"

"What about the fucking army, man?"

"You must've taken orders there all right."

"You talking about Nam. Nam was different." After a pause he said, "It was like being in clink."

Strickland waited.

"I mean it wasn't like clink but it was like clink because you can't say what it's like, either. It's like living a different life. A different planet. Nothing connects up between nothing in it and the real world, so how do you ... Shit, I don't know. It was like a movie."

"Like a war movie?"

"Never mind. Like going to a fucking movie. Never mind. Fuck it."

"Was it—were you ever in danger?"

"Was I ever not?—You mean was I ever in the shit?" His grin disappeared. "Twice."

"Ever ... hurt?"

"You mean psychologically?"

"I meant physically."

"I'm here, ain't I?"

"... Ever get hit in the head, fall down, lose consciousness? Ever been in the hospital?"

"Naw." He struck the pillar pose again and chuckled. "Solid."

"Ever done any drugs?"

"No," he said quickly. "Why?"

"Oh, you never know. Just asking." After a minute, Strickland said, "I do a little coke from time to time."

Mike was impressed. "No shit. You get high?"

"You know. Once in awhile."

"... Wanna get high now?"

Strickland pursed his lips, then laughed.

Q. Is this the kind of disorder that would be treatable, by drugs for example?

A. That question I think indicates a rather unfortunate assumption about the state of the pharmaceutical art today. To be frank, drug treatment is not a very advanced form of therapy—more akin to faith healing than science. We have a lot of different chemicals that seem to have a lot of different effects on a lot of different people but most of the time we don't even know how they work, let alone why. The brain is an incredibly, unimaginably dense and complicated lump of circuitry. A great physiologist once compared it to the Milky Way—so try to imagine a galaxy of little stars doing an incredibly complicated yet very meaningful dance at almost the speed of light. Then try to imagine a bunch of humans trying to choreograph that dance with nothing but microscopes and prescription pads at their disposal. Pharmacology is trying to return to equilibrium this amazingly turbulent electrochemical galaxy by smuggling a few more

chemicals across the blood–brain barrier, adding a few more ingre-
dients to the soup haphazardly. It's like copyediting a million-page
manuscript by randomly inserting five percent more vowels—or
trying to improve the fuzzy picture on your television by adding,
you know, five percent more red or blue.

Q. Dr. Strickland, do you get paid by the hour?

A. Why—yes, I do.

Q. Uh-huh. What do you make, sixty dollars an hour?

A. That is my rate, yes.

Q. Is the meter running while you are in court?

MR. MASSICK: Now I'm afraid I'm going to have to object,
your Honor. That's argumentative, the way it's framed.

THE COURT: All right, sustained.

A. The fact is that I earn what is—

THE COURT: Now just a minute, Doctor. The objection was
sustained.

A. Oh. Sustained. Thank you.

THE COURT: Perhaps you could rephrase the question, Ms.
Lattimann.

Q. Do you get sixty dollars an hour, Professor, for the time you
sit here on the witness stand and testify?

MR. MASSICK: Now I do apologize Your Honor but on second
thought I'm also going to have to object to the substance of this
question on grounds of relevance, I think.

MS. LATTIMANN: I'm willing to strike that last question, Your
Honor.

MR. MASSICK: Well, thank you.

THE COURT: The jury will kindly disregard Ms. Lattimann's
question.

Q. Professor, you yourself as a psychologist are not allowed to
prescribe drugs, are you?

A. That's a little like asking the candlestick maker if he is allowed to sell pastries. It's not my line of work. It's not what I do.

Mike sniffed and said, "Speed. STP. Crank. Goofballs. PCP once and never fucking again. Here." He held out his powdered knuckle to Strickland.

"No, no thanks. I'm good." He patted his stomach and laughed. "I'm stuffed."

Mike snorted what was left and went on, "Mescaline, at least I think it was mescaline. LSD, all that hippie shit. Weed."

Strickland looked around the room. The surfaces were all mirrors and light. "Marijuana?" he said. "I've never smoked marijuana. This is a beautiful environment."

"There it comes." Mike rolled his head around on his neck and rotated his shoulders. He slapped Strickland on the back and said, "Vamos, amigo. You can't get shit like we got in the army anymore but we'll find you some kind of shit somewhere."

Out in the street, Strickland confided, "I like being happy."

Q. Could Mr. Burger be cured by means other than drugs, or will he always have this problem?

A. He can, I believe, like any of us, be helped to realize that emotional arousal, including various forms of anger, has a mediating, cognitive element, and is therefore capable of being sublimated or redirected. He could, I think, with the aid of a skilled therapist, be led to adopt a task-oriented or problem-solving attitude instead of an ego-oriented one. I'm sorry: to answer your question as briefly as possible, I would say that yes, absolutely, he could learn to not take things personally, to control his anger—to use his brain.

Q. And how long would that take, Professor?

A. It is difficult to say.

Q. And how many times would he blow up, and how many more people would he be likely to beat to death before he had learned to as you say not take things personally?

Mike and Roz and their friends waiting to be seated at The White Grape.

Antonio DiRosa coming in with his group, asking Roz, Is it a long wait?

Roz looking at him meaningfully with moist eyes, and with moist lips saying, Depends what you're waiting for. Roz looking at Mike defiantly.

The maitre-d' saying, Ah, Mr. DiRosa! Your party's table is ready.

Mike clenching his fists, gritting his teeth.

DiRosa, passing by, stopping to whisper, I'm gonna fuck your wife till she screams.

"Huh?" said Mike, passing him the joint.

"Nothing." Strickland puffed at it with an air of responsibility. Then he sat back.

"It's like," he said, "I can feel my peristalsis."

"Totally." A shrewd look came into Mike's eyes. "It's like a total proclivity, right?"

They were in a once-sumptuous hotel room, but the white carpet and leather furniture looked like they hadn't been cleaned since they were installed. There were a few other people in the room but they appeared to be asleep, despite the loud music.

"Proclivity?"

"Yeah, you know what I mean, like a proclivity to swear."

Strickland blinked. "You read my report."

"So that's like a, a proclivity to swear, that's like, what, I say fuck a lot, is that it?"

"Hell, it's not a judgment, Mike. Of course you swear a lot—relative to myself and other people of my particular … cultural and socio-economic background. But if I'd lived the life you've lived, no doubt I'd probably cuss a lot too."

"Man," said Mike, "you don't know shit about my fucking life."

Mike jumped up and punched a street sign.

"Sometimes I feel like I'm not even anywheres," he said. "Like I'm not even, like there's not even … anything. You know what I mean?"

Strickland considered, then said, "When I hold my eyes open it feels like the wind is blowing right into my skull."

"Man," Mike said, "you should shave that fucking beard off. It makes you look like a fucking A-rab."

"That's quite a statement, coming from a man of … of a minority group."

"You mean a nigger?"

"No."

Mike laughed at him. "See, I can be a racist but you can't get away with it. Actually I'm not a racist—some of my best friends are ragheads!"

After a moment, Strickland laughed too.

"I'm not even really a nigger," Mike said. "My old man was a fucking wetback."

He smashed a street sign thoughtfully.

They were in another bar. Mike returned to the table.

"Okay, so she wants to play it that way? Okay."

"She does, huh?"

Mike whistled restlessly for a minute. "Man," he said, "I promised myself I was gonna get all the fucking pussy I can while I'm still
in the world."

After a long pause, Strickland said slowly, "I think my wife is
having an affair."

"Man, what you fucking looking at?," Mike muttered. Then
he shouted it across the bar: "Man, what you fucking looking at,
man?"

"What are *you* looking at?" came the reply.

Mike rose, as if lifted by a crane. "I'll look at whatever the fuck I
feel like, my friend."

"Oh my," Strickland giggled.

"I'm not your friend and if you want to look at my woman then
you can take a fucking photo."

Mike started across the room with the poise and footing of
someone crossing a rope bridge.

"Mike …"

"Maybe I'll buy one," Mike suggested. "She sell them after her
strip show?"

"Fuck, man, you better back off, man."

"Yeah? Or what."

"I'm just telling you now, you better just about back the fuck off,
man."

"Mike, come on, this is stupid." Strickland looked to the woman
for support, but she was watching the argument with the disengaged
engrossment of a referee.

"You think you can tell motherfuckers what they can and can't
look at, motherfucker?"

"Now you're getting in my face and that's something I don't
like."

"All right, both of you, this is silly, childish—"

"Yeah, what about this, you like this?"

Mike shoved the guy.

"That's ENOUGH!," Strickland screamed.

They looked at him.

"I mean, I mean, what are you doing, Mike? Have you forgotten that you're out on, I mean out on fucking bail?"

"Oh *yeah*, you mean for *killing* that fucker?"

"Come on," said the woman, "forget this shit."

"Watch your back," the man muttered as they left.

Mike laughed and clapped Strickland on the shoulder. "Dan my man! You see that fucker's face?"

"I mean, what do you want to go and get all worked up for? How am I supposed to … What are you thinking?"

"Aw shit, man. Come on now, don't be like that. That was some fucking A-1 shit right there, admit it. Admit it."

Mike shook him by the shoulders till he smiled.

In the cafeteria, Strickland, hungover, said, "And can I get a salad instead of the fries?"

"Sure, but it costs a dollar."

"That doesn't make any sense. The side salad costs less than the side fries."

"Man, I just do what they tell me."

"Yeah," Strickland muttered, "that's what they said at Belsen."

The anxious young man said, "And I can't even drive anymore because of the yellow lights. I know it's stupid, but whenever I stop for one I feel like I should have gone through and whenever I go through I feel like it was really too late and I should have stopped. And green lights are no good because they could turn yellow at any moment so I'm constantly re-evaluating whether—"

Strickland rubbed his neck and said, "I've got an idea. Why don't we jump straight to the relaxation exercises we've been working on."

Strickland looked in the mirror and touched his beard.

Someone said, "The main thing is you don't treat sex like a big deal, or make more of a secret of it than any other thing that they don't understand yet."

"But you can't deprive them completely of television—it's ostracizing."

"Milgram, Asch, Schachter ... All the best experimental work has been done with stooges."

"My twelve-year-old boy now. Our bathroom light switch is outside in the hall, and Alfie and his little pal would turn off the light when his fourteen-year-old sister took a shower, so of course she has to come out in the buff, which is the point. Well, when Frank and I had had about enough of her caterwauling I told her: That's enough now, open that door, and I hauled the two little hoodlums in by the ear and I said: There! Get a good eyeful! That's a perfectly ordinary female naked body and nothing to get so excited about, is it? And to *her* I said: And that's a perfectly ordinary couple of twelve-year old boys with a perfectly natural and ordinary curiosity and nothing to get so riled up about, is it? You're not the bloody queen."

"I don't know, maybe we've handled ours with kid gloves."

"Oh but you *gotta* handle kids with gloves!"

Strickland, beardless, went to the punch bowl.

Trace said, "Oh, all over the place. I collect them."

Martie said, "And they're all polar bears?"

"I love polar bears. I love how white and fluffy they are."

Strickland went away from the punch bowl.

*

Someone said, "It's the only time in your life when you get to stand in front of a roomful of people who are guaranteed to know less than you. I can tell them *anything*—and they have to believe it."

Someone said, "I know that guy! You mean the Resto-Rage guy?"

Martie said, "I guess that's what the newspapers call him ..."

Someone said, "Childhood is just an example of Stockholm Syndrome."

Everyone laughed.

Nigel said, "I don't get it."

Everyone laughed.

Strickland said, "That doesn't make any sense. I thought Stockholm Syndrome was when you gradually over time started to sympathize and identify with your abductors. But with children the process is exactly the reverse."

No one laughed.

Trace said, "Sit still. See if you can keep your eye open while I lick your eyeball."

Martie was watching them from across the room.

Strickland laughed and said, "Yuck!"

One of the women cried, "Let's pick keys already—I want a goddamn drink already."

Trace pressed herself against Strickland and said, "What do we do?"

Strickland said, "Just make sure you pick last."

The women lined up and withdrew keys from a convoluted Chinese teapot.

Trace said, "Oh, you go ahead, dear."

Martie said, "No no, that's fine, you first."

Nigel said, "Wait a second. Who's actually left? Just Dan and I?

Well, we can't very well let you and Martie go home together, can we heh heh?"

Strickland grabbed the teapot and turned it upside down. Nothing came out.

"I knew it."

Nigel pushed his glasses up his nose and said, "Guess we forgot to put our keys in, hey pal?"

Strickland punched him on the chin.

Nigel took a step back.

"Ow," he said. "What was that for?"

Strickland looked at his wife, then left the room.

Trace said, "Where's he going?"

Nigel called, "Are you okay to drive, buddy?"

Martie went to the window and said, "Don't be stupid."

Strickland drove.

"Glasses up with their ring finger?" he muttered.

"I'll have a little chat with Mr. Daniel."

But the bartender didn't recognize him.

"A little chat with Mr. Daniel, please."

"Mr. Daniels, you mean."

"No," said Strickland, "there's an apostrophe."

Strickland parked on an embankment and looked down at Los Angeles.

Then he drove home.

Martie was sitting in the kitchen over a cup of coffee.

"Good," she said when he came in.

Strickland went to the window. "Your friend give you a ride home?"

"No. *Your* friend. Nigel was drunk. So were you."

He turned around. "The guy is a ... He pushes his glasses up with his ring finger, Martie. His *ring* finger. Any other finger would make sense—"

"What about *her*? She collects polar bear knick-knacks."

"We didn't even sleep together."

"Oh no?"

"No." After a pause he said, "It's worse than that."

"You like her."

He sat down at the table. "I liked the idea of liking someone again."

She slapped him, then laughed through tears at the look on his face.

He tried to slap her, but she blocked him, then slapped him again. He reeled back, knocking his chair over. He righted it, then pushed it across the floor at her. She jumped out of the way, grabbed the nearest thing to hand—half a loaf of bread—and threw it at him. He swatted it out of the air and ducked the toaster which followed.

"You're crazy!"

"*You're* crazy!"

She emptied the cutlery drawer onto the floor at his feet. He tore the dish tray out of the dishwasher and threw it at her legs.

Ben sat up in bed, in the dark.

"I wasn't sleeping with him either!"

"Oh, come on!"

"For someone with such a big brain you can be a real idiot. I only kept going with him because he was the only one who said we didn't have to!"

The phone rang.

He said, "Is that true?"

"I'm not getting that," she said.

"Well, neither am I."

They sat at opposite ends of the table, the floor around them scattered with broken dishes.

Martie said, "Why can't we make each other feel like that again?"

"You mean anymore?"

"I mean again."

He touched her arm.

She said, "I don't know what I want."

"Maybe that's because you don't want anything."

The phone rang again.

Martie returned and said, "That was the hospital."

In the bright, cluttered waiting room, Martie said, "Atrocious the way these places are run. Like a bus station."

Strickland frowned and nodded. Ben wriggled in his lap.

A doctor entered and Martie stood up.

"Mrs. Esposito?"

She sat down and muttered, "Do I look like a Mrs. Esposito?"

"They're doing the best they can."

"That's what they said at Auschwitz."

"Mr. and Mrs. Endicott?"

"Can she hear us?"

Melanie said, "I can hear you."

The doctor said, "She'll be a bit groggy for the next twenty-four hours or so, but no harm done."

"Thank you," said Strickland.

"A … psychologist will want to talk to the three of you, before she checks out."

"I am a psychologist," said Martie, "and so is my husband."

"Then you'll understand."

"I understand that you must have a bloody good union here."

The doctor left and Martie sat down beside the bed.

"Oh, you stupid, stupid girl."

"Leave me alone."

Strickland said to Ben, "Let's wait outside."

"What were you thinking? You little idiot. You stupid, stupid, stupid, stupid, stupid—"

In the waiting room, Ben ate dirt out of a potted plant. Strickland slapped his hand.

"You … You'll spoil your appetite."

The boy looked at his father in amazement, then started to cry.

After a long pause, Massick shifted his bulk behind the desk and said, "With all due respect, I think you've got the wrong end of the stick on this one, Doctor. I don't believe I ever said anything about insanity."

"But," said Strickland, "you're pleading insanity. You're pleading Mike not guilty by reason of insanity."

"That's a technicality. What we fundamentally have here is a jury trial. That means twelve bozos deciding guilty or not guilty. Simple as that. Never mind this by reason of insanity bushwah. Juries don't understand it. Remember, they're laymen—another word for bozos. Every day of every year a jury somewhere finds a crazy man guilty and a guilty man crazy. If they like you, they find you not guilty. If they don't, you're going to jail. Simple as that. What sort of people do they dislike? Monsters. Weirdos. Madmen. Sickos. People *not quite right* in the old nobby-noodler. People they fear and hate because they don't understand them—because no one was able to *help* them understand them. In other words, the very sort of people who should be in a mental hospital. They're the ones who get sent to jail. What sort of people do they let off? I'll tell you. People they feel sorry for. People they recognize. People like them. People who did what they would have done themselves in the same circumstances. So you see. This isn't about sane or insane, or even guilty or not guilty. There is no guilty or not guilty in this case—the guy did it. All there is is a yay or a nay. Is this guy a bad guy, or is this guy a good guy. All you have to do is show them that this guy isn't a bad guy."

"But I don't think Mike belongs in a mental hospital."

"Neither do I. Neither does he. I know and you know and probably even he knows that he'll be a lot more miserable in the nuthatch than in the slammer. In the slammer he'd have regular exercise and phone privileges and conjugal visits and a shot at bail. In the booby hatch—who the hell knows? And they might keep him in longer than he would have spent in jail anyway because they won't be able to figure out what's wrong with him. But what can we do? The guy wants a trial and is entitled to a trial. He wants to go before a jury of his so-called peers and what does he want? He wants them to give him the thumbs-up. He wants them to say he's not a bad guy. Do you think he's a bad guy?"

Strickland said, "No."

"All right. There we are. So tell me, Doctor. What's the story?"

"Story?"

"Why did he do this thing? What was he thinking? If they're going to understand him they're going to need the story. What made him do it?"

"I don't know."

"Then you haven't done your job."

Roz opened the door. "Oh," she said. "He ain't here."

"I need to talk to him."

"Well, I don't know. I should just about guess he's probably at work."

Q. Professor, can you offer any scientific evidence that your psychological diagnoses are in fact correct?

A. Well, in my clinical opinion, I would say that as a general rule one knows one's diagnoses are correct when the treatment offered for the diagnosed disorder is effective. I think it would be difficult for anyone to go on practicing psychology if they were wrong most of the time.

Q. You are familiar with the practice of bleeding, Professor, which was practiced for two hundred years even though it was ineffective and wrong?

A. If that is a question, then yes, I am familiar with it.

Q. Did the doctors or barbers or whoever performed those bleeding or leeching operations know they were wrong, Professor, or did they believe they were helping their patients?

A. If you mean is it possible that I am wrong even though I think I am right, yes of course, but the same could be said for anyone at any time in human history.

Q. That is very generous of you, Professor.

A. I think perhaps you could stop calling me Professor now.

The bar was not open yet. He knocked on the front door, then went around to the back of the building, picking his way past garbage cans and garbage.

On the back wall, someone had spray-painted the words SPICK KILLERS.

He knocked.

A large man opened the door and looked at him.

"Is this ... Does Mike work here? Mike Burger?"

The large man closed the door.

"Good union," Strickland muttered. He was picking his way back through the garbage when the door opened again and Mike came out.

"Shit, man. What the fuck?"

A group of men were seated around a pool table covered with piles of paper. One of them rolled a toothpick back and forth in his mouth without seeming to move his tongue. They all looked at Strickland as if they had been waiting for him.

Mike shook his thumb at Strickland and said, "Aw, shit, this guy's okay. Friend of mine. We'll be in the back, okay, Andy? Shit."

Strickland waited in a dirty, derelict kitchen stacked to the ceiling with cases of alcohol. Mike came in holding a VCR in one hand, its power cord dragging behind like a tail.

"Here," he said. "I wanted to give you this."

"A VCR?"

Mike pulled at his teeth and said, "Roz said I should get you something, you know, so I thought: shit."

"Thank you," Strickland said. "Actually, we don't own a television."

"Aw, fuck it. Pawn it if you want. You know how women ..."

"We've been thinking of buying one, though. And now we could rent movies. It's very thoughtful."

"Aw, fuck off, man. It was just an idea."

Strickland put the VCR down on the edge of a dusty grill. "Listen, Mike."

"But you should blow out, man. You shouldn't really ought to be down here right now anyway."

"I'm dropping your case, Mike."

"Come back some night, I'll run you up a tab."

"I said I'm dropping the case. I just came from Massick. I'm not going to do it."

"Huh?"

"I'm not going to testify. Go to court. Say that you're insane. I don't think you're insane."

"Insane?"

"I can't do it. I'm sorry. It wouldn't be honest. I want to help you but … Jesus, my life is more fucked up than yours right now. I have no right to sit in judgment on … anyone. I'm sorry."

"But it starts next week. I'm on trial *next week*."

"I know. I'm sorry. But it wouldn't be right. I don't think you belong in a ment—I don't think you have a psychol—I don't think you're crazy and it would be dishonest, unprofessional, and, and, and wrong for me to pretend otherwise. And probably illegal."

"You saying you ain't gonna testify."

"That's what I'm saying."

"But man, I'm going to court next week!"

"I heard you the first time. I don't think you heard me."

Mike put his hand delicately on a stack of Jack Daniel's boxes, as if it were the head of a child.

"I understand if you're angry."

"What the fuck are you talking about?" He was breathing heavily. "You talking about quitting?"

"I am quitting."

"Man, what the fuck you *talking* about? Who said you could quit? Who the fuck hired you? Who the fuck pays your bills?"

"Well," said Strickland, "Massick."

Mike began tapping the lowest box in the stack with his shoe; bottles tinkled. "Let me just get this straight here for a minute. I gotta go and get my ass dragged into court next fucking week and you want to blow off?"

"I was hired by Massick, and I never promised that I would— Everything was contingent on whether or not I, on the results of— I'm sorry it took so long, but these things take time."

Mike kicked the box; glass broke.

"Man, what, the fuck, you talking about! Who you think hired Massick, man? Who the fuck you think pays *his* bills?" He kicked the box again. "Not me! That's for sure as fucking sure. You think I got money? I don't got shit. It's that motherfucker out there who's got the money. I don't got shit, I ain't shit, unless that motherfucker says I'm shit."

He punched the top box and the whole stack came crashing down. Jack Daniel's came gurgling out of the boxes and spread slowly across the floor.

"There! That's what I'm talking about! Now who the fuck you think's going to pay for *that* shit? It sure, as fuck, ain't gonna be fucking Massick!"

He began kicking and stamping on the fallen boxes.

"And I sure, as fuck, ain't going, into, fucking, clink again, and getting my other, fucking, kidney, cut the fuck out, by one of that spic, fag, DiRosa's, fucking, brothers!"

Panting, fists clenched, he turned on Strickland.

Strickland took a step back and said, "I don't think this is a very intelligent way to discuss this."

*

As the sound of breaking bottles reached them, the men around the pool table looked at one another, then at the man with the toothpick. The man with the toothpick took the toothpick out of his mouth. He placed it on the edge of the table. He said, "Shit."

Mike went limp when the door opened, which allowed Strickland to get out from under him and grab him by the throat.

"What's all this fuss?" said the man with the toothpick.

Strickland let go. They got to their feet.

"You need some help with this ... friend of yours?"

"Naw, Andy," said Mike.

Strickland tugged his shirt into place. "We're fine, thanks."

The man with the toothpick said to Mike, "You need to take a little time out?"

Mike said, "Naw, Andy."

"Let me see. How about this. Take yourself a little time out. Work whatever this shit is out. Just be back before first rush. Then clean this fucking mess up."

Out in the street, they shuffled towards Strickland's car, blinking and shielding their eyes from the sun. Strickland had the VCR under one arm.

"I just about had you there," Strickland said.

"Aw man, forget that."

"No kidding. Another two minutes ... Did you like that hold?" Strickland cocked his free arm to show which hold he meant.

"You fight like a fucking school kid. Kicking a guy's fucking legs out."

"That's because I haven't been in a fight since school!"

They stood next to the car, looking down at the city as the sun set.

"So what am I supposed to tell them?" said Strickland. "I can't—
I won't lie."

"Shit, man. Who the fuck said shit about lying? Tell them the
fucking truth. Tell them that asshole got what he fucking asked for."

"Mike," Strickland said. "What happened on July ninth?"

"Man, what the fuck do I know from July ninth? How the fuck
do I know what I'm doing July ninth or tenth or any other fucking
day? That shit's a long time ago."

"You know what day I mean."

"Man, you mean the night I *killed* that motherfucker, say so."

Mike Burger and Antonio DiRosa in the foyer of The White Grape,
shouting into each other's faces.

Man, what you fucking looking at, man?

What you think *you* looking at?

I'll look at whatever the fuck I feel like, my friend.

I'm not your friend and you better back off, man.

Yeah? Or what.

I'm just telling you now, you better just about back the fuck off,
man.

"Nobody talks to me like that, man."

Strickland said, "But what did he say?"

You think you can tell motherfuckers what they can or can't look at,
motherfucker?

Who you calling motherfucker, motherfucker? Go fuck your
own mother.

Mike's friends, who have been holding him back, suddenly
meeting no resistance.

*

"Some punk piece of shit spic motherfucker tells me to fuck my mother, what the fuck you expect me to do? Take that shit lying down? Fuck that. Nobody says shit about my mother, man."

Mike got back in the car. Strickland joined him.

"She got enough of that fucking shit when she was alive."

"All right," said Strickland. "All right, all right, all right," he said. "Tell me about your mother."

Q. Are you familiar with the phrase begging the question? Strike that. How do you know when your treatment has been effective? Do you do follow-up studies? Do you get other psychologists to assess your results? Do you in fact make use of any of the tools of science? Analysis, comparison, evaluation, validation—do these play any part in your clinical work, Dr. Strickland?

MR. MASSICK: Now I do beg Your Honor's pardon but—

A. Let me explain something to you, Ms. Lattimann—

THE COURT: Now just a minute, Doctor. There is I believe going to be an objection to what was clearly a compound question.

MR. MASSICK: Thank you, Your Honor.

MS. LATTIMANN: Your Honor, with all due respect I would appreciate it if you left the objections to the defense counsel. I have my hands quite full enough without—

THE COURT: Ms. Lattimann, I would advise you to stop right there. Anyone can see that that was a compound question and therefore improper. You may rephrase, provided you limit yourself to one question at a time.

DR. STRICKLAND: May I say something, Your Honor?

THE COURT: Jesus and Mary. No you may not, until you are asked a direct question.

DR. STRICKLAND: It seems to me I was asked several, and it seems to me that everyone else in this court is given a chance to speak up whenever they like whereas I am not even allowed to elaborate on my answers, when it should be obvious to anyone with a, it should be obvious to anyone that there are some questions that cannot be answered with a simple yes or no, and I would also like to say for the record in respect to Ms. Lattimann's, well I don't know, I want to say argumentative and sarcastic question that yes—

THE COURT: I will decide what is argumentative, Doctor, thank you.

DR. STRICKLAND: As a matter of fact I do know what begging the question means, and furthermore that if she means to imply that my method is not scientific because I do not use double-blind studies or choose to hop my patients up on speed or downers or goofballs—

MS. LATTIMANN: Mr. Massick, perhaps you could please control your witness.

THE COURT: Ms. Lattimann, it is not for you to make requests of that nature to Mr. Massick.

DR. STRICKLAND: You give a hundred people a drug in a double-blind placebo-controlled study and lo and behold, sixty of them seem to do a little better, so the drug works, and a hundred doctors start prescribing it to a hundred patients each, but what about the forty it doesn't help, or makes feel worse? That's modern medicine. The individual is swamped by the average. And that's what you'd have us turn psychology into, Ms. Lattimann. Let me tell you, there is more wisdom, and compassion, and insight in one good case study of one unique and troubled person than in any number of tables of figures added up and smoothed over by mathematical frippery ...

THE COURT: Thank you, Doctor, that will do nicely.

DR. STRICKLAND: All right, Ms. Lattimann, we all see what you're trying to do. You want to discredit psychology as a science? Fine. I'll do it for you. Not just clinical psychology but I'll throw in experimental, and popular, and social and personality and depth and all the other kinds of psychology for free. They're all bunk. Of course they are. They're just stories we make up to explain why we do things, but none of us even knows why we do things ourself so how can we expect to make a science out of why everyone does everything that they do?

THE COURT: This is not the way things are done in a court of law, Doctor.

DR. STRICKLAND: You think if you find it in the DSM then it's science? Do you know anything? Yes, let me ask you some questions for a change. Did you know, Ms. Lattimann, that the manual was produced by committee consensus? That means they chatted about the different categories and decided by vote what should be included and what should not—isn't that correct? And isn't it true that there were disagreements, and that in fact a few years ago, wasn't there a big outcry when the Committee on Nomenclature voted that homosexuality was not a mental disorder, and wasn't that controversy resolved by sending ballots out to members of the American Psychiatric Association and having them vote on whether or not homosexuality is or is not a mental disorder? Now, that is not a scientific procedure, is it, Ms. Lattimann?

MS. LATTIMANN: Your Honor, I trust that you will instruct the jury correctly when the time comes to strike this tirade from the record if you are not going to clear the courtroom now or hold Dr. Strickland in contempt of court.

THE COURT: Ms. Lattimann, the next person, male or female, white or black, witness or counsel or juror or bailiff, who tells me how to do my job, will be the one held in contempt of court. As for you, Professor, Doctor—

DR. STRICKLAND: All right. Just let me say one more thing. Ms. Lattimann wants to quibble over definitions and diagnoses. It should be clear by now why I do not. Call it impulse dyscontrol or explosive personality type or any of the hundreds of things it's been called. None of the names says anything. A label isn't an explanation. The point is this. Could Mike Burger have acted differently? Could he have conformed his conduct to the law? My answer, in my professional, clinical opinion, is no. He could not. Not when you know who he is, what he has been through, how he relates to the world. A man in a restaurant told him to fuck his mother. So he beat him up, and the man died. He had no choice, when you consider his upbringing. His father was a violent, hateful man who beat his wife when their children—*her* children, he called them—acted up, or acted out, or did not behave exactly as he wanted them to behave—that is, as blocks of wood. Mike Burger as a child saw his mother thrashed till she was black and blue for *his* mischief, for *his* misdeeds. So when Antonio DiRosa told him to fuck his mother, something snapped. Maybe DiRosa became in that moment Mike's father. Maybe the man's unfortunate choice of words seemed to accuse Mike of himself being his father, or like his father. In either case, he was not a child any longer and he was not going to stand for anyone insulting or harming his mother anymore. So he attacked. What else could he do? Now tell me, Ms. Lattimann. Where are you going to find any of that in a textbook of psychological disorders?

THE COURT: Now we've simply got to have some kind of order and reason here. This isn't the way things are done. We've got to have order, or we'll be left with nothing but chaos.

MIKE BURGER: I'm sorry, man, but that's a load of fucking shit. I hated that bitch.

The judge cleared the courtroom.

SIX WEEKS LATER

The anxious young man said nothing for a long time. "It helps me sleep, too."

"Well, that's fine," said Strickland. "Just, you know. Be careful. Those things can be addictive."

"I guess."

"... Should we work on relaxation?"

"I don't know. I guess I'm probably relaxed enough already."

"Well ... I'm moving to a new office. So, if you want, we can meet there from now on."

The young man looked around his kitchen. "I don't mind."

Melanie and Ben helped Strickland carry boxes from the interview room out to his car.

"Blind corner!"

"Beep beep, coming through!"

"Oops—head-on collision!"

The phone rang. Melanie ran to get it.

"It's ... the *police*," she whispered.

They both looked at the box in his hands. On top was the VCR that Mike had given him.

"Joy ride," the cop explained. "Probably dumped it hours after they grabbed it. Drove it halfway into an aqueduct, otherwise somebody'd've spotted it sooner."

Strickland looked at the car. "And this—you're sure it's mine?"

The cop handed him the registration. "Glovebox," he said.

On the little stage, Ben said, "In the skirts of Norway, here and there, sharked up a list, of lawless res-o-lutes ..."

Beryl stood at the back of the room, squeezing her hands.

Later, alone with Strickland, she cried.

"They were terrible. *So* terrible! I always thought bad acting was bad directing, but those children ... They're not even believable when they're being themselves!"

Strickland told his class, "Don't ask them how they are. Don't ask them how they feel. Though their problems come from inside, they don't feel it that way. Ask them how *life* is. Ask them how the *world* is treating them."

The girl in the black turtleneck wrote everything down.

Strickland sat at his new desk in his new office, thinking.

He wrote something down, sighed, and rubbed his neck.

"Despite its appearance," he muttered, "it is actually a reaction to distressing feelings of weakness, Ms. Lattimann ..."

There was a tap at the door.

"Mind if I come in?"

Martie sat on his couch and said, "Such an unbearably tedious woman. Her only contact with the outside world is the six-o'clock news, and she only watches that so she can have something to be afraid of. The other night—this is good, you'll love this—she heard some pundit say that the only reason there's a recession is because everyone says so. You know: everyone is told there is a recession, so they don't spend anything, and so there is a recession. Oh, she puzzled over this for nearly the entire hour. She couldn't understand why we didn't just call it something else, use a different word— something 'upbeat,' she said. As if, instead of a recession, we could all agree that what we were in the middle of was actually a *carnival*, and if everyone just said it and believed it, it would come true ..."

They chuckled. She sighed and said, "It's actually quite endearing, though, if you think about it."

*

Strickland was about to ring the doorbell again when at last he heard footsteps coming from inside the house. The chain was eventually unlatched, the locks unlocked, and the door opened.

"Oh!" said the little old woman. "It's Danny!"

"Hello, mother."

Strickland said into his tape recorder, "We tell ourselves we're not going to be like our parents."

"I'll make tea," she said. "Aren't you cold in only that? Oh, but you shouldn't have come all this way, not just for a visit."

"I was in the neighborhood. How are you feeling?"

"Oh, bosh."

"But when the time comes, you find your primary concern is not what a robot you're turning your kid into, but how to keep them alive long enough to someday hate your guts."

"Sit down. You always look flushed after that drive. Let me make you something to eat. No, sit down. And turn that nasty thing off. It's nothing but bad news. Did you hear about this young man who tried to shoot the president? Maybe he did shoot the president, I don't know, they don't tell you anything. It's beyond me why anyone would go and do a thing like that. Why, the man was only inaugurated last month. He hasn't had a chance to do anything to deserve it yet. Not that I think shooting anyone is the answer to anything, but you would think you could at least wait and see what he actually *does*. Shooting a man like that a month after his inauguration! It doesn't make any sense. Why would someone go and do a thing like that?"

Strickland frowned and shook his head.

NOTES ON SOURCES

*And we, all of us, are interpreters, 'hermeneuts'—
creatures who pan for sense in the muddy waters of
human transaction, and who, if we are interested in
people, collect this sense into the bundles of remembered event, belief, and fantasy that constitute the
human biography.*

*The psychologist's musings may eventually take on
a formal shape—in flow charts and formulae—and
may be checked systematically against the evidence;
conversely plain men may achieve an intuitive depth
of insight that professional psychologists lack. But both
are hermeneuts, and their efforts to achieve understanding are essentially of the same sort.*

Liam Hudson

THERE ARE TWO REASONS to cite one's sources: to parade one's erudition, and to escape accusations of plagiarism. Psychologists, no doubt inspired by both motives, usually cite; fiction writers, whose pride and identity are so tied to notions of their creativity and originality, usually don't.

I hope to escape accusations of plagiarism.

In almost every case, I have modified the original author's original words—sometimes slightly, sometimes radically. Assume that every quotation in this book is inaccurate and wrong. Consult the original before requoting.

Where a number of editions are in existence, possibly with different paginations, I have included the total page count in parentheses. This should permit you to track down the quotation in any edition without too much trouble. Simply divide the cited page number by the total, and multiply the result (a fraction) by the number of pages in your copy. This will at least give you some idea where to look.

Frontispiece: Freud, "Schematic diagram of sexuality," in The Complete Letters of Sigmund Freud to Wilhelm Fliess. (Translated and edited by Jeffrey Moussaieff Masson. Belknap, 1985.) p. 100.

5   Epigraph: William James, "The Consciousness of Lost Limbs," in *Essays in Psychology*. (Harvard University Press, 1983.) p. 214.

Reaction-Formation

11   Epigraph: Freud, *The Interpretation of Dreams*, in *The Standard Edition of the Complete Psychological Works of Sigmund Freud*. (Translated and edited by James Strachey. Hogarth, 1953.) vol. 4, p. 113.

25   *'The play of shine and shade on the trees as the supple boughs wag.'* Walt Whitman, "A Song of Myself," §2.

30   *'what is unclean and disturbing and should not be part of the body'*: Freud, "Character and Anal Erotism," in *Standard Edition*, vol. 9, p. 172.

34   *"Respiration becomes shallow and rapid ... involuntary rhythmic contractions ..."* This jumble is actually taken from Havelock Ellis, *Psychology of Sex: A Manual for Students*. (Emerson Books, 1936.) pp. 19-28 (of 377).

48   Alfred Adler. *The Practice and Theory of Individual Psychology*. (Translated by P. Radin. Harcourt, Brace, 1929.) pp. 187-190 (of 352).

57   *Perhaps if I could have lain with Bunny ... I wanted to lie with him now!* Lytton Strachey, "Monday June 26th, 1916," in *Lytton Strachey by Himself*. (Edited by Michael Holroyd. Heinemann, 1971.) p. 140.

57-58 *"I imagined myself reading ... what would happen in the end."* Ibid., p. 150.

58   *And then the vision of that young postman ... really might, if I had the nerve, come off*. Ibid., pp. 140-141.

Eat the Rich and Shit the Poor

59   Epigraph: H. K. Nixon, *Psychology For the Writer*. (Harper & Brothers, 1928.) p. 1.

80   *"And bring us some bread,"* said Mr. Custard. In Hervey Cleckley's excellent *The Mask of Sanity* (C. V. Mosby, 1950), there appears on page 61-62 the following scene:

"Boastfully he told me that he was, in addition to all his other parts, an artist of remarkable ability. He asked to be given a loaf of bread, stating that he would mold from it creations of great beauty and worth. On getting the bread he broke off a large chunk, placed it in his mouth, and began to chew it assiduously, apparently relishing the confusion of his observers. After proceeding for a length of time and with thoroughness that once would have met with favor from advocates of Fletcherism, he at last disgorged the mess from his mouth and with considerable dexterity set about modeling it into the figure of a cross. Soon a human form was added in the customary representation. Rosettes, intertwining leaves, garlands, and an elaborate pedestal followed. The mixture of saliva and chewed bread rapidly hardened. By the next day, it had become as hard as baked clay. It was indeed an uncommon production. The whole piece was very skillfully and ingeniously shaped, dry, firm, and as neatly finished as if done by a machine. It was, furthermore, one of the most extravagant, florid, and unprepossessing articles that has ever met my glance. Max presented it with an air of triumph and expectancy that seemed to demand expressions of wonder and gratitude beyond reach of the ordinary man."

I wanted very much to use this scene, but found that I could not get Custard to sit still long enough.

Paddling an Iceberg

99   Epigraph: Jim Bird, *Self-Help? Self-Harm! The Seven Myths of Self-Help.* (Chapman Loebb, 1999.) p. 50.

102   *"You will become what you are."* Nietzsche, *The Joyful Wisdom,* §270.

103   *The individual is ... adding to the first act of stupidity a second.* This is a jumble of four separate quotations from Nietzsche: (1) *Twilight of the Idols,* "Morality as Anti-Nature," §6; (2) *Human, All Too Human,* §39; (3) and (4) *The Wanderer and His Shadow,* §38 and §323.

103-104   *"Whoever despises himself still respects himself as one who despises."* *Beyond Good and Evil,* §78.

104   *...gloriously, angelically wronged.* Cf. Nietzsche, *Human, All Too Human,* §62: "Coarse people who feel themselves offended tend to take as great a degree of offense as possible and to relate the cause in greatly exaggerated terms, simply in order to be able to revel thoroughly in the feeling of hate and vengeance that has been aroused."

104   *Whoever respects himself must still despise himself as one who respects.* Perhaps this is the meaning behind another of Nietzsche's beautiful little parables: A sage asked a fool the way to happiness. The fool answered without delay, like one who'd been asked the way to the next town: "Admire yourself, and live on the street!" "Hold on," cried the sage, "you require too much; surely it suffices to admire oneself?" The fool replied: "But how can one constantly admire without constantly despising?" *Joyful Wisdom,* §213.

105   *... he enjoys himself in Paris.* Schopenhauer, *The Wisdom of Life.* (Translated by T. Bailey Saunders. Willey Books, no date.) Chapter II, p. 14 (of 124). This observation also finds an echo in Nietzsche: "'Taking joy in a thing' is what we say, but in truth we are taking joy in ourselves by means of the thing.'" (*Human, All Too Human,* §501.)

107   *... a philosophy fit only for slaves, for it taught men to embrace the status quo.* Henry James, cited in Robert D. Richardson, *William James: In the Maelstrom of American Modernism.* (Houghton Mifflin, 2006.) p. 53.

107-108   *"It is important ... affects digestion adversely.* Peale, *The Power of Positive Thinking.* (Prentice-Hall, 1952.) pp. 27-28 (of 276).

108   *"Ask yourself whether you are happy, and you cease to be so."* John Stuart Mill, *The Autobiography of John Stuart Mill,* p. 78 (of 170). Here is the quotation in context:

"I never wavered in the conviction that happiness is the test of all rules of conduct, and the goal of life. But I now thought that this goal was only to be attained by not making it the *direct* goal. Those only are happy (I thought) who have their minds fixed on some object other than their own happiness. Ask yourself whether you are happy, and you cease to be so. The only chance is to treat not happiness, but some goal external to it, as the purpose of life. Let your self-consciousness, your scrutiny, your self-interrogation exhaust themselves on that; and if otherwise fortunately circumstanced you will inhale happiness with the air you breathe, without dwelling on it or thinking about it, without either forestalling it in imagination or putting it to flight by fatal questioning."

This is the best piece of advice I have ever read.

109 *"The will, as Nietzsche would be the first to admit ... 'self-referential subroutines'*
   ... " Barton Q. Barnard, from the introduction to *The Will and The Won't: Nietzsche and the Myth of Decision*, by James R. Bird. (Clapham University Press, 1993.) p. xxi.

110 *"The sum of the inner movements ... one calls his soul." Daybreak*, §311.

110 *... the great writer could be recognized: The Wanderer and His Shadow*, §97.

Nietzsche also said that to improve one's style is to improve one's thoughts, and nothing else. In other words, you cannot say exactly what you mean until you figure out exactly what you think, and most of our thoughts cannot even be thought clearly unless they are clutched with words: "I caught a notion on the way, and hastily took the readiest, poor words to hold it fast, so that it might not again fly away. But it has died in these dry words, and hangs and flaps about in them—and now I hardly know how I could have had such happiness when I caught this bird."

As someone who put a high value on saying exactly what you mean, Nietzsche deplored verbosity and pleonasm: "The half-blind are the mortal foes of authors who let themselves go. They would like to vent on them the wrath they feel when they slam shut a book whose author has taken fifty pages to communicate five ideas—their wrath, that is, at having endangered what is left of their eyesight for so little recompense." He even formulated a "draconian law" against such authors, which stated that a writer should be treated as a criminal "who deserves acquittal or pardon only in the rarest of cases: that would be one remedy against the increase of books." This may not be practical, but one must admire the sentiment.

"In the mountains," he wrote, "the shortest route is from peak to peak, but for that you must have long legs. Aphorisms should be peaks, and those to whom they are spoken should be big and tall of stature."

See *The Wanderer and His Shadow*, §131; *Joyful Wisdom*, §298; *The Wanderer and His Shadow*, §143; *Human, All Too Human*, §193; and *Thus Spoke Zarathustra*, p. 67 (of 343).

Psychology reveals evasions

as the human psyche

C.P. Boyko's new story collection is as full of odd secrets

C. P. BOYKO

◆ One of the most unfairly slept-on books of 2012, C.P. Boyko's *Psychology and Other Stories* (Biblioasis) tackles mental health and the professionals who assess it from six diverse yet tightly controlled angles. These are stories with many moving parts and a range of styles and settings, from tender coming-of-age tales to intra-family corporate takeovers. But they all have psychologists and psychiatrists circling the periphery, and it's rarely clear whether any-

stories seemed to require a little bit more space, so I gave it to them."

Boyko grew up in Saskatchewan, and earned degrees in English literature and psychology from the University of Calgary. *Psychology* neatly combines those two disciplines, and Boyko says the same impulses drew him to both as a student: "a fascination with the way people's thought processes work, [their] motivations and personalities".

Yet Boyko's own motivations ard personal motivations ard personal-ity prove to be a little harder to pin down. On the phone he's cautious, even cagey; about basic biographical informa-

readers will realize it also contains the keys to many of its own locks. The book's pleasures, in other words, are self-contained. Don't skip the "Notes on Sources" section at the back—or, for that matter, the entry on "Notes on Sources" in "Notes on Sources". A blurb on the back cover from one Hubert T. Ross ("Very revealing") feels out of place until you realize that in the dedication, Boyko refers to Ross as his own psychiatrist.

I had a feeling that Boyko wouldn't be eager to confirm or deny this man's existence to me. And I was right.

"Again, I think that if I comment too extensively on them [the hidden biographical information references], I deprive other readers

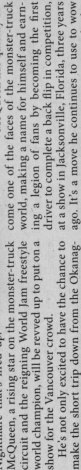

Monster truck driver rolls over competition

I n the car-crushing, gear-grinding, dirt-chewing world of monster trucks, it's as close as Cam McQueen ever gets to a home game. So when the 34-year-old from Kelowna roars out onto the floor of B.C. Place Stadium as one of the headliners of the Maple Leaf Monster Jam Tour on Saturday (January 26), it won't just be the 540-cubic-inch, 1,500-horsepower engine of his behemoth Northern Nightmare that's fired up.

He's not only excited to have the chance to make the short trip down from the Okanag-

Sports
Jeff Paterson

an and I had a bunch of family and friends that had come down to watch," he recalls fondly. "Now that we're back in Vancouver again, it's fun to relive that first experience in the truck. It was definitely a little nerve-racking. I didn't have any practice, so I just strapped myself into the seat and it was showtime. But once I fired up the motor and the adrenaline started pumping, there was no holding back."

McQueen has quickly become one of the faces of the monster-truck world, making a name for himself and earning a legion of fans by becoming the first driver to complete a back flip in competition, at a show in Jacksonville, Florida, three years ago. It's a move he continues to use to wow

back in 2008, he tells the *Straight* in a telephone interview from his Kelowna home before heading back out on the road as part of a three-month North American tour. "I had been working to try to get into this sport for quite a while, but the company that was putting the shows on had plenty of drivers and didn't need me. I was actually working for another company in Las Vegas when I got the phone call asking me if I could be in Vancouver, and I said, 'Heck, yeah.' That was my first true Monster Jam show that I ever did."

McQueen jumped at the chance to drive one of the mighty machines that night, and he hasn't looked back. And as he rose through the ranks, rolling over parked cars *and* his competition, he eventually earned the opportunity two years ago to get behind the wheel of his own truck. Now he's the very proud man behind the wheel of Northern Nightmare, the only Canadian-themed truck out on tour.

Although he lives his dream, travelling the world, the hard-driving McQueen maintains he will always have a soft spot for Vancouver.

"It was a big show, especially for my first time in a real competition to roll the truck out into the stadium there and see all the fans,

boundaries of both man and machine to see what they can dream up next.

"We're always pushing the envelope," he explains. "The back flip was kind of a benchmark in our sport. It had been a while since something new like that had been seen. It was something the sport kind of needed to push it that much further, and now it's not that the back flip is old news but it's been seen enough that, as drivers, we're thinking, 'What else can we do to raise the bar?' It's always changing, and that's one of the exciting parts about our sport."

The Monster Jam shows consist of two types of competition: speed races and freestyle, where drivers get the chance to perform stunts of their choice. McQueen drove Northern Nightmare to the freestyle title at the world finals in Las Vegas last spring, and he has his sights set on defending the championship later this year. In order to qualify, he first has to earn enough points at individual shows like the one he'll compete in at B.C. Place. And with the tour coming back to town, McQueen is ready to go full throttle; because in the world of monster-truck shows, bigger is better, and the size of the

stadium here giv
put the pedal to t
"The floor in Va
gest we see throug
we get a big floor s
which means mor
ger jumps and mo
diness in his voic
to play around co
we often perform
er when you can k
And it's great to b
ing and keep the
ately, that is our g
Obviously, m
everyone, and M
But he's amazed

noteworthy for their length. In a world where fiction tends to get corralled into either short stories or novels, Boyko's work exists in a lovely middle ground. The pieces in *Psychology*—none of which, it should be said, are actually called "Psychology"—clock in at an average of 50 pages; "The Blood-Brain Barrier," a brilliant look at the headaches of being an expert witness in a murder trial, runs for nearly 80. Every subject, from the self-help book industry ("Paddling an Iceberg") to Sigmund Freud's experiments with cocaine ("The Inner Life"), is given ample room to stretch its legs.

"To be honest, I just don't see the hard distinction between stories and novels," Boyko says, reached by phone at his home in Victoria. "I hear people talk about them as distinct entities, with totally distinct characteristics, and requiring distinct skills. To me, really, the only factor that differentiates them as a group is length. These

C. P. BOYKO

avoids giving interviews to the press as much as possible, and believes everything you need to know about his work is contained on and between its covers. The rest, even when it comes from the author himself, is just speculation.

The design and promotion of *Psychology* also attempt to sever any connection to its real-life creator. Boyko's biography on the back is intentionally evasive, and there are no acknowledgments or author's photograph. There's barely even an indication that this isn't Boyko's first book—his acclaimed debut collection, *Blackouts*, was released under the name Craig Boyko in 2008.

Here's the thing, though: I understand where Boyko is coming from. *Psychology and Other Stories* is a mysterious, rich, and extremely compelling collection. But careful

tant pause, I don't really remember." He love to get into this stuff And I guess I could, off the record, but that would be kind of silly, because you've got a job to do. But, yeah, I don't really want to give away the secret of those things—or even assuming that there is any secret to be given away. It's just a question of wanting to leave some ambiguity and uncertainty, which is actually part of why I write fiction, not essays. It's amenable to ambiguity, and multiple interpretations. If I say what my interpretation is, that already cuts out that possibility for other readers.

"Anyway," he adds, taking a breath, "that was a long way of saying 'no comment.'"

> MICHAEL HINGSTON

C. P. Boyko will appear alongside fellow authors Barbara Lambert and Bradley Somer at the Vancouver Public Library's central branch on Wednesday evening (January 30), as part of the Vancouver Writers Fest's Incite series.

111 *"If you don't give in to your true self, your true self will give in to you."* Jim Bird, *Letting Go: How To Stop Striving and Start Living!* (Chapman Loebb, 1998.) p. 215 (of 325).

111 *"Smiling is not a panacea—but it is a good cure for a frown."* Ibid., p. 20 (of 325).

111 *"I know, I know, you're thinking ... It applies to everyone."* This sample of Bird's catechistic style is actually taken from his third book, *The Power of Powerlessness: Letting It Happen To Make It Happen.* (Chapman Loebb, 2000.) p. 48 (of 309).

111-112 The two "striving index" self-quiz questions are from *Letting Go,* pp. 191 and 194 (of 325).

112 The beautifully absurd diagram is from p. 117 (of 325) of *Letting Go.* Adapted slightly.

114 *You are a piece of fate ... Why would you want to be?* Ibid., pp. 174, 15, 205, and 302 (of 325).

118 *"101 ways to score points with a woman."* John Gray, *Men Are From Mars, Women Are From Venus.* (HarperCollins, 1992.) pp. 180-185 (of 286).

118-119 Gaddis, *The Recognitions.* (Harcourt Brace, 1955.) p. 505 (of 956).

123 *"The drive towards self-improvement ... divided we fall.* Bird, *Self-Help? Self-Harm!* p. 105.

127-129 This long quotation is from *The Power of Powerlessness,* pp. 176-179 (of 341).

The reference to "Your golf game" here is peculiarly reminiscent of a passage from W. Timothy Gallwey, *The Inner Game of Tennis* (Bantam, 1974): "A 'hot streak' usually continues until the player starts thinking about it and tries to maintain it; as soon as he attempts to exercise control, he loses it. To test this theory is a simple matter, if you don't mind a little underhanded gamesmanship. The next time your opponent is having a hot streak, simply ask him as you switch courts, 'Say, George, what are you doing so differently that's making your forehand so good today?' If he takes the bait and begins to think about how he's swinging, telling you how he's really meeting the ball out in front, keeping his wrist firm, and following through better, his streak invariably will end. He will lose his timing and fluidity as he tries to repeat what he has just told you he was doing so well." p. 8 (of 178).

129 *"Using the power ... in an instant!"* Anthony Robbins, *Awaken the Giant Within.* (Simon & Schuster, 1992.) p. 35 (of 538). (Italics and exclamation mark mine.)

129 *... even bad music and bad reasons sound fine when one marches off to fight an enemy.* Daybreak, §557.

137 *... knack of being themselves.* Cf. Nietzsche, *Assorted Opinions and Maxims*, §387: "We always stand a few paces too close to ourselves, and always a few paces too distant from our neighbor. So it happens that we judge him too much wholesale and ourselves too much by individual, occasional, insignificant traits and occurrences."

140 *I would only believe in a God who knew how to dance. Thus Spoke Zarathustra*, p. 68 (of 343).

140 *She liked herself, and wanted to change.* Cf. Nietzsche, *Assorted Opinions and Maxims*, §339: "As soon as it reposes in the sunlight of joy, our soul involuntarily promises itself to be good, to become perfect, and is seized as though by a blissful shudder with a presentiment of perfection ..."

140-141 *The great physicist Schrödinger ... a true continued self-conquering.* Many of the words in this section are Schrödinger's. But here, as elsewhere, I have not hesitated to condense, expand, change words, reorder sentences, and otherwise distort the original text. To have been rigorous about enclosing in quotation marks all those words and only those words that Schrödinger actually wrote would have left the passage looking like a bristling hedgehog. The other option, to completely paraphrase his ideas, was even less appealing, for Schrödinger's prose is often unsurpassable. See *Mind and Matter*, in *What is Life? With Mind and Matter and Autobiographical Sketches*. (Cambridge University Press, 1992.) pp. 99-101.

141 *Deciding what to be, becoming what we are, is a true continued self-conquering.* Or, as Bergson put it: "To be conscious is to change, to change is to mature, to mature is to go on creating oneself endlessly. We are the sculptors of the moments of our life; each of them is a kind of creation. And just as the talent of the sculptor is formed under the very influence of the works he produces, so each of our moments modifies our personality. It is therefore correct to say that what we do depends on what we are; but it is necessary to add also that we are, to a certain extent, what we do, and that we are creating ourselves continually." *Creative Evolution*. (Translated by Arthur Mitchell. Macmillan, 1919.) pp. 7-8 (of 425).

A third reason to cite one's sources just occurred to me: the joy of sharing good writing. After all, it's so much easier to quote well than to write well.

142 *The living being is only a species of dead being. Joyful Wisdom*, §109.

143 *The patience of the bricklayer is assumed in the dream of the architect.* Gael Turnbull, "An Irish Monk."

143 *"doomed by determinacy"*: A catchphrase of Barton Q. Barnard's that crops up in several of his works; but see, for example, his overweeningly titled *The Brain Code Broken: What Science Reveals About Dreams, Personality, Sex, and Free Will.* (Chestermeare University Press, 1991.) *passim.*

145-146 *Deceived by the apparent smallness ... from our proper course.* Jim Bird, *Self-Improv-ment: The Art of Getting Everything You Really Want By Giving Up Wanting Everything.* (Chapman Loebb, 2002.) p. 258 (of 399).

147 *"Everything good is on the highway."* Emerson, "Experience."

Signal to Noise

149 Epigraph: F. Scott Fitzgerald, *Tender Is the Night.* p. 126 (of 274)

171 *... she manufactures her own unhappiness."* This witticism is found in Peale's *The Power of Positive Thinking*, p. 73 (of 276).

180 *"There's only one God in heaven."* Carlton Brown, *Brainstorm.* (Farrar and Rinehart, 1944.) p. 233. Though this line is not quite plagiarizable, I mention the book here, not so much because it inspired certain minor details of my story, but because it is the best memoir about mental illness I ever expect to read. Highly recommended.

The Inner Life

185 Epigraph: Joseph Collins, in the introduction to Jane Hillyer, *Reluctantly Told.* (Macmillan, 1935.) p. ix.

187 *The psychic effect ... which it belongs.* Sigmund Freud, *The Cocaine Papers.* (Edited by Robert Byck. Stonehill, 1974.) p. 60.

188 *"increase the reduced functioning of the nerve centers."* Ibid., p. 64.

188 *"the third scourge of humanity"*: Quoted in Ernest Jones, *The Life and Work of Sigmund Freud.* (Hogarth, 1953.) vol. 1, p. 104 (of 454).

188 *by mouth cocaine was harmless, under the skin sometimes dangerous.* Ibid., vol. 1, p. 105 (of 454).

188-189 *"unjustified fears" ... increasing the dose."* Cocaine Papers, pp. 109 and 117.

189 *"advisable to abandon ... nervous disorders."* Ibid., p. 175.

189 *"These injections ... himself cocaine* injections." Freud, *Standard Edition*, vol. 4, p. 115.

179 *"song of praise to this magical substance"*: Jones, vol. 1, p. 93 (of 454).

190　What I saw in her throat ... *date of the dream.* Freud, *Standard Edition*, vol. 4, p. 111.

191　Injections of that sort ... *given by injection.* Ibid., p. 117.

192-195　*I am toying now with a project* ... This and several quotations that follow come from *Letters of Sigmund Freud.* (Edited by Ernst L. Freud. Basic Books, 1960.) April 21, 1884, pp. 107-108; June 29, 1884, p. 115; May 17, 1885, p. 145; January 18, 1886, p. 193; January 20, 1886, p. 195; and February 2, 1886, pp. 201, 202, and 203.

195　*The effect ... ward off fatigue.* Freud, *Cocaine Papers*, p. 61.

198　*I had begun to suspect ... was a masturbator.* Freud, *Standard Edition*, vol. 7, pp. 78-79. In fact, this reference does not appear under "cocaine" in the index volume of *The Standard Edition*.

199　*"in the nose ... in other organs."* Quoted in Freud, *The Complete Letters of Sigmund Freud to Wilhelm Fliess.* p. 71, footnote.

199-200　*Swellings of the nasal mucosa* ... This long sentence and the one that follows it are close enough to direct quotations to need a citation: Max Schur, *Freud Living and Dying.* (Hogarth, 1972.) p. 66, footnote. Frank J. Sulloway, *Freud, Biologist of the Mind.* (Basic, 1979.) p. 140.

200　*"The number of symptoms ... in the nose.* Quoted in Freud, *The Origins of Psycho-analysis.* (Edited by Marie Bonaparte, Anna Freud, and Ernst Kris, translated by Eric Mosbacher and James Strachey. Basic Books, 1954.) p. 5.

200-201　*Both Freud and Fliess ... also constantly prescribed.* Jones, vol. 1, p. 339 (of 454).

201-210　*"I am now making this diagnosis ... what to do then."* This, and all but one of the quotations that follow, are from *The Complete Letters to Wilhelm Fliess*: May 30, 1893, p. 49; January 24, 1895, p. 106; April 20, 1895, p. 126; June 12, 1895, p. 132; October 26, 1896, p. 201; June 18, 1897, pp. 252-253; November 16, 1898, p. 334; March 8, 1895, p. 117; May 21, 1894, p. 74; December 3, 1897, p. 284; and September 27, 1898, p. 329.

202　*"let the biographers worry, we have no desire to make it too easy for them!"* Freud, *Letters*, April 28, 1885, p. 141.

The Blood–Brain Barrier

223　Epigraphs: Meyer Levin, *Compulsion.* (Simon and Schuster, 1956.) p. 342 (of 495). L.S. Hearnshaw, *Cyril Burt, Psychologist.* (Hodder and Stoughton, 1979.) p. 261 (of 370).

218 *Do you have any objection to me calling you Professor?* Thomas Szasz, *Psychiatric Justice*. (Macmillan, 1965.) p. 204.

228 *"If I said to you a table and a chair ...* Parts of this interview are adapted from Ronald Markman (with Dominick Bosco), *Alone With The Devil: Famous Cases of a Courtroom Psychiatrist*. (Doubleday, 1989.) pp. 88-89.

238 *N O T A L*: This rather striking typo is borrowed from Jay Ziskin, *Coping With Psychiatric and Psychological Testimony*. (Law and Psychology Press, 1981.) vol. 2, p. 240. My courtroom dialogue owes much to the sample case in volume 2, which reads almost like a novel. Highly recommended.

241 *Orson Welles*: Dialogue from the movie *Compulsion* (1959), based on the novel by Meyer Levin, which was itself based on the famous Loeb and Leopold case.

266 *great physiologist*: Charles Sherrington, *Man On His Nature*. (Cambridge University Press, 1951.) p. 178 (of 300). In a famous passage he compares the awakening brain to "an enchanted loom where millions of flashing shuttles weave a dissolving pattern, always a meaningful pattern though never an abiding one — a shifting harmony of subpatterns. It is as if the Milky Way entered upon some cosmic dance."

267 *Is the meter running while you are in court?* Ziskin, *Coping*, vol. 2, p. 334.

273 *"The main thing is you don't treat sex like a big deal ..."* This sentiment is Freud's: "What is really important is that children should never get the idea that one wants to make more of a secret of the facts of sexual life than of any other matter which is not yet accessible to their understanding." "The Sexual Enlightenment of Children," in *Standard Edition*, vol. 9, p. 138.

280 *I think it would be difficult for anyone to go on practicing psychology if they were wrong most of the time.* Ziskin, *Coping*, vol. 2, p. 55.

Notes on Sources

293 Epigraph: Liam Hudson, *The Cult of the Fact*. (Jonathan Cape, 1972.) pp. 163-164.

297-301 The citations to the works of Jim Bird—and Barton Q. Barnard—are fictional; Jim Bird and Barton Q. Barnard are fictional.

So, of course, are all the characters in this book; so, for that matter, am I.